PRAISE FOR LAURIE LUCKING

"*Common* is a well-told tale of true sacrificial friendship with a dash of sweet romance and a sprinkling of fairy tale magic. Teens and adults alike will enjoy this engaging coming-of-age fantasy."

    —Carrie Anne Noble, award-winning author of *The Mermaid's Sister*

"*Common* is a lovely coming-of-age story with a sweet romance that will have you holding your breath in anticipation."

    —Julie Hall, USA Today Best-Selling author of the Life After Series

"Engaging and intriguing! Laurie Lucking's *Common* pulled me in and kept me riveted from beginning to end. I look forward to seeing what she comes up with next!"

    —Katie Clark, author of the Enslaved Series

"Laurie Lucking's *Common* quenches a spot in my heart that craves fairy-tale romances. With a dashing prince and a fearless heroine, you'll find yourself turning pages late into the night, unable to put this sterling debut down."

    —Lucette Nel, author of *The Widow's Captive*

"*Common* deserves every point on each of its sparkling five stars. I truly loved it, regardless of the fact that it's a lot more romance-heavy than I normally read. The book taught me a lesson about expanding my boundaries, and that a great story is simply a great story and can be thoroughly enjoyed regardless of whether or not it's squarely set in your favorite genre. I feel silly for ever being so picky!

"If you're looking for a relaxing, heartwarming story you can dive into headfirst, I highly recommend that you grab a copy of *Common*. You won't regret it!"

—Jamie Foley, author of the Sentinel Trilogy

"*Common* chambermaid Leah Wellstone is shy, loyal, and brave—and relatable—a refreshing change from the better-than-everyone-at-everything warrior heroines. The romance between Leah and Prince Rafe is delightful, and the ending perfect for lovers of fairy tales—or for anyone who enjoys a good romance. I look forward to reading more from Laurie Lucking."

—Elizabeth Jane Kitchens, author of *The Rose and the Wand*

"Although *Common* contains all the staples readers of romance novels love, it is not just another Cinderella story. Filled with surprises that make readers eager to discover what comes next, *Common* is a fairy-tale romance unlike any other."

—Lauricia Matuska, author of *The Healer's Rune*

"*Common* pulls readers into a fantasy world of forbidden attraction, unforeseeable twists, and memorable characters. Plan on staying up all night reading—you won't be able to put it down!"

—Sara Baysinger, author of the Black Tiger Series

"*Common* is a new fairy tale, full of wonderful characters and a storyworld that pulls the reader in. Exploring the themes of loyalty, faith, and self-worth, Ms. Lucking's debut novel shares Leah's struggle to save the royal family and her friend Rafe against insurmountable odds. Carve out some time for this delightful story— once you start reading, you won't be able to stop until it's over!"

—J.M. Hackman, author of the Firebrand Chronicles

"Lucking is an amazing fantasy writer! Anyone who enjoys a bit of romance in their books will enjoy this well-written story of courage and triumph. It's nice to have a story with an HEA. Those are a scarce thing nowadays. I truly enjoyed this story and cannot wait to read more from Ms. Lucking in the future. Five stars from me!"

—Deanna Fugett, author of *Ending Fear*

"A shy servant girl, a handsome prince, a forbidden love, an evil sorcerer. Pair that with a group of mystic nuns and what could go wrong? This debut novel from Laurie Lucking has all these things and more! If you love a Cinderella tale with a bit of dark magic, *Common* is the story for you."

—Pam Halter, award-winning author of *Fairyeater*

"This book was a fun, romantic, and exciting read that sped time up. I'm hooked and can't wait to read what Laurie Lucking writes next."

—Sarah Armstrong-Garner, author of *Sinking*

"Are you looking for a young adult fantasy with memorable characters, bold adventures, and a sweet romance? Laurie Lucking's delightful debut, *Common*, ticks all of these boxes and more. Get ready to be won over by plucky heroine, Leah, as she adapts to challenging circumstances and falls in love unexpectedly along the way."

— Jebraun Clifford, award-winning author of "Beyond the Stars, Past the Moons" in *Encircled*

"Gripping and beautifully written, *Common* is an adventure in friendship and real love. The ending had me so enthralled, I feared my reader-heart would be ripped in two. I couldn't put it down! Highly recommend it."

— Desiree Williams, author of *Illusionary*

TALES OF THE MYSTICS
BOOK TWO

ALSO BY LAURIE LUCKING

Common

Tales of the Mystics, Book One

Traitor

Tales of the Mystics, Book Two

Coming Soon:

Scarred

Tales of the Mystics, Book Three

Mystic

Tales of the Mystics, Book Four

Traitor

TALES OF THE MYSTICS
BOOK TWO

LAURIE LUCKING

Love2ReadLove2Write Publishing, LLC
Indianapolis, Indiana

Published by Love2ReadLove2Write Publishing, LLC

Indianapolis, Indiana

www.love2readlove2writepublishing.com

ISBN-13: 978-1-943788-55-2 (Paperback)

ISBN-13: 978-1-943788-56-9 (Ebook)

LCCN: 2021932771

Library of Congress Cataloging-in-Publication Data is on file at the Library of Congress, Washington, DC.

This is a work of fiction. Names, characters, incidents, and dialogues are products of the author's imagination and are not to be construed as real. Any resemblance to actual events or persons, living or dead, is entirely coincidental.

Cover Design by Sara Helwe (www.sara-helwe.com)

To Dad,
For so many laughs and memories
and for always believing in me

CHAPTER 1

"*E*xiled to *Delunia*?" I gripped the edge of my chair before I could topple out of it.

When Papa asked me to join him in his study, the nervous twitch of his brow hinted something was wrong. But I'd expected a scolding about the cost of my latest gown or a request to admonish my sister Sophia about her flirtatious behavior or loose tongue.

Not this.

Papa adjusted his collar. "Not exiled, Penelope. It is a betrothal. A joyous occasion."

Oh, yes. My last engagement had been such bliss.

"The emperor and his son are thrilled to be making the alliance." He adopted his best diplomatic smile, spreading his hands across the polished surface of his desk.

I swallowed a scoff. Of course they were. The benefit would be entirely on their side. How could Papa even consider it? Delunia was miserably hot, the people were loud and unrefined, and they didn't speak any form of Sandrinian.

And it was thousands of miles across the sea from my beloved Trellich. From the entire continent of Sandrin.

The nightmare my life had become over the past year was about to get even worse.

"Won't the voyage take weeks? Will I ever see you again?"

"Only one week, if the weather is favorable." A ripple pricked through Papa's confidence. "But it is a long journey, I can't deny it. We won't be able to visit often, but I'm sure every few years or so . . ."

Every few years. I'd almost prefer to separate from them forever than to become a stranger to my own family. "But why? How could anything they're offering in an alliance be worth sending me so far away?"

He hesitated for a beat. Two. "They trade many valuable materials, and it would certainly be in our best interest to support and encourage those relations."

"We have valuable items to trade as well," I argued. "They can't match our textiles, nor our gemstones. Isn't that reason enough for the Delunian royal family to foster our trade agreements?"

"Their navy is formidable, the best on the Toan Sea. It wouldn't hurt to have such might on our side, especially"—he glanced away, avoiding my gaze—"since our relations with Imperia have become more strained than ever."

"Imperia?" I gritted my teeth. The very name made me want to shudder. "They wouldn't cause trouble now, not with the new trade agreement in place."

A knot on the dark wood of Papa's desk consumed his full interest.

I swallowed a huff of frustration. "Surely, they wouldn't defy an agreement they so recently—"

"They didn't sign the agreement, Penelope." Papa's gaze collided with mine, roiling with frustration and concern.

"What?"

"I received their response last week." He massaged his forehead. "They do not wish to enter into negotiations with us at this time."

My stomach sank so quickly, I expected to hear a thud on the floor. They refused to sign because of *me*. Our improved alliance was supposed to be sealed by my marriage to Raphael, the Imperian Crown Prince. Instead, I'd gotten mixed up in a treasonous—murderous—plot.

"You're ashamed of me. That's why you're sending me away." I curled my fingers into the smooth material of my skirt.

"Of course not, dearest." He leaned back against the curved wood forming the back of his chair. "I, too, misplaced my trust in the Duke of Brantley. He managed to fool us all." He straightened. "But people will talk, and this marriage might give you a chance for a fresh start."

A fresh start. Was such a thing possible? Another fiancé. A new country to explore. More opportunities to squander, relationships to destroy.

I gnawed at my lip. *No, I mustn't think like that.*

The Duke of Brantley fooled even his dear friends, his own king and queen. I'd never step foot beyond Glonsel Palace again if my every thought anticipated future mistakes.

"Do you know anything of the Delunian prince?" I channeled stern tension into my legs, drawing on every last reserve from my etiquette training to sit still rather than fidget.

Papa smiled, apparently pleased by my feigned interest. "I met him when he was just a boy. A stout little fellow, clearly gentle-hearted and eager to learn. His father has spoken highly of him in his letters. Says he'll make a fine husband, and one day, emperor."

As though a father's word could be trusted on such a subject. Especially when he sought to convince us to agree to the marriage.

But Papa looks so hopeful . . . "That is—comforting, I suppose. How old is he?" I pressed my lips together to prevent them forming a grimace. *Please, Luminate, don't let him be ancient.*

"Only a few years your senior. Nineteen, I believe."

That, at least, was a relief. "Then I am to be an empress."

The word tasted foreign—equal parts intriguing and distasteful —on my tongue.

"Indeed. And what a lovely one you'll be." Papa stood, rounded his desk, and placed a warm hand on my shoulder. "You shall be missed, child, more than I can say. But I do think it's for the best. You've an entire lunar cycle to prepare for your departure, so take some time to get adjusted to the idea."

An entire lunar cycle. He spoke the words as though they described a vast length of time, not the span of four weeks.

I rose, tucking my hands behind my back to hide their trembling. "I have much to think on and prepare. I'd best—"

"Of course."

I hardly registered his reply before he clenched me tightly to his chest. Burying my face in his velvet doublet, I shut my eyes against welling tears. I'd be with my family for a lunar cycle yet, and they'd visit every once in a while. We could always write letters that would take weeks to travel across the Toan Sea . . .

A whimper escaped, and Papa clutched me tighter. *Please, don't make me go.*

"Delunia? What an excitin' prospect! Hardly anyone from Trellich's traveled there, I'd wager." My lady's maid, Victoria, fiddled with a knot at the back of my corset.

"True. I was there once, as a child, when my family attended Emperor Tertius's coronation. I confess, I've never had any wish to return."

"I'm sorry 'tis't what you'd hoped for, m'lady."

I hardly knew what I hoped for anymore. But another marriage—especially one in Delunia—certainly wasn't it.

"It's my duty as a member of the royal family. Again. Though it's entirely unfair that little Dominick gets to stay in

Trellich and prepare to rule, while my chief value lies in my marriageability to other kingdoms as a token of peace."

The knot finally gave way, allowing my lungs to expand more fully than they had all day.

"And what a peace I accomplished with Imperia." The mutter escaped my mouth before I could hold it back.

Victoria gave my arm a sympathetic squeeze before helping me into my nightdress. "If I may, Your Highness . . ."

I sank onto the edge of my mattress. "Say anything you like, Victoria."

While most of the girl's talk was idle gossip, she'd earned my trust by staying by my side after Nicholas—the Imperian nobleman I'd been much more eager to marry than the prince —and his accomplice, the infamous sorcerer Lord Damien Lessox, had been arrested and I'd been sent home in disgrace.

Based on the dark, suspicious looks members of the Trellan court had cast upon me ever since, it appeared she and my father and sisters were the only allies I had left.

Perhaps Papa's plan truly was the only way to lighten the shadow darkening my name and reputation.

Her shoulders rose with her deep inhale, sending her thick braid of light-brown hair slipping to her back. "Ye've been sulking for months, princess, and it pains me to see it."

Victoria took a few steps closer. "That Duke of Brantley had the looks and charm to turn the head of every young lady in both Trellich and Imperia. The entirety of Sandrin, I'd wager. No maiden who's honest with herself would fault you for developin' an attachment. Those who shun ye now are just jealous he never paid any mind to 'em, or have likely been searchin' for an excuse to look down upon ye for years, knowin' they'd never have yer beauty or position."

I choked back my surprised laugh. How novel to have someone speak to me so plainly rather than skirting around unpleasant subjects with a hasty bow or curtsy.

She swallowed. "I hope I caused no offense."

"None at all." I patted the bed beside me, and she hesitantly perched on the white bedspread, her hands restless in her lap. "I find it refreshing, when so few people are honest with me. Especially now."

"We all make mistakes, princess." She offered a slight smile. "Even you ought to be allowed one every so often."

I avoided her gaze. My first love, the greatest adventure of my life, was now relegated by everyone—even my lady's maid —into the category of *mistake*. How could I cast aside my memories from Imperia when they hovered over me like a storm cloud? When I still longed for . . .

I blinked, as though the simple gesture could clear my head of thoughts of him. Nicholas sat rotting in the Imperian dungeon. I could hardly marry him now.

Angling to face Victoria, I patted her knee. "What a treasure you are. You shall be very much missed."

But did I have to miss her? Would it be asking too much?

Inhaling sharply, I sat up straighter. "Please know you're under no obligation whatsoever. I'm happy to give you the highest recommendation to any of the ladies at court, or perhaps you could attend one of my sisters."

She bit her lip and raised a brow.

I blew out a breath. "What I'm trying to say is, I won't hold it against you in the slightest if you choose to stay in Trellich, but . . . would you consider accompanying me to Delunia?"

Her hand flew to her mouth. "Do ye mean it, m'lady? All the way to Delunia, what an experience!" She bounced, shaking the bed. "Ye know, they say the Delunian gentlemen are very handsome, with dark eyes and bronze skin. And the dresses there are so beautiful, all those beads and colorful fabrics. Do they even call 'em dresses, do ye think?"

I giggled, the sound a bit croaky from lack of use. "I believe they're called *etanas*, but I know nothing of the handsomeness, or lack thereof, of Delunian men."

Her eyes narrowed almost to a glare before widening. "I apologize for lettin' my tongue get ahead of me."

"I don't mind in the least. And I hope you're right about those Delunian gentlemen."

The statement sounded forced, even to my ears. I hadn't the slightest interest in Delunian gentlemen, least of all their prince.

"Does that mean you're willing to go with me? Papa estimated the sea voyage alone will take a week, not to mention the time to get to the coast. I remember little about the Delunian palace, and of course few of them will speak Sandrinian."

My words tumbled over each other in a torrent. Much as I'd regret talking her out of it, I needed to ensure she had the choice I was being denied.

"M'lady." She paused in her fidgeting, but a palpable energy pulsed from her. "Ye know I have no family to hold me here. Delunia will be different, yes, and no doubt we'll face some challenges. But ye've always been a kind mistress, and I'm eager to see as much o' the world as I can. I wouldn't miss this chance for anything." She rose from the bed and skipped around the room, gathering my gown and stockings and replacing them in my wardrobe. "Just think of it—me, travelin' across the Toan Sea to Delunia!"

My face relaxed into a smile as I watched. I wouldn't be alone. Victoria would serve as a companion and reminder of home, and apparently even provide the spark of enthusiasm for Delunia I lacked.

In the midst of her twirls and jumps and squeals, Victoria had managed to turn the pallor of my uncertain destiny a little less bleak.

～

Dominick set out across the sitting room, his waddling steps hasty, as though slowing down would cause him to topple all the way instead of just slightly. I extended my hands to him. Recovering from a tumble, he took several more steps and reached me. I scooped him into my lap, snuggling him close.

Once I arrived in Delunia, I wouldn't see my baby brother for years. He'd be a different child—a mischievous boy instead of a fumbling toddler—the next time I saw my family.

I squeezed him tighter, but he started to squirm. "Out. Out."

"Oh, all right. Keep exploring, little one." With a final pat on his dark hair, I released him.

Sophia leaned on the edge of her chair, her eager gaze upon me. "What do you think, Pen? Wouldn't it be perfect?"

She'd been conversing with Vivienne and Papa, but my mind wandered elsewhere.

"Wouldn't what be perfect?" I asked.

Her tightly-wound curls vibrated with indignation. "Weren't you listening?"

"I was distracted by Nicky." Among other things.

"Hmm." Her eyes softened as the chubby-cheeked prince toddled past. "Well, I received a letter from Ayla this morning. She's invited me to visit in three weeks! Just in time for Gael to return home from his tour of the Upper Flynnite border."

She smoothed her skirt, splotches of dark pink blossoming on her cheeks.

Vivienne raised a brow at me, and I passed a hand over my mouth to cover my grin. Sophia had been breathlessly anticipating a proposal from Prince Gael of Lower Flynn for months. Perhaps Ayla, his twin sister, was in on the plan.

"That's wonderful news."

"Of course it is." Her folded hands squirmed in her lap. "But don't you see? The timing is ideal—you may accompany me to Lower Flynn on your way to the eastern port."

"Oh. I hadn't—"

A crash cut my words short.

"Prince Dominick!" Nicky's nursemaid hiked up her skirts and ran to him.

I jumped to my feet and craned my neck to look behind the couch on which Vivienne sat. He'd felled a thin round table and now sat banging a small marble bust of our great-grandfather, King Duncan, against the floor.

I rushed to his side to recover the statue while Vivienne set the table to rights. "No, Nicky. That's not a toy."

Papa stood behind us, fists on hips. "Leave the boy alone."

I backed away as he tousled Nicky's hair, chuckling.

"Why shouldn't my heir take an interest in his ancestors? In his position? As in all things, he shows great aptitude."

I forced myself to pause. *Inhale, exhale.*

Papa exercised such perception and balance in every other matter. But somehow Mama's death only moments after Nicky's birth had produced a colossal blind spot when it came to my youngest sibling.

"But, Papa, he might hurt himself. And I don't believe Great-Grandfather's likeness was intended for such rough treatment."

"Here, Nicky." Vivienne crouched at my side. "Come sit in my lap, and we'll look at it together."

"He's fine as he is." The humor in Papa's voice had given way to gruffness. "A boy needs a little rough play, not always to be coddled by his sisters."

I placed a hand on his shoulder. "Perhaps, but if he doesn't learn caution, Glonsel Palace will someday be bereft of all its treasures."

He shook off my touch, turning to me with narrowed eyes. "The palace's treasures are all to be his one day, are they not?"

Vivienne's flinch mirrored mine. Three young women supplanted by a two-year-old because of his gender.

"Yes, but—"

"I'll hear no more." His voice lowered to a harsh whisper.

"The boy lost his mother. Not a single embrace, not a single memory. I'll take nothing else from him."

My stomach clenched as though I were to be the next recipient of Nicky's brutality. Papa's actions sprang from love, from a desire to protect and shelter. But what kind of a child would such treatment create?

I lowered my head respectfully. "Of course, Papa."

Sophia looked up from the letter she'd been re-reading as I returned to my seat. "See, Pen? It's all right here. We'll depart on the twentieth, reach Lower Flynn on the twenty-third, then after a few days, you may proceed to the port. I believe Papa said a ship departs on the twenty-eighth."

I blinked, trying to take it all in. "That does sound lovely, but I'm afraid I was planning to depart from Torquil Harbor."

"In Imperia? The voyage from Lower Flynn would be shorter." Sophia pursed her lips. "I'm sure you can easily change your plans, and this way—"

"No, I—I have a stop I want to make in Imperia."

In truth, I hadn't given the details of my journey much thought. My specific route hardly mattered if I couldn't alter my final destination. But the prospect of leaving Sandrin behind—rarely, if ever, to return—gave rise to a sudden, inexplicable draw toward Imperia. Toward the pieces of relationships I'd left in shambles in my haste to return home before they decided to lock me in the dungeon alongside Nicholas.

I shivered, even as the nebulous idea hardened into resolve.

Papa rounded the couch, anger displaced by concern. "What stop is that? Do you think it wise to return to Imperia, after . . . ?"

I set my jaw. "Perhaps not, but I believe it is necessary."

"But why?" Vivienne regarded me with a somber gaze.

"I—" The plan felt shaky in my head, ludicrous to say aloud. "I'm not ready to give up on the trade agreement just yet. They might be more willing to negotiate in person."

Perhaps I might even see Nicholas . . .

A tremor accompanied the thought. From anticipation or foreboding?

Papa sank into his armchair. "I would not put you in danger, Penelope. In spite of our official apology and recent overtures, they seem determined to shun us."

"But we were counting on that agreement to settle things between us, especially now that we won't be connected by marriage."

Papa glanced to the nursemaid hovering behind Nicky. "Yes, well—"

I pulled back my shoulders, strangely determined to proceed down this questionable path. "We mustn't allow them to hold my actions against our entire country. If this betrothal is truly to be a fresh start, I need to put my history with the Imperian royal family behind me. I will no longer hide behind an official statement from our palace."

Papa's sigh ruffled his beard. "If that is your wish, I won't stop you."

CHAPTER 2

*P*apa's deep voice rumbled through our dining room. "Thank you, Luminate, for this food and this new day. Amen."

I raised my bowed head in unison with the other members of my family. Papa bit off the end of a thick slice of bacon with a noisy chomp. Sophia and Vivienne each raised a fork to sample their eggs. Selecting a ripe purple berry, I popped it in my mouth.

I ought to cherish these few private meals left with my family. But my upcoming voyage to Delunia had cast everything into shadow, its inevitability making the remainder of my time in Trellich feel equally precious and futile.

Tart juice burst across my tongue as I chewed. Did the people of Delunia pray to, or even acknowledge, the Luminate as their creator? I'd never studied our religious texts as devoutly as my tutors wished, but I had found a certain peace in our weekly observances in the palace chapel. Peace that came in shared prayers with my family and the knowledge that a being far beyond what I could comprehend was looking out for me.

Is He, though?

The berry plopped into my empty stomach like a pebble. My dismal fate marched toward me at an unrelenting pace, and no higher power had lifted a finger to intervene. But if the Luminate viewed me in the same light as everyone else did — reckless, unfaithful, traitorous — He probably felt no obligation to intervene.

Did He even care what happened to me anymore?

I grasped my knife and spread butter across my biscuit, but the action accentuated rather than hid the trembling in my hands. Perhaps it didn't matter that Delunia held no regard for the Luminate. Perhaps He preferred for me to travel far away, making clear His judgment against my perceived wrongdoing.

"Is there anyone in particular you'd like to invite, Penelope?"

My head snapped up. Papa regarded me expectantly from the head of the table.

"Invite to what?"

Sophia snickered. "Surely that biscuit doesn't require *all* your attention, Pen."

"To your farewell dinner, of course." Papa's smile held an air of amused patience.

Heat blazed in my cheeks. "Farewell dinner?"

Sophia gave an exasperated sigh.

"You must have so much on your mind." Vivienne's gentle voice came from my left. "Papa was suggesting we hold a banquet to celebrate your engagement and give people a chance to say goodbye."

"I see." I took a sip of orange juice to forestall the horror flooding my mind from making its way to my face. "I appreciate the thought, Papa, but I don't think that will be necessary. Few among the noble families would wish to bid me a personal farewell, and it might be best not to publicize that I'm being sent away."

Papa's fork clinked onto his plate. "But I view the matter in the opposite light. If you were to slip off to Delunia without fanfare, people would imagine you'd left in disgrace and broken your ties to Trellich for good. A banquet celebrating your engagement and our strengthened alliance with Delunia will be just the thing to demonstrate our pride in you and our hope for the future of our two countries."

If only they truly had any pride in me. "That does make sense, but I still don't—"

Sophia interrupted. "Pen, we must have a banquet! I've already decided on a style for my new gown."

Papa directed a dark look at her.

Vivienne dabbed at her mouth with a napkin. "You might be surprised who will want to say goodbye. And a send-off dinner might be a nice memory for all of us."

Sophia's whining I could easily withstand, but Vivienne's wisdom and compassion were much harder to resist. One glance at the determination lining Papa's face, and the last hint of protest died on my lips.

"All right. If you really want to plan something, I won't stop you."

Papa laid his napkin on the table with a flourish. "Excellent. I shall speak with Mrs. Floram about the arrangements."

I blew out my sigh slowly, silently. While well-intentioned, this dinner would feel more like a funeral than a celebration.

It's important to Papa. A successful banquet will bolster the royal family's reputation. We must demonstrate Trellich's confidence and strength.

The refrains chorused through my head time and again as I approved guest lists, place settings, and menu selections. At least they provided distraction and purpose as I felt increasingly like an outsider in my own country, with little to fill my thoughts aside from misgivings for the future.

The day of the banquet arrived, carrying with it all the activity of a large palace event. But instead of the usual hum of excitement, the atmosphere held a distinctive cynical quality—a dissonant note within a familiar chord.

Did everyone in Glonsel Palace feel it, or was it merely a reflection of my own unease?

By the time I retired to my chambers to dress, my insides simmered like a pot of water threatening to boil over and burn me from within.

Victoria chattered with remarkable energy as she fussed over my dress and hair, oblivious to—or perhaps compensating for—my despondency. When she finished, my spirits drooped as though I'd just returned from a taxing social function, not simply survived the preparations.

I surveyed the results in the tall oval mirror in the corner of my dressing room. The cherubs carved into the top edges seemed to stare at me, disdain in their wooden expressions. I shivered in spite of the heavy layers of material hanging from my frame.

"What do ye think, m'lady?" Victoria's reflection appeared next to mine as she adjusted the neckline across my shoulders.

The palace seamstresses had clearly taken to heart their instructions to design me something grand for my send-off. Tiny gemstones dotted taffeta of the deepest blue, making it sparkle like the night sky. The bodice hugged me as though they'd sewn it right over my corset, and my flouncing skirt would hardly fit through doorways.

Victoria had wrangled my hair into an endless array of curls, some piled atop my head, others dangling in perfect spirals against my neck. The diamond tiara adorning my brow completed my appearance as a dark queen of the night.

Or empress, in my case.

"Absolutely beautiful. Thank you." Best not to say anything more.

She squeezed my arms, her smile soft. "Ye'll certainly give them an impression to remember."

I stepped into the hall, swallowing against the bittersweet

tang coating my mouth. My last formal banquet in Trellich. I'd never have to face these people again. At least, not until I was married to the Prince of Delunia. But would the future we toasted tonight provide a better life, free from the weight of judgment surrounding me? Or would I long for the Trellan court—furtive glances, contemptuous gossip, and all?

I made my way down the grand staircase, striving to appear stately as I inched down every step to avoid tripping on my skirt. Papa would never be truly proud of me now, but I could at least avoid embarrassing him further.

"Princess Penelope, there you are." Mrs. Floram, our head housekeeper, bustled to my side. "You look lovely this evening, Your Highness." She swept into a deep curtsy.

"Thank you."

"Your guests are beginning to arrive, so if you would accompany me to the front hall to greet them—" She gave a deferential sweep of her arm.

My guests. I choked back a bitter laugh. No one attending this banquet cared two straws about my impending departure, aside from what gossip they could glean from it.

I drew as deep a breath as my tight stays would allow. "Of course."

I plastered a smile into place as we strode into the well-lit front hall. Candles lining the walls made the polished floors gleam.

"Oh, Princess Penelope, what a sight!" The Earl of Veringham's daughter dipped into a graceful curtsy. "Such a splendid dress, and I simply must know how your lady's maids accomplish such wonders with your hair!"

Her own hair was pulled into a high chignon, prominently displaying the low neckline of her violet gown.

I bobbed my head. "I thank you, but I hardly know myself. She seems to outdo herself every time."

"Just one, then? How curious, for I'm sure you could afford more. Even I have two."

My jaw stopped just short from clenching. "Only one will accompany me to Delunia."

"Ah, I suppose not many wanted to stay after . . . and, well, a voyage to Delunia is hardly for the faint of heart!" She flapped a hand to her chest. "Thank goodness you'll have one, at least. Heaven knows the help you'll be able to find there."

"I'm sure I'll manage."

She unfurled an ivory fan. "I must let you attend to the other guests. But what a shame your Duke Nicholas can't be here to appreciate you in all your splendor, hmm?"

With a wink and a few flicks of her fan, she glided into the next room.

My wooden smile faltered. How dare she? The gall, to mention Nicholas so flippantly while he wasted away in an Imperian dungeon.

"Princess, how lovely!"

I nodded to the elderly gentleman ambling past. "Thank you so much for coming."

"Why, Penelope, you sly thing."

I started at a pinch to my elbow. "Charlotte, how good of you to come."

"Of course I wouldn't miss it." The Countess of Felten bounced on her toes. She couldn't have been many years older than myself. "But how could you not write to me about this new engagement? What a disappointment to hear of it from old Lady Carthal, of all people. Engaged to a second prince already." She shook her head, swaying her blonde curls. "Has ever a young lady been so fortunate?"

My mind reeled as I inclined my head to passing guests. I would've hardly applied the word *fortunate* to my situation.

"It has taken me some time to get used to this new development. I would've scarcely known what to write." Not that I would've owed *her* a letter, in any case. "But yes, I suppose it is advantageous that my father was able to arrange this marriage so soon after — "

Her grin turned conspiratorial. "I suppose the swifter the better. Perhaps news of your little mishap hasn't reached Delunia yet."

I blinked. "We have no intention of deceiving—"

"Of course not, of course not." She straightened the large ruby pendant hanging from a golden chain around her neck. "What a pity you have to go so far away, but I suppose no one here would take you now. Oh, there's my husband! Isn't he handsome in his new necktie?" She waved a gloved hand. "I must rejoin him, but make sure to stop by and see me at dinner." With another squeeze to my arm, she was off.

Was this how everyone viewed the engagement? That I was fortunate anyone would take me at all? Removing a handkerchief from my reticule, I dabbed a bead of sweat from my forehead.

Every conversation tracked a similar pattern.

Young ladies approached me as though we were friends, as though they cared I was about to sail across the Toan Sea, followed by a flippant comment about the duke or my two engagements, then flouncing off in a manner that indicated they were all too happy to leave my side, thrilled to have something to hold over me.

My store of smiles and polite conversation had worn thin by the time we were ushered into the dining hall. At least there I would be placed between Papa and Sophia.

A small salad of intertwining green and purple leaves sat at my table setting, arranged on a fine china plate. On the edge lay three slices of marshmelon.

Mist dampened my eyes. *My favorite*.

What would I be eating in Delunia? Would anyone care enough to learn my preferences?

Sophia prattled about the disappointing lack of young gentleman in attendance as we took our seats. I bit back the temptation to cut her off with a sarcastic remark. I couldn't let careless words cause us to part on bad terms.

I kept my eyes on my plate, avoiding the range of curious to disdainful gazes from the gathered aristocracy. *Only three courses left, then I'll never have to see any of them again.*

I started at the surprising sense of release that accompanied such a thought. For the first time, I allowed the possibility to trickle through my mind—maybe my leaving for Delunia truly was for the best.

Papa stood, clinking his spoon against his goblet to get everyone's attention. The ensuing silence hummed with anticipation. I adjusted my posture, lifting my shoulders as though a puppeteer tugged at an imaginary string above my head. No tears or scowls or uncertainty. Only refinement, poise, grace.

He gave a standard welcome and words of thanks. I stared at a point just beyond the crowd, shifting my gaze to each corner on occasion, a practiced smile glued in place.

". . . with our new ally across the sea. The strengthened partnership between our countries will increase our peace and prosperity for generations to come."

Papa's chest puffed out as it always did in preparation for the conclusion of a speech.

"In this, we do not lose a princess but rather gain a future empress. An empire! And so we send Princess Penelope forth with our gratitude and the blessings of the Luminate, our ambassador and pioneer as we forge ahead into a new era."

He motioned for me to stand.

I flattened my palms on the table in case my trembling legs wouldn't support me. For a fleeting moment, I almost believed him. I could accomplish so much good for our people, establish a strong, beneficial relationship between our nations. The decadent scents, lavish decorations, and clamorous cheers all buoyed my spirits.

Then my eyes landed on the taunting gaze of a stately woman. Nearby, a father glared cold indifference, his daughter's lips curved into a mocking smirk.

Sweat dribbled down the back of my neck as a cold wave of familiarity crashed over me, dousing the flicker of hope.

King Frederick had given just such a speech when announcing my betrothal to Prince Raphael.

Two countries' hopes had ridden on the success of that marriage, while I'd merely played the part, acting as a dutiful fiancée to Raphael until Nicholas could bring his plans to fruition.

No wonder none of these people believed I would succeed. They might clap to appease Papa, but every last one of them knew the truth of my situation: I was a traitor being sent as far away as possible, not a heroine.

I'd never been so eager to board a ship and cross the sea in my life.

CHAPTER 3

"*M* 'lady?"

I blinked, catching Victoria's concerned gaze behind me in the vanity mirror. "I apologize. I must've been lost in my own thoughts."

The days following the banquet were passing in a nauseating push and pull of painfully slow and disorientingly fast. I couldn't wait to separate myself from the gossips, those who crowed over my demise while smiling to my face.

But to launch myself into the unknown, to leave my family and everything that was familiar and beloved . . .

"Nothin' to apologize for." Victoria paused in her efforts to wrangle a wayward curl and patted my shoulder. "I was merely askin' about yer trunks. We're bringin' along all yer jewels and personal effects, o' course."

I tried not to wince. Items had been disappearing from my chambers for days as Victoria and other palace staff tucked my life away into a series of flat-topped trunks, as though my identity were fading away, piece by piece.

What portions of it would still be intact by the time we reached Delunia?

"But I wasn't certain how many of yer gowns ye'd like to

bring along." Victoria scratched at her chin. "Ye'll likely get a new wardrobe in Delunia, since their styles're so different."

She bounced on her toes, as though the prospect was pleasant rather than off-putting.

"But o' course ye'll need somethin' for the journey, and enough gowns to get you started until —"

"I want them all."

She started. The words had come out more harshly than I intended. "All?"

"Yes." *Let them think I'm vain or self-important.* My desire to impress the Delunian royal family wasn't nearly strong enough to overcome my nostalgia. "Even if they don't get much use, they're the dresses I've worn to balls and dinners and . . . they hold many memories."

She pressed her lips together, her eyes softening. "O' course."

"Besides, they won't be of much use to anyone here."

My lips remained parted as a thought arrested me — the envious look in Sophia's eyes when I wore my jade-green gown. And she so loved the dress my maids in Imperia fashioned from silk the color of deep-red wine. My blue-gray taffeta would suit Vivienne's quieter nature, and perhaps something in lavender . . .

"On second thought, I will select a few dresses to give to my sisters. But I'd like to take the rest."

Victoria nodded. "Very good, m'lady. I'll see it taken care of."

∾

"Mama? It's me, Penelope."

I'd spent my last three days in Trellich saying goodbye. To my beautiful dappled mare, Priseya. To the grevel tree over the river I'd climbed as a girl. To the chipped bench in a secluded corner of the gardens, surrounded by crimson bells and farendons. To the overstuffed chair in the library where I'd daydreamed of romance and adventure. To the nursery, where I'd played and fought and giggled with my sisters.

Now I knelt at Mama's grave in the cemetery outside our palace chapel. The stone marking her final resting place loomed above, its delicate carvings pristine. Papa had spared no expense, insisting Mama's memory receive the respect she deserved. A monument fit for a queen.

But aside from the name inscribed in scripted letters, I'd never found it to have any connection with her. The spray of lilies of the sunrise I'd set before me scented the breeze.

"I'm sure you know this already. If you're aware of anything now, you probably know everything . . ."

Even after two years, I wasn't sure how to conduct myself at Mama's grave. It wasn't as though she could hear me, yet to remain silent didn't feel right either.

"What I mean to say is, I'm going to Delunia to marry the emperor's son. Do you have any recollection of Vander? I don't. But Papa is so eager to pursue this new alliance. You know how he can be."

If she'd been at any of our family dinners over the past month, she would've directed an exasperated—but equally adoring—gaze at Papa and made a flippant remark about "your father and his politics." Then changed the conversation to music or fashion or gardening.

A ghost of the conspiratorial grin we would've shared lifted the corners of my lips. "I—I'll be an empress someday, Mama."

Why did the words make me feel timid and weak instead of powerful?

"I know I haven't visited in a while. A long while. But I'm leaving tomorrow, and I wanted to say goodbye. Again."

Memories washed over me, soured by guilt. My last visit to the cemetery was before I'd left for Imperia, my head filled with dreams of Nicholas—strategies for arranging our private trysts, what I'd write in my next letter, which gown to wear when I'd see him upon my arrival in Imperia.

Since returning, I hadn't had the heart to face her.

"Would you have sent me away?" The question floated into the void, never to be answered. "Somehow I don't think you would, not if I didn't want to go. And I *don't* want to go. I want nothing to do with Delunia."

At least here I could be fully honest. And yet . . . even Mama couldn't have saved my reputation or regained any measure of respect for me in Trellich.

How disappointed she would've been to learn of my duplicity with Nicholas. At least I'd been spared from failing her along with the rest of my family. But had she witnessed my disgrace from whatever vantage point she had in heaven? Had she disowned me right alongside the Luminate?

Regret enveloped me in fetters so tight I could hardly breathe. "Oh, Mama, I only wanted to marry the man I loved. If only things could've turned out differently . . ."

I pressed my face to the ground, letting the spiny blades of grass absorb my tears. As though I could hide from such celestial scrutiny.

When my legs became numb and soreness nipped my back, I sat up. My handkerchief could dry the moisture from my face, but I'd likely need a bath to erase the grass stains. My eyes fixated on her stone. My mind stilled, my lungs inhaled deeply—anything I could do to capture this place, any remaining wisp of her essence.

"Goodbye, Mama. I love you and miss you. Always. But I'll be gone for a long time. Possibly . . ."

I couldn't bring myself to finish the statement aloud.

Possibly . . . forever.

❧

I plodded into our small family dining room, noting every imperfection in the marble floor, each swirling carving along the edges of the table and chairs. Who knew if—no, I had to think of it as *when*—I'd ever see it again?

The rest of my family trickled in, and we ate, sadness hanging over us like a thick pall.

Only Dominick seemed undisturbed, throwing his food to the floor with reckless abandon as his poor nurse tried to convince him to behave in a series of desperate whispers and gestures. I didn't have the heart to interfere. Papa would only remind me it was Dominick's palace anyway; he was welcome to adorn the rugs with steamed carrots as he liked.

Better to leave on good terms with everyone.

Sophia let her spoon clink into her bowl. "I still can't understand why you would want to step foot in Imperia again, Penelope. Won't it be dreadfully uncomfortable to see Rachel —that is, Leah—again?"

I kept forgetting Leah had been Sophia's lady's maid for a time under the pseudonym Rachel. A lady's maid no more— now a princess. Prince Raphael's wife.

According to our messengers, the marriage had taken place only a month before. I cringed. My trip would be perfectly timed to witness the peak of their wedded bliss.

I swallowed the bite of chowder in my mouth. Erma, our head cook, had taken the initiative to make a selection of her best dishes, but her efforts had been sadly wasted on me. Every mouthful tasted like powder and churned my stomach.

"Yes, I'm sure it will be most uncomfortable to see her once more."

"How vexed I was when she disappeared like that, with hardly a word, only to discover she'd fooled us all!" Sophia waved her goblet, threatening to spill its contents. "She had such a knack for embroidery, and my other lady's maids had become quite fond of her, you know."

How vexed I was to find she'd used her position as your lady's maid to snoop through my private chambers and find my letters from Nicholas.

Which she'd then apparently posted to Prince Raphael as evidence of Nicholas's plot to overthrow the Imperian royal family. Our engagement had ended temporarily, until Lord Lessox put Raphael, along with the king and queen, under a spell to force the marriage to go forward. If Leah hadn't recruited a group of mystics to overpower the sorcerer . . .

I couldn't think of her without my head swirling into a confusing mix of awe and resentment.

I focused on Sophia, swallowing a laugh at her look of consternation. "I confess I'm not looking forward to spending time with Leah—or any of them, in truth—but I do feel the visit is necessary. I had a hand in causing our alliance with Imperia to crumble, so it's only right I be the one to repair the damage."

Vivienne nodded solemnly. "You're very brave, Penelope."

Anxiety, uncertainty, trepidation—many emotions coursed through my veins, but bravery wasn't one of them. "Prince Raphael will be surprised, of course, but he isn't vindictive. I think he at least will be willing to see me."

"Prince Raphael." Sophia released a little sigh. "I've heard he and Leah are so deeply in love. A prince defying his parents' wishes to court a commoner. Such a romantic story."

I nearly choked on my bread. Romantic, indeed. If only I hadn't been cast as the villain.

"You must pass along my regards, of course." Papa speared a piece of buttered asparagus on his fork. "I do appreciate your efforts to salvage our trade agreement, no matter how thankless the task might be. The makings of a good diplomat." He nodded approvingly.

"Of course, Papa." I was so tired of political machinations, yet I was about to dive more deeply into the fray than ever.

"You know, he believes in you. We all do." Vivienne's soft

voice was barely audible over Nicky's victorious cry as he landed a dollop of potatoes on his nursemaid's apron.

I leaned closer to respond, letting Sophia distract Papa's attention with details surrounding her trip to Lower Flynn. "You're sweet, Vivienne. But I think he's mostly grateful he no longer has to ponder what's to be done with me."

"That's not true." She shook her head, lips pressed together in a stubborn frown. "All those things he said at the banquet—he meant every word. He wouldn't be sending you if he didn't."

My mouth sprang open to protest, but I let it die in my throat. I glanced to Papa, where he slid his upside-down fork over the tabletop, as though drawing a map.

Following his initial shock and disappointment at the nature of my return from Imperia, he'd loved and supported me throughout the past year, even as friends and acquaintances kept their distance. He'd stood a little straighter ever since he'd sprung the news of my betrothal on me, a posture of pride rather than defeat. Maybe she was right.

"Thank you." I released my fork so I could squeeze her hand. "I can't tell you how much that means to me."

She gave me a sad smile. "We will miss you very much, Pen."

I studied the girl at my side. Shy, smart, just on the brink of womanhood. Would I have the opportunity to see the person she'd become? Could letters alone convey such a momentous journey?

"I will miss you too. Immensely."

CHAPTER 4

*D*orendyn Castle loomed ahead, ever closer as the carriage bounced us forward. Ever since I'd bid my family farewell, my mind had assumed a trance-like state. My movements were automatic, my responses succinct.

None of this could truly be happening. And if it were, I wanted no part of it.

The castle's lighter exterior and large windows gave it a welcoming look, less regal and imposing than Glonsel Palace. No longer welcoming to me.

The invisible belt curling around my insides cinched another notch tighter. What was I going to say? I hadn't even written a note to give them warning of my coming. I'd intended to, but every time I sat at my desk, the blank page taunted me.

> *Dear King Frederick and Queen Beatrice,*
>
> *I know you'd prefer never to see me again, since I participated in the Duke of Brantley's plan to murder you. You have my sincerest thanks for not throwing me in the dungeon. But I'd like to discuss our proposed trade agreement and hoped you might extend your hospitality for my last two days on the continent of Sandrin before I depart for Delunia for yet another engagement.*

Hopefully (and regretfully) yours,
Princess Penelope

I mentally crumpled the imagined missive and shrank back into my seat. What had I been thinking? I couldn't face them after everything that'd happened. If the glares and disdain had been uncomfortable in Trellich, here they'd be overpowering. Would they spare me from the dungeon a second time?

But Nicholas was in there, somewhere. Could I draw so close without attempting to see him?

Hope still lingered, frail but palpable. If I faced this place again, would the dark shadow that had enveloped my life over the past year finally lift?

Victoria had given up trying to converse with me by our third day on the road. She leaned forward, eagerly taking in the sights and sounds surrounding the Imperian royal palace. So like our last journey to Imperia, when I'd hoped to be spotted by passersby who might admire the beauty and elegance of their prince's betrothed.

Now I trembled each time our carriage caught someone's eye. Would anyone recognize me? If so, would they merely sneer? Or perhaps alert a guard, or even throw something?

I pulled the hood of my cloak farther over my face.

"Here we are, m'lady."

Marcus, one of the guards who would accompany us to Delunia before returning to Glonsel Palace, held open the carriage door. Our other guard, Edmund, had traveled ahead to the seaport with the majority of our luggage.

I blinked at the hand Marcus extended. "Oh. Thank you."

My feet alighted on the ground. We'd stopped just in front of the main entrance, in plain view of rows of windows on every floor. Had I reached the point at which I couldn't turn back? Or could I hop back into the carriage and . . .

"Welcome to Dorendyn Castle." A heavyset woman bustled forward, her graying hair subdued into a knot at the nape of her neck. The head housekeeper—Clara. "I had no knowledge we were expecting guests, but you're clearly here to see—" Her words came to an abrupt stop as she caught a glimpse of my face from under my hood. "Princess Penelope."

"It was very rude of me to give no notice of my visit, I apologize. But I'd so appreciate if you could let the royal family know of my arrival and my wish to speak with them when convenient."

The straightforward request and calm poise of my tone took me by surprise. On the inside, I shook with the trepidation of a child about to face a scolding.

Her jaw shifted, her eyes unfocused as if looking within. At last, she folded her hands. "Of course, princess. If you would follow me."

I did as she asked, docile as a lamb being led to a lion's den.

"Princess Penelope?" Footsteps sounded behind me in the small room off the entrance hall where I'd been deposited to await a welcome from my hosts. Or a dismissal.

"Leah." One look at her lace-trimmed gown brought it all rushing back. I squared my jaw. "That is—"

"I still prefer just Leah." Cheeks tinted pink, she dipped into a stiff curtsy. "It is you . . . I thought perhaps Clara was mistaken. We heard nothing of your arrival. I fear we haven't prepared . . ."

"No. It was a decision with little preparation. I understand if you can't accommodate me."

Of course they *could* accommodate me. Whether they'd be willing to was a far different question.

Leah—Princess Leah—attempted a smile. "I hope you've been well?"

"Yes, I thank you."

I took a moment to study my former lady's maid. Pretty in

her finery, but ill at ease. As though the clothing fit her physical form, but her presence couldn't quite fill it.

I thought back to my time at Dorendyn Castle. Leah had appeared quiet and well-mannered before she'd had the gall to spy on me—tracking me to a private interview with Nicholas and reading my correspondence.

I winced. The analysis wasn't entirely fair. Her spying had been a matter of life or death, not mere pettiness or curiosity.

She regarded me with pursed lips, her eyes wide with uncertainty.

Of all the people to be greeted by first. I swallowed. "I trust you've also been well?"

"Oh, yes. There's been much to learn, of course, but Queen Beatrice has provided many tutors. Our wedding was lovely, and Rafe . . ." She looked at the floor, her voice trailing off. "What—what brings you to Imperia?"

I loosened the ties of my cloak, overcome by sudden warmth. "I am to marry—"

She raised her brows.

"—a Delunian prince."

Leah's mouth opened and closed. "I see. Congratulations. I wish you joy in your marriage and new life."

"Thank you. And I offer my congratulations to you and Raphael as well." My words sounded as much like condolences as hers. "Before I journey overseas, I thought I might . . ."

The door behind us opened. Prince Raphael's gaze landed on Leah first, taking on a warmth it'd never held for me.

She darted toward him. "There you are! I asked Clara to send someone to fetch you, but I wasn't sure where you'd gone after tea."

He took her hand in both of his. "My apologies. I should know better than to sneak off to the stables without telling anyone." He straightened his surcoat. "Now, what could've produced such an urgent summons?" His eyes collided with mine. "Penelope—"

Seeing a ghost couldn't have produced a more sickly pallor. "I must apologize." For so much.

The king and queen of Imperia had perhaps deserved an attempted overthrow—haughty, self-important, and determined to keep their servants uneducated and subdued—but Raphael had always treated me with respect and consideration, albeit without any desire to become my husband.

I coughed into my handkerchief. "That is, I never should've presumed to stop in unannounced."

The shock left his face, replaced with practiced chivalry. "Guests are always welcome. It's been too long since we've had any contact with your family. Knowing Clara, she already has a room prepared. I fear my parents are away at present, but we expect them back later this afternoon. Upon their return, I shall request an audience on your behalf."

"That's very kind, thank you."

His grim expression confirmed he knew as well as I that arranging an opportunity to face King Frederick and Queen Beatrice was hardly a kindness. But I'd made it this far.

I had to at least attempt to complete my mission.

The guard nearest me cleared his throat. "Their Majesties, King Frederick, Queen Beatrice, Prince Raphael, and Princess Leah, are ready to see you now."

I nodded. As Raphael had predicted, Clara had wasted no time preparing a guest chamber for me. I'd spent the past two hours soaking in a bath, being fussed over by Victoria, and pacing until I'd likely worn a stripe into the thick woolen rug.

The summons had come both agonizingly late and far too soon.

In unison, the guards hauled open heavy doors to the throne room, and one announced, "Princess Penelope of Trellich."

As though one of the most infamous personages in the country needed an official introduction.

The temperature in the room seemed to dip, as though I'd traveled to the northernmost tip of Trellich instead of south to Imperia. I approached the dais and lowered into a curtsy before raising my head.

How strange to be a lowly supplicant, when once I'd sat in the very throne now occupied by Leah.

"Good afternoon, Your Majesties. I'm grateful you've taken the time to see me. My father and sisters send their regards, and—"

"To what to we owe the pleasure of your visit, Penelope?" The queen's stony gaze left no question whether she found any true pleasure in my presence.

My jaw clamped so quickly I nearly bit my tongue. If we were glossing over any pretense of civility, I might as well get to the point. "I set out for Delunia in a few days. You may have heard of my betrothal to their prince."

My pulse sent a rushing stream of blood to my head. Why had I thought this was a good idea? Discussing my new engagement with the family who'd hoped to wed me to their own son . . .

The queen's tone was stiff. "Indeed. We send our best wishes along with you. One can only hope this marriage will better suit your tastes."

My confirmed suspicions pricked my chest like pins. They'd refused to sign the trade agreement out of spite.

Aimed directly at me.

Raphael darted a glare at his mother before offering a sympathetic smile. Dear Raphael. I'd never relished the thought of marrying him, but he'd been a true friend and ally. Chivalrous to his core.

I doubted I'd be so fortunate a second time.

Keeping my gaze fixed on the prince, I forced my voice out once more. "Before I set out, I wanted to return to Imperia to personally appeal for the beneficial nature of the trade agreement devised by my father and your emissaries. I feared perhaps the unfortunate misunderstanding between us last year caused you to view the proposal in a less favorable light."

"Misunderstanding?" Queen Beatrice's shrill register could've caused dogs to howl.

I held my breath for three heartbeats. *Be humble, Penelope. For Papa. For Trellich.* "Of my own creation, I fully concede. I know my father has issued a formal apology from the Trellan royal family for my conduct, but I'd like to add my own regrets. I should've never agreed to the Duke of Brantley's plan . . . I should've warned you of his intentions—I made many grievous mistakes, all while a guest in your home." Pressing my lips together, I lowered my head. "I'm very sorry."

The king shifted his feet. "Quite gracious of you, I'm sure."

Queen Beatrice flicked her fan open and strode down the dais steps. "If that is all, I'm afraid we're late for a meeting with King Frederick's council."

"Would there be a better time to further discuss the trade agreement?" She couldn't get rid of me that easily. "I can provide a breakdown of the estimates provided in the original proposal, along with—"

"We shall take it under advisement, but I can promise nothing." She arched a silver brow. "Your input, however, will not be necessary."

A physical blow would've been less painful. I curled my toes in my slippers, forcing my posture to remain upright. "I understand. Thank you for your time. I wouldn't want to cause further interruption to your day."

Leah stepped forward, her expression in equal parts determined and skittish. "But of course you'll stay the night, and you must join us for dinner."

The queen hissed out a breath as she turned Leah's direction but offered no contradiction. Leah must've earned more respect from her than I'd guessed.

"We shall see you then." She swept out of the room, King Frederick in tow.

Raphael watched them go, then moved to Leah's side and took her hand. Some unspoken communication seemed to pass between them before they descended from the dais.

"I must apologize for my parents' behavior. The near uprising has taken a toll on them, and they still haven't—" Raphael's boot squeaked on the marble floor.

"You have nothing to apologize for." I reached out to touch his arm but let my hand drop. To the extent I ever held any claim over him, it was gone. "I should be grateful they were willing to see me at all. But if you'd consider pleading the cause of the trade agreement with them, I truly think . . ."

"Certainly. I have no quarrel with Trellich."

Perhaps I haven't entirely failed, after all. "Papa will be relieved to have one Imperian ally, at least."

Discomfort dampened his attempt at a reassuring smile. "More than you might think."

Leah fingered the emerald pendant resting at her throat. "I do hope you'll stay for as many nights as you like. You may find them more welcoming over time, in a less formal environment."

My fist clenched in the folds of my skirt. The former servant—my lady's maid—who'd gained my confidence only to betray me, now regarded me with pity, reveling in her elevated station. How the little traitor must be enjoying . . .

I swallowed, pinching my eyes shut. She wasn't the only traitor in Dorendyn Castle.

"Thank you." The words squeezed from my lips as though through a vice, but they left a strange lightness in their wake.

Leah blinked. "You're very welcome."

"Not just for the invitation to dinner."

She took a step back, her eyes wide. "Oh, I . . ."

Raphael curled a protective arm around her waist.

"I wish things had gone differently, I confess, but if not for you —"

Images of the prone, lifeless bodies of Queen Beatrice, King Frederick, and Raphael forced themselves into my mind's eye.

The lump in my throat constricted my voice to a whisper. "I never wanted them dead, and if our plans had reached fruition, I'm not sure I could've lived with myself."

Leah squeezed my wrist, a sheen highlighting the green in her eyes. "I hope you know I never meant you any harm. If there'd been another way . . ." She dropped her hand. "Well, we wish you the best in your new adventure."

"Truly." Raphael's gaze held only a fraction of the brilliance he reserved for his wife. "Though it may be slower coming from my parents, know that in our eyes you are forgiven. We hope you find what you're looking for in your upcoming marriage."

Blinking back tears, I dipped into a curtsy and made a hasty retreat.

I hoped I found that too.

~

I shifted in my seat. The dining hall of Dorendyn Castle brought back so many memories. Forced conversation with Raphael and his parents. Stealing glances at Nicholas as he duped King Frederick into trusting his counsel.

My eyes were still tempted to roam the table, hoping he might be in attendance. I shook my head. Nicholas was in the dungeon, floors below. Could he sense I was near?

Pushing a small stack of boiled carrots around my plate, I glanced up. Mercifully, the king and queen had seated me as far from themselves as possible. Leah sat across the table, animatedly talking with a lively dark-haired woman they'd introduced as Sister Eleanor.

To my left, an older woman called Sister Rochelle wore a matching black dress and headpiece.

Leah's gown was a deep crimson, catching dark highlights in her red hair. Her arm movements seemed stilted, as though her corset laces were drawn too tight.

I suppressed a smile. Compared with what she'd worn her entire life until the past year, she must've felt like she was drowning in the heavy layers of fabric.

She met my gaze. "Here we seated you next to Sister Rochelle but didn't think to tell you the news. Sister Rochelle is traveling to Delunia as well, and we believe the two of you will be aboard the same ship."

My fork dropped from my fingers, clinking to the floor. They were sending a spy? "That certainly is news."

I ducked beneath the table to retrieve my fork, my palms tingling with sweat. How long did they plan to keep an eye on me? Until my marriage? Or for the rest of my life?

I took a slow sip of wine before turning to Sister Rochelle. "I understand you sisters tend to live a quiet, secluded life. What brings you to Delunia?"

Perhaps if I sniffed out their scheme right away, they'd change their minds.

Her motherly smile made my chest constrict. "How kind of you to ask. I've lived at our manor almost my entire life. The mountainside is a beautiful, peaceful setting, and I've been so blessed to maintain my childhood home for so many fellow nuns. But my travels with Leah made me a bit restless. There's so much of the world I haven't seen, and my influence only stretches so far in seclusion."

Sister Eleanor patted her lips with a napkin. "Knowing Sister Val and your Mabel, no doubt everyone will stay organized and well cared for. But I'm certain you'll be greatly missed."

"Thank you. Lately I've felt a great call from the Luminate to embrace work as a missionary." Sister Rochelle folded her hands in her lap, looking every bit the devoted nun. "He is not well known among Delunians, and many of their regions are poverty stricken. In time I may even start a school."

"How very noble. I hope your endeavors meet with success." *And keep you busy enough not to meddle with my affairs.*

I bit my lip. Perhaps it truly was coincidence she and I happened to be traveling at the same time to the same destination.

Even so, I preferred to keep my distance from anyone so connected with the Imperian royal family.

CHAPTER 5

*S*ister Eleanor seemed immune to the unease among our breakfast companions. The animated woman's headpiece swayed around her like a living thing as she spoke. "I confess I'm quite envious of you and Sister Rochelle, getting to see a whole new corner of the world."

"There will be some interesting sights, I'm sure." I bit into a sausage wrapped in breading, one of the Imperian foods I would miss most. "But in many ways I would've preferred to stay home."

It was disconcerting, the way her open gaze coaxed me to share my honest thoughts.

"Change is certainly never easy. But it is in those unsettled times in our lives when the Luminate can show up in the most surprising ways."

I held back a scoff. No doubt the Luminate would make plenty of future appearances in the lives of Sister Rochelle and Sister Eleanor. Even upstanding Leah and Raphael. But I could only assume He, along with the rest of Sandrin, couldn't wait until I sailed as far away as possible.

She apparently took my silence as encouragement to continue. "Of course you needn't be a nun or mystic to share the Luminate among the Delunian people. Sister Rochelle will be doing admirable work, but in such a large country, she can only do so much. *You* will be their future empress."

"I—" Was she poking fun at me? Her expression offered nothing but fervor and sincerity. "I'm not sure I'd be the most qualified person to instruct on such a subject."

"Not instruct, my dear." She laughed as though I'd told a joke. "Demonstrate. Introduce others to Him by the faithful way you live your life."

Many mystics lived in seclusion, but surely one who served as an adviser to the royal family was aware no one would hold *my* life as an example of faithfulness. Enlightening in its failures, perhaps, but not its virtues.

I took a long sip of water. "I shall give it some thought."

"I hope you do. A people who have lost sight of their creator cannot help but fall into despair."

I nodded, my jaw clenched tight. To imagine I could preach about the Luminate in either word or deed was nothing short of ludicrous.

I scraped the last bite from my plate, a question revolving through my mind: Why had I bothered to come here? Merely to subject myself to the king and queen's snubs, Leah and Raphael's excessive adoration for one another, and the mystics' sermons about the Luminate?

I needed to escape. Rising, I set my napkin on the table. "Please, excuse me."

I directed my curtsy toward King Frederick, who dismissed me with a terse nod.

Leah caught me before I reached the door. The way Raphael's gaze followed her was almost comical. How had I never noticed when she was my lady's maid?

"I can't help but feel our hospitality has been sorely lacking."

I suppressed a snide retort. "Not at all. The meals have been delicious, and you've been very kind to accommodate me on such short notice. I don't hold you responsible for who does —or doesn't—choose to speak with me."

I gave the slightest tilt of my head in the direction of the king and queen, who had barely acknowledged my presence since our audience the day before.

Leah tugged at her beaded collar. "Would you be interested in an outing of some sort? A horseback ride, perhaps, or —?"

"No, thank you. I . . ." My rote refusal trailed off. Could I pose my true request?

The king and queen certainly had no interest in helping me, and perhaps it'd be better to ask Leah than Raphael.

"Actually, there is something." I lowered my voice. "This will likely strike you as odd, but I hoped I might be allowed to spend a little time in your dungeon. That is, if Nicholas is still housed there."

They wouldn't have executed him . . . would they?

Her narrowed eyes widened. "Ah. I see. I believe he is still there, though I'm not sure whether . . ." She darted a glance at the table. "Come with me." Gripping my arm, she pulled me out the door and down the hall.

The idea of Leah acting as a spy suddenly didn't seem quite so absurd.

We arrived at the top of a stone staircase flanked by guards. Releasing my arm, Leah approached the guard on the right and held a whispered conversation.

He frowned as she spoke but nodded, giving me a wary appraisal. "This way, princess."

I shuffled to his side.

Leah leaned close before I descended the first step. "I'll give you some privacy, but you can find me here when you've finished your visit."

"Thank you."

Dizziness made my head swim, my lungs unable to take in enough air. I was about to see Nicholas again, after a year apart. In a dungeon.

I shuddered against the cold air and dank smell as we reached the bottom of the stairs. They expected people to survive in such squalor? I exhaled through my nose. I'd never visited the dungeons at Glonsel Palace; they likely didn't boast any improvement.

The bars blurred in my vision as we passed cell after cell. I kept my gaze firmly planted on the dusty ground beneath my feet, having no desire to make eye contact with any of the criminals within. My heart stuttered amid its frantic pace.

I could've easily been locked up right beside them.

Chills ran down my spine, and I quickened my pace to catch up with the guard. The stench grew worse the farther we walked, until I choked on every lungful of air. A snort sounded as I removed my handkerchief and held it over my nose.

The guard slapped his stick against the nearest bar, filling the confined space with a reverberating clang. I set my jaw against the urge to gasp—best not to provoke further reactions from the inmates.

The guard stopped so abruptly, I nearly crashed into him. "Here he is. Nicholas Alberle."

Nicholas Alberle. Said with a sneer, implying a man of the lowest caliber, the scum of the earth.

My first inclination was to shout at the impudent man. A lowly guard didn't have the right to even speak the name of one so superior to him—a highly respected duke of Imperia— let alone with condescension.

But Nicholas was a duke no more. And certainly not respected. The change in circumstances tore through my chest as though I'd been struck by lightning from within. I was in a dungeon to visit the man I loved, the man I'd planned to marry.

Bile rose in my throat, and I almost begged the guard to take me out of the vile place.

Then he was there, pressed against the bars. "Pen, is that you?"

I swallowed and turned. "Yes, Nicholas. I'm here."

His hair had grown past his ears and hung in greasy clumps. An unkempt beard and mustache gave him the wild look of a woodsman, and tan baggy clothing hung from his wasted frame.

I willed my expression to stay steady, not to betray the revulsion vying for prominence against the pity his situation aroused. How differently things would've turned out if only I'd convinced him to give up his treasonous schemes.

He attempted one of his winning smiles, his eyes lit with confidence. "At last, the sight I've longed for all these months. I knew you'd come for me, darling."

I shifted, my shoes crunching against the dirt. "I'm so sorry it had to end like this. It pains me to see you in such terrible conditions, but I'm afraid I've only come to say goodbye —"

"End? Goodbye?" He quirked a brow, as though I were flirting with him. "Certainly not, Penelope. I know you wouldn't abandon me after all we've been through together."

Abandon him? My mind struggled to piece together my expectations for this visit versus the bizarre reality. I'd anticipated contrition, sorrow. Despondence, even. Hardly a plea for my continued affection.

"Have they set a date for your release?"

His chuckle held a dry edge. "From what I can tell, they don't intend to. Pleading my cause has hardly been effective, as you can well imagine."

With a glance at the hovering guard, he motioned me closer and dropped his voice to a whisper.

"But now that you're here, you may advocate on my behalf. Unleash your irresistible charms and the allure of those dark eyes on that prince you became so fond of and see what you can negotiate." The curl of his lips had a seductive tilt.

I stepped back. Was that how he saw me? As a conniving coquette who used her beauty to manipulate everyone around her?

"Prince Raphael is married to Princess Leah, whom he adores. If my so-called allure ever had any effect on him, I highly doubt it would now."

He scoffed. "I've seen this Leah, and she's nothing to you. In love or not, Raphael is a man, after all. And if you do fail to attract him, you can always draw on your friendship. The alliance you still hope to foster between our fine countries."

"But what could I possibly assert on your behalf? You planned to kill them and take the throne. What reason could they have to trust you?"

"Ah, Pen. Always playing the innocent. Recall that you, too, were in league with our little plot. The only reason I didn't argue for your own incarceration was I assumed you'd be of more use to me from the outside." He crossed his arms, leaning lazily against the bars. "Besides, every royal family has some history of murder and treason. Danger comes with the territory of having so much power."

I stared at him, my mouth agape. *This* was the man I'd been enamored with? So much so that I'd risked everything for his selfish ambitions? A man who flippantly considered murderous plots to be something every royal family should expect to contend with. Who was only glad I hadn't been imprisoned because I might be useful to him?

The butterfly that'd flitted about my chest ever since I'd dreamed up the idea to travel to Imperia stilled. Curled into itself, as though to hide within its cocoon.

"You know that's not fair." I lowered my voice, eyeing the guard who fiddled with his keys, pretending not to listen to every word we said. "I never had any desire to kill the Imperian royal family. That was entirely your idea, not mine."

Nicholas raised his palms in an appeasing gesture. "Penelope, my dear." His expression melted into one of contrition and longing. "I apologize so much time in this revolting dungeon has made me coarse. I could never wish such a fate upon my bright, flawless flower. Please, dearest."

He extended his fingers through the bars. Reluctantly, I inched forward and enclosed them in my hand.

"I'm simply desperate to be with you once more. To once again dream of a future together." He stroked my thumb, his tone wheedling.

Could a future with Nicholas still be possible if his release could be negotiated? He had nowhere to go, as his dukedom and property had been bestowed upon another. He might return with me to Trellich . . . *no*.

Papa arranged my marriage to the Delunian prince. I wouldn't let him down a second time.

Extracting my fingers, I shook my head. "I'm sorry, Nicholas. That future no longer exists."

"But—"

"Please, let me speak." I squared my shoulders. "I will consider putting in a good word for you with the Imperian royal family. But even if you gain your freedom, a marriage would not be possible. My father has secured Trellich's alliance with Delunia by arranging my betrothal to the emperor's son, and I depart in two days."

"Delunia?" He looked more offended than heartbroken. "Surely you can find a better match than with one of those savages."

I choked back a laugh. Filthy and locked in a prison, he still held his characteristic disdain for nearly all other men. An unexpected impulse to defend my future husband rose with my anger.

"It may not be what I would've wished for, but I'm sure they'll treat me well. Regardless of how I feel about Delunia, I've brought enough shame upon my family and will not repeat that mistake."

He snickered. "Ah, poor Penelope. Gone are your days of fun and intrigue. I see that now. So dutiful and honor bound. Well, enjoy your life of dull obligations at the side of a husband who doesn't hold your interest. Perhaps another young lady might be persuaded to do more for my cause."

Rage turned my vision red. How dare he? I spluttered a moment before setting my jaw. He didn't deserve my pity or my anger. "Goodbye, Nicholas. Enjoy your lodgings—I expect they'll be your home for a long time to come."

I stormed back down the hall, barely registering the guard's footsteps as they caught up with mine.

He wasn't even bothered I was going to marry another man? Only that I wasn't going to help him regain his position in society. *Another lady* might be persuaded . . .

My teeth clenched so hard they grated together. Despite all his vows of fidelity, my suspicions had been justified after all. The joy and sorrow I'd amassed as I prepared for our reunion disintegrated into ash, clogging my chest.

The man I'd loved was foul, vicious. How had I never seen it before?

I scoured my memories for evidence of goodness, kindness. Some indication his nature was more than he'd revealed in this encounter. But I found only flirtation, warm looks, stolen kisses. Nothing of substance.

What a fool I'd been to risk everything for such an undeserving scoundrel. Never again.

A low moan jolted me from my dark musings. I turned toward the sound. The man within the nearest cell arched his back in agony, his cry louder this time.

Even as I flinched, I drew closer.

The guard drew up beside me. "Careful of that one, miss. He can turn violent."

"Who—who is he?"

"Why, that's Lord Damien Lessox. Famous sorcerer."

Lord Lessox. Our "comrade in the north" as Nicholas had referred to him. Now he convulsed, gripping his hair.

I couldn't stop staring. "What's the matter with him?"

The guard shook his head. "Stark raving mad. Almost sad,

really. But just what he should've expected, getting so entrenched with dark magic."

Lord Lessox wrapped himself into a ball, muttering frantically. With an effort, I pried my gaze away and walked forward. My legs quaked, thankfully hidden under the folds of my skirt.

I'd been allied with that man. Allowed his dark magic to touch the Imperian royal family. How much further would it have spread if our plan had succeeded?

My feet trailed the guard's in stilted motions. Right foot forward. Pause. Left foot forward. Pause. Again and again until we emerged into the bright corridor.

Leah stood to the side, conversing with a pretty maid. Upon seeing me, the maid dipped a brief curtsy and waved farewell to Leah, who gave her a broad smile.

"That was Olive, one of our kitchen maids. She's just become engaged to a stable hand who—" Leah's brows lowered as she studied my face. "I'm so sorry, prattling on when you've just been . . . was it so bad?"

"I don't know what I expected, but"—I licked my lips, gritting my teeth against the urge to cry—"he is not the person I remember."

Sympathy shone in her eyes. "It must've been hard to see him like that. A walk in the gardens might help, or I could have the servants draw you a bath."

"No." I shook my head. "You've been very kind. Much more so than I deserve. But there's nothing left for me here. I must find Victoria and Marcus and have them gather our things."

A line creased her forehead. "Are you sure? We'd be happy to—"

"Thank you—for everything. But yes, I'm sure."

I couldn't leave this all behind soon enough.

CHAPTER 6

The *Ismena* stood tall, dwarfing the surrounding rafts and fishing boats. Stately masts pointed to the sky like long, thin fingers. Round windows dotted the planks just beneath the deck at regular intervals, reminiscent of an enormous necklace.

Conscious of Victoria at my side, I straightened my shoulders. Just because crossing the sea was a new, dangerous venture didn't mean I had to face it like a coward.

Victoria and Marcus had accepted our sudden departure from Dorendyn Castle and the resulting stay in a village inn without complaint. Now our carriage hurtled us toward Torquil Harbor.

I blinked into the mist hovering in the air, my head filled with the tangy scent of saltwater. The ocean sparkled in endless blue, waves lapping at the sand and jumping over each other like a playful litter of kittens.

Nothing to be intimidated by. As long as we met with no storms, the hold didn't spring a leak, the wind didn't topple the ship like one of Nicky's toy soldiers . . .

The carriage halted, and I clutched my skirt to steady myself.

"Here we are, m'lady." The gleam in Victoria's eyes only increased when Marcus extended his hand to help her down.

I hoped my hand didn't shake too badly in my own descent from the carriage.

Following a quick bow, Marcus hoisted a trunk and set off toward the ship. How did he know where to go? I glanced around the bustle of activity on the dock. Everyone seemed to have a direction, a purpose. Even Victoria helped our driver arrange a stack of valises and hatboxes.

Only I stood frozen, uncertain of my purpose. My future course.

Above, sailors unfurled one of the *Ismena's* white sails. It billowed in the wind, as though impatient with the necessity of waiting for boarding passengers. If only the ship would break ties with its anchor and drift out to sea without me aboard.

But what was left for me here? Sidelong glances, whispered asides, and . . .

"M'lady?" Victoria touched my arm, pulling me from my reverie.

"Ah, Victoria. Is the luggage all settled?" Hopefully, I sounded more confident than I felt.

"Yes, m'lady. Marcus has located Edmund, and they're makin' sure it's all delivered safely. But they want us to be among the first to board, that we might get settled in our quarters before departure."

"Of course."

Suddenly, the dirt beneath my feet seemed precious, invaluable. Once I'd boarded the *Ismena*, how long would it be before I stepped on solid ground again?

∿

The ship rocked back and forth, my stomach lurching along with it. I fought to steady my breathing, but my nose wrinkled at the cabin's stale air.

Across the cabin, Victoria snored softly. How she could be so at ease with every change, every disruption, every form of travel, I'd never know.

Each creak and groan of the surrounding timber made me twitch. So little separated us from the fathomless ocean below. So much could go wrong so quickly.

Sighing, I sat up and edged out of my hard cot. This was only my first night at sea. How would I survive an entire week?

I stumbled to the small circular window. Outside, tiny pinpricks of light dotted the night sky. Perhaps some fresh air would clear my head.

Turning the door handle as quietly as I could, I peeked out. Edmund paced away from me to the end of the small corridor. Easing the door closed behind me, I tiptoed in the opposite direction and dashed up the stairs. At least the constant sounds that made it impossible to sleep made it easier to slink about.

At the top, I gulped fresh air. The salt irritated my nostrils but felt strangely refreshing. The deck looked different at night. In the pitch dark, with only an occasional sailor manning a mast or wheel, one could almost imagine the *Ismena* was occupied by ghosts rather than people.

Shivering, I pulled my shawl closer around my shoulders. I made my way to the edge, clutching the rail when a gust of wind broke the ship's steady rocking motion. The sky's inky blackness stretched in every direction, its brilliant stars mirrored in the murky water. The giant ship seemed so small all of a sudden. And myself that much smaller. Perhaps—

"Could that be Princess Penelope? What an honor to have you aboard our ship." The sailor sauntering toward me smiled, but something in his tone sped my pulse.

My fingers tightened around the cold moist rail. "Thank you. I needed a breath of fresh air, but I think now I'll—"

"You only just got here." He closed the remaining gap

between us. "You looked so lonely, I thought p'raps you were hopin' for a companion." The arch of his brows gave the comment a suggestive air.

"Certainly not. In fact, I prefer solitude." Better to discourage his impertinence from the start.

He scratched his chin. "That's not what I've heard."

I inhaled an indignant gasp. "Please bear in mind whom you are addressing, sir. Your princess has no wish to be accosted with idle gossip."

"Everybody knows your story, princess." He spit the title with such venom, it sounded like a curse. "Isn't just gossip."

"I shall retire to my cabin." I reluctantly released the rail, hoping he couldn't see the way my hands shook. "One more word from you, and I'll make sure you're reported to my father."

He grasped my arm. "I'm afraid your father's gettin' farther away every moment. Besides, I thought you liked men with a rebellious side."

Had I truly stooped low enough to be an object of ridicule across the entire continent of Sandrin? Among common sailors? I tried to pull away, stumbling on unsteady legs.

"You'll be hanged for treason if—"

"What's going on here?" In that moment, the gruff baritone was the most beautiful sound imaginable.

The sailor sneered at the newcomer. "Just makin' the princess here feel welcome."

"Princess Penelope?" The lean gray-haired man peered into my face, then hastily bowed. His expression sharpened as he turned to the sailor. "Your attentions were clearly far from welcome. Depart at once before I alert your captain."

The sailor stormed off, grumbling under his breath.

"Are you all right, Your Highness?"

I raised my head, which had drooped to my chest upon the sailor's departure. "Yes, I . . . I'm fine now. Thank you."

My rescuer clicked his tongue. "Incredible what they think they can get away with on the open water. Such insolence."

"I'm afraid those weren't the first insults thrown my way of late." My jaw clenched shut. I'd meant to keep the thought to myself.

His fingers curled into a fist. "They shall be the last if I have anything to do with it, at least on this voyage."

I'd almost forgotten what it felt like to have someone outside my family take my side. "You are very kind, Mr. . . ."

"My apologies, my lady. Sir Colin Headrick, at your service." He swept into a dramatic bow.

I bobbed a curtsy. "It's a pleasure to meet you. Despite the circumstances."

"The pleasure is all mine, princess." His gaze held respect, none of the flirtation or flattery that would've accompanied such a statement from Nicholas. "I'd heard a member of the royal family would be taking part in our voyage, though I didn't put much stock in it until now. But have you no guards? Surely you must have some kind of protection against ruffians like the man who just accosted you?"

Hopefully, the dark masked the heat rising to my cheeks. "I slipped past him. I merely wanted some fresh air and a quiet place to settle my thoughts—it hadn't occurred to me there'd be any danger in such a short venture."

"For a young lady, I'm afraid danger can be anywhere."

I crossed my arms over my chest, overtaken by a sudden chill. "So it would seem."

"Please, allow me to escort you to your cabin. I won't be able to rest until I'm certain you're safe for the night."

My heart warmed to this fatherly man, whose gallantry stood out all the more in comparison to the rough sailor. "Thank you, I would appreciate that." My steps faltered. "Although, my guard will likely be cross with me . . ."

His chuckle reminded me so much of Papa. "You'd prefer I distract your guard so you may re-enter your cabin in peace?"

The surge of giddiness made me feel like a delinquent pupil. "Would you?"

"It is my honor to save you from any threat, Your Highness. Both hostile and well-meaning."

My shoulders sagged in relief. "I owe you a great debt, Sir Colin."

"Think nothing of it."

～

Raising my face to the sun, I closed my eyes and let myself forget for a moment that I was in the middle of nowhere, heading toward an uncertain future. With Sir Colin's help, I'd managed to sneak into my cabin the night before, unnoticed by Edmund.

A smile ghosted across my lips. What a comfort, to know someone other than my paid guards still thought me deserving of chivalry. Worthy of protection.

Footsteps slapped the damp boards on deck. I opened my eyes and continued walking. I'd scrutinized every sailor I'd passed on my morning stroll but fortunately had yet to encounter the scoundrel who'd threatened me.

"May I accompany you?" Sir Colin's voice was every bit as open and gallant as at our first meeting.

I turned, offering a bright smile. "Good morning, Sir Colin. How good to see you again."

He bowed, eyes crinkling with good humor. "Ah, you do remember. I'd half wondered if you were sleepwalking last night or merely an apparition."

"Unfortunately, the events of last evening were very real." A shadow dampened my high spirits. "I recall every detail."

He nodded. "I'm grateful I arrived before any further damage was done."

"As am I." I lightly placed a hand on his offered arm.

"Come to think of it, what were you doing out so late? That is, if you don't mind sharing."

"I don't mind at all." He strolled on, apparently unperturbed by the direct question. "I too was having trouble sleeping. The curse of old age, you know—utter weariness combined with a complete inability to repose comfortably. And there's something about the stars, especially at sea." He raised his free hand, indicating the sky. "Their vastness, their sheer numbers. It makes our own existences, our own problems, so much less consequential somehow."

"I know what you mean."

We continued on in silence. Large white clouds drifted above, their pace nearly as leisurely as ours. My lungs expanded, some of the freest breaths I'd taken since leaving Glonsel Palace.

"I confess, I'm surprised to see you traveling alone, princess." Sir Colin tilted his head.

I blinked, dragging my mind from its tranquil haze. "Not entirely alone. My lady's maid accompanied me, and of course my guards." We shared a conspiratorial grin.

"But no family?"

The wound in my heart reopened, as though a bandage had been torn off. No family, indeed. "It would be a long, tedious journey for my sisters, only for them to turn around and return home. And my father has much to occupy him at present and would not wish to separate from young Dominick."

He gave a curt nod. "Of course. Perhaps it is best—think what a target the ship would be with the entire royal family aboard."

Yes, at least they were safe. A gull called above us before swooping toward the water.

"Have you ever been to Delunia?"

He raised his brows. "Oh yes, Delunia is as much home to me as Trellich."

"Truly?" My heart lifted a notch. "You enjoy it there, then?"

"You might say it's grown on me. I've studied their language and culture for over half my life. The Delunian people are hardy; they have a certain pride about them. Distinctions of rank don't seem to hold such importance. The royal family keeps their distance"—he gave me a sideways glance—"but others aren't so concerned. Something about the heat and humidity, I think. When you all sweat together, it creates a certain bond."

I giggled but squirmed beneath my dress's thick layers of fabric. Could I adjust to such a climate?

"But you've been there yourself, have you not?" he inquired.

"Not since my childhood. My memories are few, and very hazy."

"I see." He inclined his head to a gentleman dressed in a loose-fitting tunic and trousers walking the deck in the opposite direction. "An interesting choice for a marriage alliance, if I may say so. Such a distance from home."

I squinted into the brilliant sunlight. "I believe the distance was a primary advantage, in my father's opinion."

"Ah." He gave my hand a quick pat. "Do remember, princess, that you're hardly the first noblewoman to fall in love with someone other than the partner selected by her parents."

I'd known him but minutes, and already Sir Colin's understanding and lack of judgment soothed my injuries like a balm. "True, though not all such loves are so intent upon murder and treason."

His hearty chuckle made my step falter. "I'll not argue on that point, but there is something to be admired about a man with ambition."

Nicolas's sly grin—so out of place in his sunken, filthy cheeks—entered my mind's eye. Nothing was admirable about that man in the least. I barely contained a shudder.

"Your husband-to-be seems a decent sort. A bit of the arrogance of his parents, perhaps." One side of his mouth quirked up. "But there's nothing like being in the presence of a beautiful young woman to give a man some humility."

I winced. Arrogance was an unwelcome trait, but one I'd certainly dealt with before.

The shield I was building against my fiancé grew another layer thicker.

CHAPTER 7

I eyed the gray clouds obscuring the sun like the thickest of draperies. *Please, Luminate, don't let it rain again.* My throat tightened. *For everyone else's sake, if not mine.*

We'd been stuck in our cabin for the past two days with rain pummeling our tiny window like a thief determined to lay hold of his quarry. Conversation, books, and endless games of spades soon grew tedious in such a confined space. By the prior afternoon, even cheerful Victoria had been set on edge.

I planted myself on a bench, daring the sky to force me indoors. After today, this dreadful journey would be half over.

"A welcome reprieve from the rain, is it not?"

I started at the gentle voice. "Sister Rochelle."

In my disquiet following my visit with Nicholas, I'd almost forgotten she too would be aboard the *Ismena*. If she'd truly been tasked with spying on me, thus far she'd done an admirably discreet job.

"I hope you've been enjoying our voyage, princess, despite the inclement weather."

I readjusted my skirt to make space for her, since she seemed determined to sit with me whether I wished it or not. "I confess I'll be grateful to return to dry land."

"Yes." She lowered onto the bench. "But the Luminate has something for us even in the most tumultuous parts of our wanderings, if we but pay attention."

I forced my sigh to release in small, silent increments. Clearly, she and Sister Eleanor spent a great deal of time together.

We sat in silence, observing the frothing ripples spreading in every direction. How easily a ship could stay adrift in this void forever, never settling on a destination. I folded my hands beneath my elbows. At least sailors had compasses and maps to set their course.

Sister Rochelle sat up straighter. "May I tell you a story, princess?"

I opened my mouth, then closed it again. It wasn't as though I had any prior commitments, and even a morality tale from Sister Rochelle was preferable to another minute spent in my cabin. I pasted on a smile. "Of course."

She kept her gaze fixed on the rolling waves—smooth, yet ever-changing. "When I was a girl—a bit older than you, I suppose—our manor prospered. We were considered one of the most influential families in our little corner of the world, and I often hosted friends or traveled to neighboring estates."

Trying not to draw her attention, I studied her more closely from the corner of my eye. This quiet woman with graying hair in a drab black frock was once a lady of means?

"I met a gentleman named Mr. Callimer at one such party. He was handsome and charming, and his family owned a fine property on the outskirts of town. Soon we were taking long walks and carriage rides together, and he'd whisk me around the dance floor for hours every time we attended a ball."

She adjusted her skirt. "I fell deeply in love, and I believed his devotion to me was just as strong. I couldn't accept quickly enough when he proposed, and our parents were thrilled with the match."

Sister Rochelle in love? Engaged? How drastically her life had changed. "What happened?"

She leaned forward, her lowered head muffling her voice. "On occasion, I'd notice his gaze straying to another attractive woman, but I trusted him so implicitly. Well, it came out that a young maidservant in his household was with child, and when she named him as the father . . . he didn't deny it."

"Oh. I'm so sorry." I gave her arm an awkward pat. "How dreadful."

"It was, for a season." She shifted to face me. "But during that time, I began to pray as I'd never prayed before, asking the Luminate for healing, for guidance. Not to feel so lonely and isolated. To take away my crippling shame."

I stared at the rail. If only I could disappear belowdecks or even lose myself in those churning waves. One glance into my eyes would certainly reveal she'd hit upon my every point of turmoil since Nicholas's arrest.

"One day, when my fervent prayers almost consumed my entire being, He responded to me. A voice of grace and hope, a presence I could trust with no fear of being abandoned or disappointed."

She breathed out a soft laugh. "No man could compare with that. I shocked my parents, not to mention every friend and acquaintance, by selling off all my dresses and jewelry to fund my education at a convent. My parents passed away during Damien Lessox's brief rise to power, and when the Imperian king and queen issued their edict against the practice of magic, I turned my childhood home into a haven for displaced mystics."

I fiddled with my sleeve. No doubt she thought I might be inspired, hearing how the Luminate used her pain to promote a good cause. But she'd come out of her romance with a clean conscience, something I could never hope for.

"Princess?"

Swallowing, I dared to meet her eye.

"I know you must be in a lot of pain, and I won't trivialize it by claiming it will disappear anytime soon. These misfortunes—heartbreaks—require a great deal of time and space for healing. Not everyone will place their lives as fully in the Luminate as I have, and there's nothing wrong with finding another to spend your life with. But every person makes mistakes and will let you down in some way. The Luminate will never stumble, will never fail you. Let Him help you rebuild."

Her words were so enticing, but before they could sweep me away, my common sense reared in protest. "Thank you for sharing your story and for wanting to help, Sister Rochelle, but I doubt the Luminate has much interest in spending His efforts healing someone who caused her own downfall."

She shook her head, but I rose, stumbling to get my footing on the shifting deck.

"I must return to my cabin. Enjoy your afternoon."

Turning away, I made for the stairs as quickly as I could, dodging everyone I encountered.

I couldn't let the tears fall until I was alone.

"I suspect the coast of Delunia will be in sight by nightfall."

"Truly?" I beamed at Sir Colin as he joined me at the ship's rail. We'd taken at least one daily stroll together whenever the weather allowed.

"You'll be back on solid ground soon, princess."

I faced him. "Is my distaste for the sea so obvious?"

A mischievous grin accompanied his wink. "I suspect the hue of your face isn't typically tinged with quite so much green."

My laugh drew the gaze of a nearby sailor. Still not the one whose face haunted my nightmares. I suspected Sir Colin had spoken with the captain after all, for the ill-mannered sailor had yet to make a second appearance.

I lowered my voice. "I can only hope the change isn't permanent."

"It may feel that way for the first few days on land, but the sensation will pass quickly."

"I'm glad to hear it." The breeze blew a curl across my face. "Where will you stay once we reach Delunia?"

"I have a residence in Ambrus, the royal city. My servant keeps things in order when I'm away. It's not a large home, but you're welcome to visit if you ever find yourself feeling homesick."

"Thank you." I'd have one ally nearby, at least. One connection to Trellich. Except . . . "Sir Colin?"

"Yes?" His grizzled brows rose almost to his hairline.

"I don't know how often news travels from Trellich to Delunia. Perhaps more than I realize, but I confess my hope was . . ." I swallowed past the pride begging me to stay silent. "I'd prefer the royal family find out as little as possible about the details of my . . . prior engagement."

Sir Colin gave a solemn nod. "You can be assured of my discretion. I doubt they'll have heard aught but a vague murmur or two. Easy to shrug off as mere rumors. But if they find out more, it will not be from me."

My sigh mingled with the thick salty air. "I appreciate that more than I can express."

His gaze moved to the dancing waves. "I shall never raise the subject again if you'd prefer, but I can't help being curious . . . did you ever hear what became of Lord Lessox? It seemed he disappeared almost as quickly as he resurfaced."

My hand slipped from the rail. "Lord Lessox?"

"He was almost as notorious in Trellich as he was in Imperia, after all, and I'd gotten the impression he was involved in . . ." He allowed his gesture to complete the statement.

I merely had to confirm what he'd already implied, yet the

painful admission faltered on my tongue. "He was, though I didn't know his identity at the time. I didn't see him until afterward."

His eyes widened. "You saw him?"

"In the dungeon at Dorendyn Castle. I'd gone to visit Nic —the former duke." Cursed heat lit my cheeks.

"Ah, of course."

Luminate bless the man for holding back any snide remarks. Heaven knew no one else would've. "Lord Lessox was raving and thrashing. They seemed to have tied him up so he wouldn't injure himself."

Sir Colin shook his head. "Such a shame."

A shame? I glanced at him, lips pursed.

"Not that he deserved a happy outcome, of course. No doubt he knew full well the risk he'd undertaken. But for any man to lose possession of his faculties in such a way . . ." He shrugged. "It must be a terrible way to go."

"True. I've been haunted by the sight ever since."

"Small wonder—a delicate creature such as yourself, subjected to the horrors of the dungeon." He patted my arm. "You're braver than most would give you credit for, princess."

My laugh caught in my throat. It'd felt more like an addition to my long list of mistakes than an act of bravery.

"In fact, one could even say . . ." He let his words trail off, glancing behind us.

Sister Rochelle approached, the sharp breeze billowing her black dress. "Good afternoon, Princess Penelope. Sir Colin."

"I—" For a moment, Sir Colin's perpetual confidence wavered. "I don't believe we've met."

"Sister Rochelle." She adjusted her headpiece, offering no explanation.

"Ah. It's a pleasure, Sister." He dipped into a hasty bow.

"Indeed. And what brings you to Delunia, Sir Colin?"

He pivoted to face her. "I am a humble scholar. My studies mostly involve comparisons between the languages and cultures of Trellich and Delunia, though I've dabbled in other subjects such as farming practices, medicine, and art as well."

"How interesting. And what conclusions have you drawn from such investigations?"

Sir Colin tugged at his jacket's lapel. "No conclusions, merely observations. I've published a number of essays and used my findings to counsel merchants, fellow scholars, and even ambassadors."

He glanced to me with a smile. "Although my energy is not what it once was, I still enjoy spending approximately half the year in each country. At this point, I'm not sure I could choose one over the other."

"I hope to make Delunia my second home as well."

Her tone seemed stiffer when addressing Sir Colin. Perhaps mystics interacted with few gentlemen. She turned to me, her steady smile giving no indication she recalled our last conversation's abrupt end.

"You shall meet your fiancé within the next day or two, Princess Penelope. What an exciting time for a young lady."

"I suppose, though also quite intimidating."

Her soft gaze locked with mine. "Know the Luminate has set you on this path for a reason. His purposes will become clear over time."

Far from the reassurance she meant to give, fear flared in my chest. Would He use my new engagement for retribution? To punish me? After the way I'd squandered my last opportunity, He could hardly be expected to direct my path toward any kind of reward.

Sir Colin cleared his throat. "It is Delunia's great fortune to have you joining its royal family, princess. No doubt Prince Vander will feel the same way."

If only the rest of the world could view me as favorably as Sir Colin.

CHAPTER 8

*W*ith a final lurch, the ship docked in the port. I stared, numb, as sailors bustled about, shouting commands to each other.

This was Delunia. My new . . . home.

The word didn't fit as I glanced to shore, where hordes of people scurried and bumped and gestured. So much noise, so many faces. Not a single one familiar.

A tweak on my arm made me jump. "Quite a sight, isn't it, m'lady?" Victoria's expression held the promise of a new adventure. "So many colors, and I do like the sound o' their language."

If only I could be half so eager. "It's a lot to take in."

She turned to me. "Our trunks're packed, and the captain said his men'll take care o' transferrin' them from the ship to our carriage."

"Thank you, Victoria."

She bounced on her toes. "Which carriage do ye think is waitin' for us?"

I scanned the row of horses, carriages, and wagons on the road above the docks. "It's hard to say. I'm not sure who is meeting us."

"I doubt the royal family made the journey, but what fun if yer fiancé is up there right now, watchin' us disembark."

Fun. Victoria was only one year my junior, but compared with her rosy outlook, I felt like a contrary old spinster. Anxiety twisted my stomach like the tightly woven ropes the sailors pulled to lower the sails. What if he was up there? My —*fiancé.*

The word had seemed peculiar enough applied to Prince Raphael, whom I'd at least met on several occasions. Now it referred to a complete stranger.

"What think you of your new domain, princess?" Sir Colin's warm tone eased the tension in my shoulders. As always, he greeted me with a respectful bow.

"I find I don't know quite what to think."

"Understandable." He pressed his lips together. "It will be an adjustment, to be sure. No doubt you'll feel just as out of place as you have on this ship—a princess among coarse men and new surroundings—but only for a time. I believe you'll come to appreciate this country just as much as I have."

"I hope so." The words escaped as little more than a whisper.

How could such a strange place, with different people, customs, and even speech, ever capture a heart that longed for Trellich? But Sir Colin shared my Trellan roots. If he'd adapted to Delunia, perhaps it wasn't out of the question for me.

He cleared his throat. "It appears the men have secured the ship, and the landing ramp is down. Are you ladies ready to set foot on solid ground once more?"

"Yes." That, at least, could be said in Delunia's favor. No matter what the country, I was eager to be free of the ship's endless rocking and swaying.

"Excellent. Then allow me to escort you."

He held an arm out to me first, then the other to Victoria. She giggled as she accepted his gallant gesture.

I gladly placed my hand on his arm, grateful for his steadying presence. My grip tightened as we strode down the ramp. I fought the urge to close my eyes against the churning water below. The moment our feet landed on the sturdy wooden dock, I released the breath I'd been holding.

Whatever lay ahead, I was grateful to put the sea journey behind us.

~

Sister Rochelle appeared at my side in her usual ghostly manner. "Well, princess, this is where we part ways. At least for now."

Did the woman's footfalls never make a sound?

Sir Colin had bid us farewell to join the servant who'd met him, repeating his invitation to visit his home whenever I wished. Now I stood to the side of the dock, trying to avoid being knocked into the sea by sailors lugging heavy cartons and barrels.

"You're not going to the royal city?" I asked.

The knowledge should've been a relief—perhaps she hadn't been sent to Delunia to spy on me after all. But there would be so few familiar faces in this new place. One more would've brought some measure of comfort.

"I'm afraid not. I'm feeling called toward the south. There is much unrest in this country, so much poverty and hardship. I'd like to help where I can and share the Luminate's light where people need it most."

"Of course. I wish you a safe journey." At least food and shelter would be provided at my destination. Who knew what kind of conditions she might be heading toward?

"And to you, Princess Penelope." She pressed my hands and gave me one of those direct looks. As though she could see my every thought and feeling. "I wish you all possible happiness in your new home and upcoming marriage."

I squirmed under her gaze. Beneath her words lurked the warning I sensed from everyone. *Make it work this time, Penelope. Don't let us all down again.*

"Thank you." I gently tugged my hands, but she held firm.

"Before you go, I have a parting gift."

"Oh?" Curiosity rooted my feet to the ground. What could this woman possibly have that she thought I might want? I glanced to Victoria, but she'd wandered out of earshot to inspect an enormous fish brought in by a nearby fishing boat.

Sister Rochelle rummaged in a pouch tied to her belt, removing a thin chain. "The sisters gave this to me when I left. A token of the Luminate's blessing and protection." She uncurled her fingers, studying the gold pooled in her palm. "But in my prayers aboard the ship, visions of you in the Delunian palace consistently came to mind."

I swallowed past a sudden boulder lodged in my throat. Mystic visions told the future and gave warnings, didn't they? Was my time in Delunia destined to be a failure before I'd crossed ten yards into its borders? "Were the visions—bad?"

"It's impossible to tell for certain." The hand that still held mine tightened in a reassuring squeeze. "But whatever is to come, I believe the Luminate wants you to have this amulet."

"I . . ." My hands fumbled to cup the necklace she deposited into them. The metal cooled my clammy skin.

A small pendant was attached to the chain. Grasping it between my fingers, I lifted it closer to my face. Soft light radiated from the clear stone at the center, almost as though it glowed of its own accord. The gold circle surrounding it was etched with a series of crosses and swirls.

Squinting, I read the words scrolled around the back: *Love surrounds you. My love will protect you.* I converted my snort to a semi-convincing cough.

Love had done anything but protect me.

Sister Rochelle watched me, her smile never wavering. "I know it's simple compared with royal jewels, but I pray you will wear it always as a reminder of the Luminate's love and blessing. Know that He will never leave you."

Too late for that. I dipped into a brief curtsy as I slipped the long chain over my head. "I certainly—that is, it's lovely. Thank you for your thoughtful gesture."

"The pleasure is all mine. Do take care of yourself, Princess Penelope. I hope our paths will cross again someday." She lowered into a curtsy of her own.

A shadow in her eyes whispered she knew something about our future paths. Something significant. I ached to ask, to receive some kind of reassurance that I should proceed into Delunia and not dash right back up the gangplank onto the ship reversing its course for Sandrin.

But she seemed to enjoy shrouding every statement in mystery. No doubt further conversation would only increase my anxiety rather than allay it.

"Thank you again, Sister Rochelle. I hope your endeavors meet with success."

"With the Luminate at my side, I cannot fail." With a wave, she shouldered her bag and set off into the bustle.

Another person walking out of my life to a destiny more secure than my own.

Victoria's sharp inhale followed seconds after mine.

Using a staggering combination of pointing, hand gestures, and flirtatious smiles to various sailors to secure their help with translation, she'd found the carriage sent to transport us to the Delunian palace and ensured our luggage would follow closely behind.

Now, after a bumpy ride over dunes and around strange orange-red rock formations, we craned our necks to take in the sight at the top of the cliff face we'd been climbing.

The Delunian palace—*Palati del Chrysos*, as they called it—

was the tallest structure I'd ever seen, stretching up, up, up toward the clouds. Gold lined every window, shining in contrast to the white stone. A pointed dome of vibrant blue topped each of its many towers, as though they'd collected the orbs from the sea sparkling in the distance.

"To think, this will soon be *your* palace." Victoria grasped the carriage window with a dreamy sigh.

I reminded myself to blink as the view of the palace crowded out the rest of our surroundings. "It is quite grand."

"Grand?" She flopped back on the seat. "It's simply breath-taking. How opulent it must be on the inside!"

Opulent, perhaps, but nothing like home. I managed a nod.

"I can't thank ye enough for bringing me along to continue in yer service, m'lady." Victoria lowered her head into a respectful bow, attempting to contain her jittery legs.

"I'm grateful you're here." Her loyalty was far more than I deserved.

We bumped along in silence as the carriage wound up curving streets to the top of the cliff. We reached a thick wall of the same white stone as the palace. Our driver paused to speak to a guard, who peered into the window with a nod. He hauled the towering gate open, and we proceeded. Inside, shops and stands lined the streets.

I flinched against the assault of so many raised voices. Women in brightly colored wraps, some with flowers in their hair, called to one another, balancing baskets on their arms. Men in flowing shirts and loose pants spoke animatedly, gesturing wide with their arms.

Words everywhere, but not a single one I recognized.

I shrank farther into the carriage. What was I doing here? How could Papa have deceived himself into thinking this was a good idea?

Nearer the palace, we passed structures that must've been houses, despite their round shape and pointed roofs. Flowers so large they hardly seemed real bloomed in every window box, and laundry swayed in the breeze, hung from fences and wooden structures formed from pillars and crossbeams.

Did Sir Colin live somewhere nearby? The thought that my friend might be near at hand eased a bit of the invisible noose constricting my throat.

At every turn, the homes became grander. Wider, with multiple stories, the architecture bore a closer resemblance to the palace than to the circular structures. Even the streets were wider and better paved, the air hushed with formality compared with the earlier chaos. Presumably this was the neighborhood where the local aristocracy resided.

Releasing a breath, I sat a little straighter. Perhaps I might fit in with *some* of these people after all.

The carriage slowed to a stop in front of a regal staircase leading into the castle. Gilded doors shone above. My pulse's tempo jumped with each of the horses' final steps. This was it. I was about to meet the man I was supposed to marry. Swallowing, I pressed my moist palms against the starchy material of my skirt. Papa said he was gentle, right? And not too old?

I started as the driver pulled open my door.

He bowed low. "Your Highness."

I took his offered hand and stepped down into the glaring sunshine. A bead of sweat trickled down the back of my neck. "Thank you."

After helping Victoria down, he pushed the door shut once more. "We'll make sure luggage finds your rooms. Jac takes you to emperor and empress where they await in throne room."

He gestured up the stairs to where a guard with a tall hat and a formal red sash hurried to meet us.

I only managed a nod, looking between the two. The sea voyage had seemed to take an age, and even the carriage ride had passed slowly. Now my future hurtled toward me much faster than my mind could process.

Jac gave me a curt bow, his breathing labored. "Your

Highness. My pleasure it is to welcome you to Delunia. Please, allow me to escort you inside."

He glanced to Victoria, brows lowered.

"I thank you. This is my lady's maid, and I would like her to accompany me."

"Yes, Your Highness." Another bow, and he retraced his steps up the steep staircase.

Victoria returned my glance with an excited smile, and we followed.

I struggled to match Jac's brisk pace as we wound through halls and up more flights of stairs. Would I ever learn the layout of this place? Large gilded mirrors lined some of the corridors, and every ornamental table held a vibrantly painted vase with flowers even larger than the ones we'd seen in town.

My fingers itched to touch one to ascertain whether they were real, but such scrutiny would have to wait for another time. I couldn't afford to lose our guide.

The guard clomped ahead in silence. Couldn't he give us a tour, or at least offer a bit of friendly conversation? But then, perhaps the few words he'd spoken were all he knew of the Sandrinian language.

My steps faltered, and I nearly tripped on my skirt's hem. It only now occurred to me that our driver had spoken Sandrinian. Had they chosen him especially for the occasion, or was it a commonly known language here?

I relived the moments on the dock, surrounded by strings of words I couldn't begin to comprehend. *If only Papa could've been satisfied marrying me off to a Trellan nobleman.*

Victoria collided with my back in our sudden halt. To our right stood a pair of tall, thin doors, painted with an intricate design of purple and yellow flowers.

The guard bowed deeply. "Your Highness."

I barely managed a nod before one of the doors was hauled open. Victoria stepped demurely aside just inside the door, and Jac ushered me forward.

"Her Highness, Princess Penelope of Trellich." The name sounded — off — on his tongue, the "Ps" with a hint of "V." With a grand bow, he motioned to me and disappeared toward the back of the room.

My legs shook as I curtsied. I rose, finally taking in the people gathered before me. Not as many as I'd feared, presumably only the royal family rather than their entire entourage.

"Princess Penelope, you are very welcome here." The wide man who'd been seated on the taller throne rose, spreading his arms wide. Black hair intermixed with white curled against his temples beneath the crown squatting on his forehead. "How good to see you arrived in safety."

"Yes, thank you. Your — Majesty." Clearly he was the emperor. My mind raced through years of etiquette lessons. Was there a proper way to address him?

Fortunately, his smile grew wider. "Your father told me you have grown into much beauty, and I see he speaks true."

"Th-thank you. You are very kind."

Heat scorched my cheeks. This was to be my new family, and they were certainly welcoming me warmly. But I wanted nothing more than to turn and run away.

"We are so happy you are here, Princess Penelope." The empress's voice was less booming than her husband's, her effort to form the Sandrinian words more pronounced. Straight dark hair cascaded down her back, her hazel eyes soft amid her bronze skin.

"I am most happy to be here." I held back the instinct to wince against the falsehood.

The emperor descended from the dais. "I am Emperor Tertius, and this is my wife, Nadia."

The petite woman glided down the stairs to take her husband's offered hand.

"I am sure our daughter Dionne is eager to make your acquaintance." He gestured to a girl several years my junior who dipped into a curtsy before turning her wide dark eyes to me. "But no doubt you are most interested in meeting our son, Vander. Your fiancé."

My throat convulsed. *My fiancé.* Of course everyone in the room, everyone in our respective countries, knew the purpose of my journey to Delunia. Yet I felt exposed, as though my innermost secret had been shouted from a rooftop.

Attempting to swallow, I turned toward the footsteps padding down the stairs on the emperor's other side. Vander lowered into a shaky bow before extending a hand to me.

Panic set my veins to boiling. What was I supposed to do now? Were there Delunian customs between engaged couples I knew nothing about?

I crept forward and dipped into a slight curtsy. After grasping my skirt one last time in a desperate attempt to dry my sweaty palm, I placed my hand in his.

He lightly pressed my fingers before dipping his head to place a kiss on my knuckles. His arm trembled as he released my hand. He raised his head, and our gazes finally collided.

Vander was stocky, only a few inches taller than me. His dark hair was cropped shorter than his father's, his wide forehead and square jawline unremarkable. Only the deep brown of his eyes held the slightest appeal.

A thread of disappointment wove its way into my mind before I cut it short. It didn't matter that Vander was plain. In fact, it was preferable. The less romantic draw I felt toward this man, the better.

Unfortunately, Vander didn't seem affected by the same indifference. A slight smile curved his lips, and his admiring gaze darted away and back to my face again and again. "It is my greatest honor to at last make your acquaintance, Princess Penelope."

I kept my breaths shallow to hold back a sigh. "The pleasure is mine, Prince Vander."

CHAPTER 9

"What shall we dress ye in today, m'lady?" Victoria bustled about my room, unpacking trunks we hadn't gotten to the night before.

I sat on the edge of my mattress, unable to clear the haze from my mind.

The room was large, white on three walls with the fourth painted sea blue. Small bulbous lanterns dangled from the ceiling, and violet curtains hung in thick swaths on either side of the window. Gold filigree lined the ornately carved vanity and desk, matching the tall posts on each corner of my bed. All comfortable and luxuriant, but too foreign to put me at ease.

Yet this was the closest I had to a home now.

"Is everything all right, m'lady?" Victoria tilted her head, a gown slung over one arm.

I blinked. I must've missed something she'd said. "Yes, of course." I forced myself to abandon the relative safety of the bed, planting my feet on the soft white rug covering half the floor. "I can't seem to get my mind to focus this morning."

Her lips tugged into a concerned frown. "O' course ye can't." She laid the dress on the bed and grasped my arm. "This is all very new, m'lady. Give yourself time."

Tears flooded my vision, as unrelenting as they were unwelcome. I pressed my eyes closed and turned away.

Victoria patted my back. "Cry all ye want. No one's here but me, and I don't mind a bit."

I glanced to her, blinking rapidly. "Thank you."

She extended her arms, and without pausing to think it over, I accepted the wordless invitation. She held me close as sobs choked through the tightness constricting my chest and throat. I didn't want this. I didn't want to be here. No matter how badly I'd destroyed my prospects and reputation, I longed for the familiarity of Trellich. For my family.

Now divided from me by hundreds of miles.

Victoria's murmurs of "It's all right, m'lady" and "Ye just have a good cry, miss" continued until, with a few last panting breaths, I stepped back and wiped my eyes.

She handed me a handkerchief, then dabbed her own moist cheeks with her sleeve.

"I'm so grateful you're here, Victoria." An unladylike hiccup punctuated my words. "If I were all alone . . ."

"It's my pleasure, m'lady." She squeezed my arm. "We'll get ye through this yet." Taking my shoulders, she guided me to the cushioned seat before the vanity's oval mirror. "Now, let's get ye washed up and dressed before the Delunian royal family thinks ye disappeared into the night."

I emerged from my chamber, the fog clouding my head thicker than ever. Victoria had applied a cream to my face, claiming it would help reduce the puffiness and swelling. Its fresh scent exuded hints of cucumber and something floral.

I glanced down to the skirt I clutched in my fingers. She'd chosen my deep-red summer dress, saying something about the heat. I shook my head and padded forward. Where was I to — ?

"Shall I escort you to breakfast, princess?"

I swallowed a gasp as a guard marched to my side, clad in the same red sash Jac had worn the day before, but without a matching hat. "I—that is, yes. Thank you."

He bowed and strolled forward, motioning for me to join him. I tried to keep track of our path as we wound through the corridors, but statues and paintings continually stole my attention.

Unlike the muted tapestries covering the walls of the Trellan and Imperian palaces, these halls were filled with colorful paintings and vases. The statues in the larger passages had a certain air of movement to them, eerily lifelike.

A clatter of silverware and excited voices preceded our entrance into what I presumed to be the breakfast room. The cacophony ceased the moment I stepped inside. I smiled my thanks to the guard, who bowed in response. If only I could follow his retreating figure back down the corridor.

Half a dozen expectant faces regarded me as I hovered in the doorframe. Emperor Tertius had said something about hosting guests. Cousins, perhaps?

I took a hesitant step forward, which seemed to rouse the group from their curious stares. Vander jumped from his seat, nearly stumbling in his haste toward me. Emperor Tertius rose as well, along with a man with wavy dark hair and lines embedded in his tan cheeks.

Vander's smile was warm. "Good morning, Princess Penelope. I hope you slept well and found your rooms comfortable."

The hope beaming from his face made my insides clench, but I couldn't help smiling back.

"Good morning. My rooms are lovely, thank you. I'm so grateful for your family's hospitality."

He studied my face. "But you do not sleep well?"

"I—" The disconcerting silence pressed in on me, heavy with anticipation. Couldn't they resume their conversations? "The bed was very comfortable, but I'm afraid I have trouble sleeping in new places."

Vander's worried expression eased. "Of course, of course. Let us hope *Palati del Chrysos* won't feel new for long."

"Yes." With an effort, I kept the corners of my lips angled upward.

He gestured to the table, and I followed to the open seat beside his.

"Good morning, princess!"

I acknowledged the greetings from the rest of the table with a nod. The visitors' conversation reverted to Delunian as servants offered me platters of egg portions with a potent smell, fruit-filled pastries, and some kind of spiced fish. The food was delicious, though with stronger flavors than I was accustomed to at the morning meal.

Vander glanced my direction several times, seemingly gathering the courage to speak. Perhaps it was my turn to make an overture.

I indicated a triangle-shaped pastry, sprinkled with powdered sugar and filled with an orange jelly. "These are very good. What do you call them?"

"I am glad you like them, princess." Relief and enthusiasm lit his expression. "Our cook calls them *trigonis*, though I'm afraid I don't know how it translates to your language. Perhaps triangle?" His sheepish grin made him appear younger.

"Aptly named, then. What is this fruit?"

"I believe it is mandarin."

I spooned a bit of jelly into my mouth. "A bit like our oranges, perhaps?"

"Yes." Vander nodded vigorously. "Though smaller and perhaps more sweet." He blushed upon catching my eye and returned to slicing an egg on his plate.

At least he's easy to talk to. Aside from the distance, Papa could've chosen worse for me.

Vander shifted in his seat. "Princess Penelope, may I . . ." He swallowed. "Would you allow me to take you on tour of the palace after our meal?"

"Yes, that would be lovely." No matter how little romance I foresaw in our future, it'd be best if we became accustomed to spending time together.

The others trickled out of the room, bowing or curtsying to me and giving what I assumed were farewells in Delunian. Vander's parents gave us a nod, his father adding a wink for Vander, then left, trailed by Dionne.

I finished my last pastry in two bites. The room suddenly felt huge and empty, making me uncomfortably aware of Vander's presence at my side. "Thank you for waiting for me. I apologize I was so late to the meal. I—"

"No need for apologies." His fingertips grazed my arm in a feather-light touch. "You have much adjustment needed here. And it is my honor to share a meal with you, no matter the time of day."

If only this poor man were getting a bride who could recip- rocate such sentiments. "You are very kind." I folded my cloth napkin on the table and rose. "Shall we begin our tour?"

"Certainly."

After a second's hesitation, I accepted his offered arm. Better to build up some goodwill before announcing I wanted a marriage in name only.

A revelation that was guaranteed to disappoint.

Vander led me through the halls to the palace's main entry- way. Had it been only the day before that Jac had taken Victoria and me across this very room?

According to Vander, every painting and fresco had a story, representing moments in Delunia's history or popular poems or fables. I smiled, nodded, asked questions. He clearly sought to make me feel at home, but his presentation had quite the oppo- site effect. With every unfamiliar myth or historical figure, my status as an outsider became more pronounced.

His narrative hit a lull in a comparatively sparse corridor lined with windows on one side.

"You know so much about the artwork in the palace. If you

ever have the opportunity to tour my home one day . . . that is, the home I grew up in"—heat stole up my neck into my cheeks —"I'm afraid I won't be able to tell you half so much about the paintings and tapestries."

His chuckle was warm and genuine. "Art is most important to Delunians, the expression of ourselves and our people in color, in stories. My schoolmasters insisted I learn the meaning of every one. It is satisfying to at last put such learning to use." He glanced to me, brows drawn. "I hope I do not bore."

"Not at all. Though I don't think your schoolmasters would be impressed by how little I'd remember if we were to revisit the same pieces."

He patted my arm. "In time, princess. In time."

A genuine smile curved my lips. "Please, call me Penelope. You are a prince in your own right, after all. No need for formalities."

"If you wish, Penelope." He returned my smile, his cheeks darkening red.

We turned a corner into what appeared to be a portrait hall, lined with large gilded frames. I paused to study a painting in which the subject held a trident and seemed to be raising the sea level. Next to it, a woman soared above a battle-field, supported by ivory wings. I scanned farther down the wall, finding each depiction more fanciful than the last.

Not a portrait hall then, yet each figure had such regal bearing, with the black hair, dark eyes, and tanned skin common to Vander's family.

"This is my great-aunt Agnete." Vander's deep voice broke into my reflections. He pointed to the winged matron.

"Your great-aunt? But surely . . ."

"She had no wings." His laugh echoed across the marble floor. "In your home, artists approach their portraits quite differently, yes? It is easy to forget."

"Well, yes. We're usually just sitting and staring forward, perhaps with an occasional smile. They're rather dull, I suppose." My gaze moved to a young man atop a horse, clad in armor except for his discarded helmet. I blinked and narrowed my eyes at the familiar face. "That's —"

"Myself, yes." Vander lowered his head. "They must seem silly, imagining ourselves as heroes or creatures of fantasy. But no Delunian painter would agree to paint one who just sits on a throne. He must tell a story, to give some drama. The scenes are meant to represent something of our inner selves."

"You must be considered very brave, then." He looked quite dashing in the painting, the severe lines of his face more suited to armor than his usual silk robes.

"The pieces are an exaggeration, of course. And the painters, they seek to put themselves in good favor with the royal family."

"Exaggerated or not, it's a wonderful painting." I studied his downturned face until he glanced up and caught my eye.

"Thank you, princess. Penelope." A hint of a smirk tugged at his mouth. "Perhaps you ought to imagine a scene you envision for a painting of yourself."

A breathy laugh ruffled the curls at my temples, more rueful than I'd intended. "Ah, but first we must come up with a positive quality to display. I wouldn't hire a painter any time soon."

His eyes sparkled with mirth, then softened. "I have not a doubt we will come up with something."

My stomach turned a half somersault before I clenched my jaw. How quickly I'd let my guard down. Flirtation had no place in this relationship. I loosened my grip on his arm.

No matter how kind and harmless this man might seem, I had to keep my distance.

∿

A knock sounded at my chamber door. I bit back a groan and sat up from where I'd collapsed onto my bed. An entire morning touring the palace followed by lunch in the stifling heat of a third-floor balcony had worn me out.

Not to mention the company of my persistent fiancé.

Victoria opened the door, her tone light and flirtatious with whomever stood on the other side. Likely a handsome guard.

Pressing my eyelids closed against a headache, I rose from the bed and straightened my skirt.

"Oh, princess, yer hair!" Victoria closed the door. "Ye've been summoned to dinner, but I can't send ye lookin' like that."

I didn't have the energy to argue as I slumped into the vanity's seat.

Victoria's humming was broken by an occasional "tsk" as she smoothed escaped strands of hair and re-pinned curls.

"There we are." She smiled at my reflection. "We must keep ye lookin' the part of future empress, after all."

Don't remind me. I stifled a cough. "I suppose."

Her smile faded. "Cheer up, m'lady. Ye're off to eat a meal of what's likely to be the best Delunia has to offer with a family eager to welcome ye."

Her assessment sent a wave of guilt flooding through my chest. *The spoiled princess brought shame upon herself, and the extent of her punishment is to marry a rich, kind prince. Poor thing.* Gritting my teeth, I stood. "You're right, as always. Thank you."

"If nothin' else, the guard they've sent to escort ye is none too difficult to look at." She winked, raising a hand to fan herself.

A year before, such a statement would've sent me into a fit of giggles and roused an inner challenge to earn the guard's admiration. My flirtation with Nicholas had begun with just such a comment from Harriet, one of my former lady's maids.

The churning in my gut warned I wouldn't appreciate my upcoming dinner, no matter how fine.

Catching Victoria's worried gaze, I attempted a playful expression as I made my way to the door. "If only I could send you in my place."

"If only." She raised her shoulders in an exaggerated sigh.

The guard was indeed handsome, with a hint of curl mussing his dark hair and an expertly trimmed beard lining his jaw.

I ignored him as we made our way to the dining hall, attempting to draw a mental map of our path through the corridors. The winding staircase at the end of the hall renewed the ache in my head as we spiraled down three stories. At the entryway, I marched ahead, determined to make as little a spectacle of myself as possible.

Before Vander could take the place at my side he seemed to think necessary any time we were within the same room, I took the empty seat across from him, next to Dionne. He resumed his chair without complaint, though his smile held a new uncertainty.

"Good evening, Vander. Good evening, Dionne." After a nod at Vander, I turned to his sister. "Your brother took me on a tour of the palace today. Did your tutors teach you as much detail about the artwork as his?"

Her raised brows bespoke surprise at my attention, but something more calculating sharpened her gaze. "My schoolmaster was same as Vander's, so yes, we talk much of palace art." She tipped her head to her brother, then glanced around the room. Leaning closer, she continued, "They do a portrait of myself next year. My hope is they show me on ship, like a—"

She fell silent as raised conversation interrupted her from the hall. The emperor and empress strolled in, followed by one of the couples who'd joined us at breakfast. Dionne sat straighter and folded her hands in her lap.

After exchanging greetings in both Delunian and Sandrinian, the newcomers took their seats, and Tertius motioned for the servers to bring out the meal.

I took a sip from my wine goblet, then turned back to Dionne. "So what was it you were hoping they would select for your painting?"

Glancing to her parents, she gave a tight smile. "It is no matter."

I allowed a servant to drizzle a dark-pink substance over the vegetables on my plate, presumably some kind of dressing. "But I'm curious—"

"How did you enjoy your view from the balcony, Princess Penelope?" Emperor Tertius's voice thundered over the clinking of silverware.

I coughed, nearly choking on the mushroom I'd just placed in my mouth.

"Yes, yes, you were spotted." He wagged his fork between me and Vander in a manner that was half teasing, half accusing. "A romantic spot for a private luncheon."

My cheeks couldn't have burned hotter if they'd lit on fire. A quick glance to Vander confirmed a similar reaction. "The balcony was lovely. Your view of the sea is spectacular. But I must confess, I found it rather warm in the sun."

The emperor's chuckle was a louder, more jarring version of his son's.

Empress Nadia nodded. "Our climate may take adjustment, but we must get you collection of *etanas*. Your gowns are lovely but not so suited to heat."

They switched to Delunian, perhaps to translate for their visitors. I gratefully returned to my dinner.

"She is correct, you know." Dionne's mutter was barely audible over the general din.

I nodded. "I suppose having lighter dresses would help." Much as it pained me to think of losing yet another connection to home. "Are your *etanas* made here at the palace? Do you have a favorite type of fabric?"

Dionne shrugged and kept her gaze on her plate.

It seemed the odd girl was determined to remain a puzzle.

CHAPTER 10

"I've a surprise for ye, m'lady." Victoria bustled in from her adjacent room, a length of cloth draped over one arm.

I yawned and set aside the book I'd been reading. "Haven't I endured surprises enough the past lunar cycle?"

"If ye ask me, one can never have too many surprises." She waggled her brows as she approached my bed.

Angling my feet to the edge of the mattress, I reluctantly cast aside my covers. During my first week in residence at *Palati del Chrysos*, I'd learned to appreciate the bed's soft cushioning and smooth, luxurious sheets. But though I could now traverse the palace's halls with a significantly reduced likelihood of getting lost, it still felt nothing like home.

"Your first *etana*!"

I caught a hint of Victoria's grin before she unfurled the cloth. She held red-purple material the shade of elderberry juice, dotted with glittering crystal beads and cut in the distinctive style worn by Delunian noblewomen: open, flowing sleeves and a high waistline.

I blinked, torn between a desire to examine the lovely

material and the urge to scrunch it into a ball and toss it out the window. "It's . . . beautiful. But where did it come from?"

She peeked over the dress. "I made it, o' course. With some help from the palace seamstresses."

"You made it?" I squinted to get a better look at the precise beading and embroidery along the waist. "But you've already had so much to do this week, waiting on me and getting settled in."

"I confess I was up till the wee hours finishin' these beads last night." She made a weak attempt to stifle a yawn. "But I was eager to finish it as soon as could be. I hoped lookin' a bit more like a Delunian might make ye feel more at home."

Strands of gratitude and guilt twisted through my chest. "You are too good to me, Victoria. And it never even occurred to me to find some help for you. Sophia and I each had half a dozen lady's maids in Trellich, and here I'm making you do all the work yourself. Shall I request a few more maids to be assigned to me?"

The excitement lighting her eyes dimmed, and she lowered the *etana*. "Are ye displeased with me, m'lady? I've done my best to keep things in order, but if there's more I can —"

"No, no. I'm not displeased at all. I'd just like to take some of the burden off your shoulders."

A shadow of a smile returned to her face. "I don't mind, m'lady. Truly. Keepin' busy, stayin' useful, it helps keep my mind off—" She sniffed and looked away. "Well, ye're not the only one who gets homesick. I've enjoyed the times when we . . . but o' course ye'll want more maids."

My lips moved, but no words formed. Victoria had every right to be as homesick as I; she'd just been far more successful hiding it. And I understood what her fond, sheepish expression conveyed. I enjoyed the time the two of us shared at the beginning and end of each day as well. It was a small piece of home, where we could almost pretend we were back in Trellich instead of a thousand miles away.

I squared my shoulders. "I suppose I'll need more maids eventually, but there's no rush. You've been doing an admirable job on your own. Why don't you take the next few lunar cycles, or however long you need, to assess other maids? Get a sense for who might work well with you, who might be a quick study in some basic Sandrinian, that sort of thing. Then, when you're ready, you can report back to me."

"Very good, m'lady."

Victoria's former exuberance returned as she cinched me into the newly made *etana* and circled about, making sure every layer fell in graceful waves. She half guided, half pushed me to the mirror. "What do ye think?"

"I—" I swallowed against the tears stinging my eyes. Whether from appreciation for her kind gesture or dismay at a reflection closer resembling a Delunian than a Trellan, I hardly knew. "It's perfect. Thank you."

She bounced and squeezed my shoulders. "Just wait till Prince Vander sees ye!"

If only I could share her enthusiasm.

My walk to the breakfast room was surprisingly quiet without the rustle of my usual petticoats and layers of skirts. I welcomed the freedom of movement and lighter feel, but my legs felt strangely exposed with only two layers of material. Outside the breakfast room, I braced myself.

Merely a new dress in a different style. Yet the change felt monumental, as though I were embracing a new identity.

Rolling my shoulders back, I proceeded through the doorway.

"Why, is this our Penelope?" The emperor staggered back in mock surprise. "In such attire, you'd blend right in with a flock of Delunian ladies."

Nadia nodded her quiet approval. "Quite lovely."

Vander beamed at me as I approached the table. Before I could protest, he'd pulled out the chair next to his. "Impossible for you to blend into any crowd, with a face such as yours."

I cleared my throat, avoiding the pleased expressions of his parents as they glanced between us. "Thank you. I'm grateful to my maid and the palace seamstresses. It took me by surprise to have a new dress so quickly."

"I propose we test whether you will feel cooler outside in such attire. Do you enjoy riding the horses, Penelope?" Vander resumed his seat and ladled a spoonful of cream onto his berries.

"Yes, I would like that very much."

In truth, I'd missed horseback riding during my journey and first week in Delunia. And this was a way we could spend time together without the close proximity of walking arm in arm.

Tertius clanked his teacup onto the table with a booming laugh. "All right, you two. One more day of this merrymaking, then, Vander, I'm afraid those reports must be looked after. Ozias has been waiting to speak with us."

"Yes, Father." Vander leaned toward me. "Ozias is our . . . hmm. The man who cares for our land, property." He gestured outward.

"A steward?"

"Steward. My thanks."

I took a sip of tea, clenching my jaw to contain my grimace. The strong, bitter tang of Delunian tea was nothing like our light fruity flavors at home. "I apologize if I've been keeping you from your duties. We needn't—"

"Father doesn't mind." Vander's grin held a conspiratorial slant. "When a need arises, he will not hesitate to order me back to work."

I sampled my eggs as Vander and Tertius discussed the upcoming meeting with their steward. As had often been the case in prior mornings, Dionne didn't join us.

As soon as we'd eaten our fill, servants cleared our plates, and we rose from the table. Vander led me from the room, offering his arm as usual.

"Does Dionne prefer to take breakfast in her room? I haven't seen her the past few mornings."

"To tell truth, I do not know." His exhalation was part laugh, part sigh. "My sister enjoys her sleep, so yes, she is absent most mornings. But she also enjoys her food. And she sometimes wishes to avoid, well . . ."

He shrugged. "I know not whether she requests breakfast brought to her, or if she finds it after the rest of us have finished." He lowered his voice, a smile playing at the corners of his lips. "I suspect perhaps she eats all the remaining pastries when we have left room. They are her favorites."

We exited a side door into the sunshine. My skin warmed immediately, forming a sheen of perspiration. But I had to admit, the *etana's* thinner material made the heat less stifling.

"I've only seen a handful of clouds since my arrival in Delunia. Does it ever rain here?" It must, if the green grass and lush plants were any indication.

"Yes, you will see plenty of rain in coming lunar cycles. This season is more dry."

I nodded. Perhaps I'd miss the sun once we reached the rainy season. But at least it would feel more like home.

"What is that you hold?"

My fingers slipped. I hadn't even noticed I'd been toying with the amulet as we walked. Bound by some honor or guilt I hadn't taken the time to examine, I wore it every day just as Sister Rochelle had requested. Instinctively, I'd kept it hidden, but she hadn't said anything about secrecy.

"A necklace. It was a gift from someone who traveled to Delunia with us. Sister Rochelle."

"Ah." A crease formed in his brow. "You traveled with your sister? You have not mentioned this Rochelle. Where is she now?"

I held back a giggle. "She is no relation of mine. We parted ways when we disembarked. 'Sister' is a term used for a woman who devotes her life to the Luminate. Are you familiar with the term mystic?"

He tilted his head. "Interesting. I have heard reports of these mystics, but they claim power from your Luminate, yes? Where there is no belief in Luminate, there is little credibility for these mystics with no magic source."

So there really weren't any followers of the Luminate in Delunia. I'd suspected as much based on the lack of mealtime prayers and the dilapidated or converted state of what might've once been churches, but this was the first anyone had raised the subject.

I slipped the pendant beneath my neckline. "From what I understand, their abilities are very real, though it's not the same as magic. They can't draw on their power at will to accomplish whatever they choose. Instead, they connect to the Luminate through prayer, and His power channels through them."

"They get response from your Luminate?" His tone radiated curiosity, unhardened by judgment.

Your Luminate. As though He'd created Sandrin but waited for some other unknown deity to take a turn with Delunia. Any wisp of a smile faded. He certainly wasn't *my* Luminate.

"Yes, at least, that is my understanding. I've never witnessed it myself. But a group of mystics overcame a powerful sorcerer in Imperia, Lord Lessox, not too long ago. I doubt a group of otherwise peaceful women could've accomplished such a thing on their own."

"Hmm." Vander tapped his chin.

I continued before he could inquire further about Lord Lessox. "The people of Delunia don't worship any kind of creator or higher power? You have nowhere to turn with prayers or supplications?"

His chuckle shook his chest. "You have seen luxury of *Palati del Chrysos.* What kind of supplications would we direct to such god?"

"You may not need to pray for material goods, but we also pray for things like safety, wisdom, or guidance." *Or forgiveness.* A tremor ran down my arms. No, there were some things not even the Luminate could be expected to forgive. "Besides, there are many outside the royal family who may wish to pray for help getting adequate food and shelter."

"True." He shrugged. "Many years ago, some Delunians did believe in this Creator-Luminate. But sorcerers' answers to requests were more tangible, more immediate. They tell us spirit sources of magic do not respond to those who worship another. My grandfather outlawed the practice of religion in order that such spirits would have no hesitation serving people of Delunia."

"Praying to the Luminate is outlawed here?"

"You need have no worry, Penelope." His fingers put a slight pressure on my arm before he let them drop. "My father does not enforce this law now that sorcerers have no influence here. You may worship your Luminate if you wish."

An inexplicable desire to cry tightened my chest. Emperor Tertius's permission to pray hardly mattered when my own failings had separated the Luminate from me behind an almost palpable barrier.

The sight of the stables produced a welcome distraction. I forced my exhale to be slow and steady. "What kind of horses do you have?"

To my relief, Vander latched on to the new subject. He chatted about breeds and temperaments until a stable boy hurriedly bowed before us.

I studied the bustling set of large buildings as Vander and the boy conversed in Delunian. *The Delunian horses must be fine indeed to earn such grand living quarters.*

"Our horses will be prepared. My apologies if I . . . would you prefer I translate such conversations?" He rubbed the back of his neck. "I am most eager to make you feel welcome. A part of things."

"Thank you, you've made me feel very welcome. But I don't require translations of every conversation, especially simple interactions with servants or stable hands."

"Yes, good." Relief lit his face. "Your horse will be beautiful, hmm, black. Like your hair." He reddened. "She has energy but is good with taking the directions. I hope that will suit?"

"She sounds perfect."

Soon, a set of grooms and stable boys returned, leading two tall horses. The sidesaddle on the black mare was a welcome sight. A thin smiling boy boosted me into the saddle, then retreated with a set of rapid bows. I passed a hand over my mouth to cover a snicker.

Vander swung himself into the saddle of a dappled gray with surprising ease. He prodded his horse forward, and mine followed.

Vander slowed his horse's gait until he rode at my side. "Hector probably fail to tell you. Her name is *Omorphia*. Like 'pleasant.'"

"How pretty."

Being on horseback again filled me with a welcome surge of familiarity, and the *etana* skirts didn't bunch in the saddle the way one of my usual ensembles would've. But the hints of cramping in my muscles were a painful reminder I was out of practice.

My hot skin welcomed the slight breeze created by our movement. I closed my eyes and leaned my head back as we passed under the shade of a tall tree.

"Observe there, Pen. Our largest garden lies just beyond that gate."

My dearest Pen. I'd successfully kept memories of Nicholas at bay since our arrival, but now his face filled my mind. Flinching, I grasped the reins. *Omorphia* danced to the side.

"I am sorry to startle." Vander reached out as though ready to rescue me. "Do you mind if I call you Pen? I thought it might be a nice, hmm, short name for Penelope. But if you don't like it . . ."

I stroked my horse's neck, hoping to calm us both. "I'm afraid I don't like it. My family does call me Pen sometimes, but I prefer Penelope."

He nodded, his expression sober. "Certainly. I mean no offense."

"Of course. It's nothing to apologize for." I inhaled deeply, steadying my racing heart. A light floral scent perfumed the air. "You said something about gardens?"

"Yes, we have gardens on several sides of *Palati del Chrysos*, but we passed the largest just now."

I swiveled to look in the direction he pointed. Beyond a row of vine-covered pillars, an array of colorful blossoms opened toward the sun's rays.

"It would be my honor to take you there sometime."

"I'd like that." I faced Vander once more, the heat in my cheeks intensifying at the ardor in his eyes. "May we see what's beyond that hill?"

Without waiting for an answer, I nudged my horse forward.

We spent the remainder of the ride in comfortable silence, with occasional remarks on our surroundings or the horses. After dismounting, I attempted to subtly stretch my legs, a task made more difficult by my *etana*'s streamlined skirt.

Vander sent the grooms away following an exchange in Delunian, presumably instructions of some kind. He turned toward me, his gaze lingering on my face.

The two handbreadths separating us suddenly felt insufficient.

"I'm afraid I must leave you here as I must have talk with our head stable hand." His feet stayed rooted in place.

"I can certainly find my way back to the palace. Thank you for taking me out today. It felt good to ride again, and *Omorphia* is a gem."

"*You* are gem, dear Penelope." He stepped closer. "I noted your beauty the moment we met, but dressed as one of us . . ." He raised his hands as though at a loss for words.

Panic twined around my heart, thicker than the vines coating the garden columns. "Well, most of my wardrobe will remain decidedly Trellan until the seamstresses complete their work. But I do appreciate the cooler fabric."

I aimed for a flippant smile and tugged at my skirt.

"Yes, it will all take the time, of course." He placed a gentle hand on my arm. "But it makes me look to the future. To how happy we will be together, when you are my wife."

Not nearly as happy as you're envisioning. "There is certainly much to look forward to. But I mustn't keep you from the head stable hand." I extracted my arm and increased the distance between us. "I'll see you at dinner."

"I will look ahead to it."

I backed away another step, then turned and fled down the hill toward the palace.

No, no, no. The word pounded a steady beat in my head as I walked. I was supposed to push him away, to ensure he wouldn't care for me. I thought I'd have more time.

But here we were, a week past my arrival, and Vander was already taking on the role of ardent suitor. I had to tell him the rosy future he imagined was an impossibility.

CHAPTER 11

"Where will you go for afternoon?" Vander extended his arm to me as we left the dining hall following a luncheon of smoked fish and boiled potatoes.

"I thought I might spend some time in the music room." I placed my hand lightly on his arm, and we set out down the hall.

As promised, the emperor had kept his son occupied the past few days, reviewing ledgers and reports and taking audiences with merchants and ambassadors. But Vander insisted on sitting beside me at every meal and escorting me to my next destination afterward. He meant well, of course, but his preference for keeping a close proximity wore on my last nerve.

My mind skipped back to another man, whose every touch I'd cherished . . . what a mistake that had been.

I quickened my pace. The sooner we reached the music room, the sooner I'd be free of his attentions.

"Perhaps I shall join you, if I may? Father has no need of me for next hour or so. You play pianoforte, yes? I should very much like to hear you."

My steps faltered. "I suppose, if you wish. But I'm afraid you'll be disappointed . . . music is not a great talent of mine."

He covered my hand with his. "Anything you play will be beautiful, it is certain."

I pressed my lips together, holding back a wince. How unfair to recoil at his kindly meant compliments, but it couldn't be helped. If only he knew . . .

I glanced out the nearest window. The sun gleamed in a cloudless blue sky. My stomach shuddered. Perhaps it was time to broach the subject I'd been dreading.

"Then again, it seems a lovely day." I gestured at the sunshine streaming into the corridor. "Since your father is able to spare you, perhaps you could show me the garden. The one you mentioned last week?"

He paused to glance out the window. "Certainly, if this is what you prefer."

He redirected our steps toward the nearest staircase. I clutched the railing with my free hand as we circled down to an unornamented side door.

Hopefully a day would come when all their spiraling staircases didn't make me so dizzy.

Once outdoors, I breathed deeply of the fresh air, but its invigoration lasted only a moment. Even in the shade, humidity made the air thick, pressing against us. I slipped my fan from the pouch on my waist with a sigh.

Vander chuckled. "Have you just the one *etana* so far? You must ask our seamstresses to make more. Or perhaps you might borrow from Dionne."

"I'm fine." I tried to keep the growl out of my voice. Considering the blow I was about to level at him, I could at least be civil. "My lady's maid has a whole set of new garments underway. I don't mind waiting."

"Of course." He nodded, avoiding my gaze like a reprimanded child, and fell silent.

We passed through a gate leading to the gardens on the eastern side of the palace. Squinting against sunlight reflecting off vibrant greens, purples, and yellows of surrounding plants,

I peeked down the path in each direction. A lone gardener knelt in the dirt near a cluster of flowers, but the area otherwise seemed deserted.

"Let's go this way." I directed Vander away from the gardener toward a set of wildflowers, each large blossom reaching toward the sky. We'd never have allowed our gardens to descend into such disarray, yet there was a beauty about it.

Spying a secluded bench, I tugged at Vander's arm.

"Do you have kitrinalis in Trellich?" Vander indicated a yellow flower, almost in the shape of a heart, as he settled on the bench.

I perched beside him, leaving ample space between us. "Not that I've ever seen. It's pretty."

"*Rei.* Yes. I don't come to gardens often enough anymore. They were some of my favorite places to run as a boy."

I almost smiled at the image of a young Vander lumbering down garden paths, perhaps chased by a nursemaid or tutor. "I always enjoyed our gardens at home."

He shifted closer and tucked a strand of hair behind my ear. "I hope I might visit them with you one day."

"Perhaps." Clearing my throat, I leaned away from his touch.

Vander dropped his hand as though I'd stung him, the admiration in his eyes changing to embarrassment. "Pen — Penelope, I hope you can have patience with me. You will be more beautiful a bride than I could've dreamed, and I consider myself most fortunate. But I have no experience with courting. I fear I fumble in my overtures as your suitor."

Guilt twined around my heart, as unyielding as corset threads. Poor Vander — so naive, so eager to please. Without the slightest inkling that his every attempt at affection only pushed me further away. He deserved so much better than what I could offer him.

But our course was set, our union important to our families and countries. He knew the political advantages as well as I. If

I couldn't give him what he wanted out of a marriage, I could at least give him honesty.

The tightness constricting my throat wouldn't allow me to swallow. "You are very kind, and inexperience with courtship is nothing to be ashamed of. In fact, I find it far preferable to the alternative."

I winced as visions of Nicholas yet again cluttered my mind —his alluring grin as he flirted easily with me and every other female he encountered.

"That is relief to hear." Vander's brilliant smile was back, further cinching the restraints compressing my chest.

"But I'm afraid . . ."

How could I say it? What words could convey my meaning without breaking his pride? His heart?

"I'm so grateful for your warm reception, and I have every intention of fulfilling the obligation of our betrothal and becoming your wife."

His brows lowered in confusion, a shadow crossing his face.

"However, it is my preference our union be a simple alliance. A friendship, perhaps, but not—" My words stumbled, tripping over each other. I paused for a quick breath. "What I mean to say is, I do not wish for any—romance—in our relationship."

Heat burned up my neck, this time not from the stifling sunshine. I looked at the ground, my hands, the surrounding flowers. Anywhere but at him.

"I see." The statement barely escaped his clenched jaw. He muttered something in Delunian and ran a hand through his hair. "I appreciate having such truth. My apologies I am not the man you hoped for, but be assured I will respect your wishes."

His meaning collided with my ribs like a fist. He thought it was because of him?

"No, Vander, please. You must understand, I made this

decision before I even met you. You have been so welcoming—charming, even—any young lady would be fortunate to be your future bride. It is for personal reasons alone that I've lost any interest in romance. How much—" I swallowed. "What were you told of me before I came?"

"Very little, only . . . ah." He nodded, a bit of hope rekindling in his eyes. "You were engaged once before. This I know."

He extended his hands as though to take mine, then retracted them.

"But, Penelope, that is no reason for this marriage not to meet with success. I know not of the reasons your former engagement did not proceed. No matter the cause, I understand you may have hesitance. Perhaps be fearful it will turn out the same. But I will keep my commitment to you. I will give you all time you need, and perhaps we may yet form a bond of love as well as this partnership you speak of."

I shook my head, my mind hardly registering the movement as it raced, trying to consider every possibility, every angle. He knew about my engagement to Prince Raphael, but not of my relationship with Nicholas. Should I tell him? No doubt it would make my wishes easier to bear, but . . .

I pictured the admiration on his face, the open expressions of his parents. If they knew, they'd all despise me.

No, to make such a disclosure would simply drag the problems I'd left behind across the sea to my new existence. The exact opposite of what I'd hoped to achieve.

I shifted against the hard wood of the bench. "I'm afraid all the time in the world couldn't change my mind. You are correct —I did have a failed engagement, and it taught me a marriage of love does not suit me."

"Do you still long for him?" His head tipped in inquiry.

"No, I never did. Which is how I know these things can't be forced, and to try would only lead to disappointment. For both of us. If we can just stay friends—"

"It is due to me, then. I am not the kind of man you could love."

"That's not what I mean." I rubbed my temples. How had this conversation gone so wrong? "I could not love any man, not now. I feel fortunate my father chose you over —"

"Thank you, there is no need for further explanation." He rose and brushed off his trousers. Only his rapid blinking betrayed any emotion. "I am well aware this marriage was pressed upon you, and as I promise, I will respect your distance. There will be much to consider, laws to consult . . ." He massaged the back of his neck. "But I will force my presence on you no longer. Good day, princess."

I flinched at the return of my formal title. "But I . . ."

He'd already rounded a corner and disappeared into the maze of flowers.

I lowered my forehead into my palms, ignoring the drips of sweat. So much for a peaceful, friendly alliance. Now he would despise me. As much as I despised myself.

Victoria pinned a final curl into place. "All prepared to make a splendid appearance at dinner." She splayed her hands over my reflection in the mirror.

"Thank you." My attempted smile faded almost before it began.

Victoria's lips quirked downward. "Cheer up, m'lady. No doubt we'll get used to eatin' fish at every meal before long."

I managed a small laugh. "They do enjoy their fish here, don't they?" I'd kept to my rooms for the remainder of the afternoon, but I couldn't avoid Vander forever. "I'll return shortly after the meal ends. I plan to retire early this evening."

"As ye like, but don't hurry yourself on my account. Take all the time ye wish to bask in the adorin' gaze of yer betrothed."

I turned away before she could see my face, my stomach heaving at the thought of the meal to come. The slight progress I'd made toward forging a home for myself among these people would be gone with one glance at Vander's stony face. And if he'd spoken of our conversation to his family . . . I shivered.

Just when I thought I couldn't feel more alone.

Vander and his father rose as I entered the dining hall. The emperor dipped into a gallant bow. Vander inclined his head, the curve of his lips only managing the slightest smile.

I hesitated in the doorframe just long enough for a brief curtsy before shuffling to my place beside Vander. "Good evening."

He pulled my chair out for me, his movements rigid.

Tertius and Nadia filled the silence with exclamations of delight at the food the servants uncovered. I watched for any sign of displeasure with me or concern for Vander, but they chatted as merrily as usual, not paying us any particular attention.

Vander must've kept his heartbreak to himself, at least for now.

My relief blended with renewed sadness for him, culminating in a pounding behind my temples.

I took a small bite of salad, pushing aside the stringy watercress stems they served so often. Vander shifted his chair farther from mine than usual, where he could wield his fork without the slightest risk of his elbow bumping mine.

Releasing a breath, I risked a glance at him. "Thank you so much for taking me to the gardens this afternoon."

He coughed, covering his mouth with his napkin.

Tertius perked up from his seat at the head of the table. "The gardens, you say? And what did you think of them, Penelope?"

"We didn't go far, but they're very beautiful." *Aside from their association with such an unpleasant memory.* "I've never seen such large, colorful blossoms."

"Indeed, the weather in Delunia does wonders for our plants. Did you have a favorite?"

"I . . ." Stalling, I took a sip of water. The many plants along our path had barely caught my notice. "I'm afraid I don't remember many names, but the large red flowers with the pink centers were lovely."

"Ah, yes, the *dalmar kardi*. I believe it means 'soothing heart' in your language." He patted his wife's hand. "Planted by your request, were they not, my dear?"

"They were." Setting down her fork, she returned his smile. "Your gardeners were so thoughtful to make space for flowers I like the most."

Remorse tugged at my stomach, curbing my hunger even further. No wonder Vander had such high expectations from his upcoming marriage with such affectionate parents as his example.

Tertius winked at us. "Perhaps we can find a flower from Trellich that might grow in this climate. I'll let you do the honors of pleading her cause with the gardeners, son." His face crinkled into a grin.

"Of course." Vander raised his wine goblet in his father's direction before taking a long drink.

Maybe it wasn't such a relief that he hadn't told his parents, after all.

CHAPTER 12

I took breakfast in my chambers the next morning. Vander's scowl from dinner had haunted me throughout the night. A certain relief flowed from the knowledge he'd accepted my wishes regarding our relationship. He'd no longer push unwanted affection on me, and I'd no longer have to pretend.

Painful as it was, I'd done the right thing being honest with him. But I had so few allies in Delunia already, and Vander's new coldness made clear my confession had lost me his friendship.

Taking a sip of tea, I winced and leaned my head back. I missed the sweet berry flavors of our beverages at home. I missed gray rainy days mixed with sunshine.

I missed Nicky's babbling and Vivienne's quiet wisdom and Sophia's humorous preoccupation with her wardrobe. Father's deep voice and quick laugh. The decorations and mementos dotting every corner of my chambers that made them so thoroughly *mine*.

The smooth gait of my horse, the greetings of guards as I walked the halls, the tapestry depicting ice-capped mountains with frost hawks soaring overhead.

My breath released in a shaky sigh. I missed everything about home. If only . . .

Sir Colin. I sat up.

Much as I appreciated Victoria's company, she'd embraced life in Delunia so fully she didn't seem to understand the extent of my homesickness. And the nature of our relative positions made it challenging to confide in her fully. But Sir Colin would sympathize with what I was going through, and he'd invited me to stop by his home any time.

Resolve formed in my mind almost before I'd had the conscious thought. *Today, I'll visit Sir Colin.*

With a new lightness permeating my mind and heart, I dressed quickly, humming a song Sophia always used to sing.

I peeked out the door of my sitting room. My two usual daytime guards stood at their posts in the corridor.

I squared my shoulders. "Um, excuse me."

Both turned their attention toward me, their postures still rigid.

"Good morning. I was hoping to go on an outing today. Would you please escort me?"

The young, handsome one Victoria had noticed on our first day nodded. "Certainly, my lady."

The other watched our exchange, brows furrowed. The first made a quick statement in Delunian, and the gray-haired guard's expression eased. "Ah. Yes, princess."

The first guard turned back to me. "Will you have need of horse or carriage?"

"Oh. I—" *Would I?* Such arrangements would only slow us down and possibly draw unnecessary attention to my jaunt into town. "No, I don't think so. Ambrus is easily accessible on foot, is it not?"

"Indeed, Your Highness." He dipped into a slight bow.

I glanced to Victoria, who was folding my nightdress. She'd been so eager to join me in this strange country but thus far had seen very little of it. "Would you care for a walk into the city, Victoria?"

Her head perked up from her task. "Do ye mean it?"

"Of course."

Guilt nipped my stomach for never wondering before now whether she'd appreciate an excursion.

"Then yes, I'd love to join ye!" She carefully set down my folded nightdress. "Just let me find my hat." She ducked into her small bedchamber adjoining my quarters, then scurried to join me in the hall. "Where are we to go?"

She tipped her hat at a jaunty angle and gave a shy smile to the younger guard as he fell into step behind us.

I choked down a laugh. "I thought I'd pay a visit to Sir Colin."

"That kind old gentleman on the ship with us? How nice."

Our slippers shushed along the marble floor as we approached the palace entrance. We emerged into bright sunshine at the top of the grand staircase.

The heat hadn't abated, yet somehow I felt freer here than within the palace grounds, as though I could go anywhere, truly get a fresh start. The palace yard brimmed with life as stable boys led horses through the pasture and washerwomen hung tablecloths to dry.

Victoria nudged me with her elbow. "Not so very different from home, is it?"

She was right. The bustle of servants, the dust kicked up in the streets, the cacophony of birdsong and hoofbeats—it all reminded me of home. The surrounding colors were more vibrant, the sun's heat more insistent, but the similarities were more striking than the differences.

We strolled through the small gate sectioning off the palace yard.

The guards exchanged a few friendly greetings behind us. Though it lacked familiarity, I rather appreciated the ability to come and go without the ceremony of large iron gates heaving open like the release of a prison door.

The newfound sense of freedom invigorated me. If I was brave enough to venture out, I could do all the exploring I wanted.

A throat cleared at my side. I glanced over to find the younger guard pursing his lips. "Princess, I am so sorry to disturb, but where would you like us to take you?"

I smiled, hoping to put him at ease. "I'd like to call on a friend who accompanied us on our journey to Delunia. Sir Colin Headrick."

"Very good." He nodded but continued to regard me expectantly. *But where does he live?*

Heat clawed up my neck as I realized his unspoken question. Of course I couldn't expect the guards to take me to Sir Colin just because I shared his name. The city of Ambrus surrounding the palace was large, likely housing far more notable aristocrats than our scholarly friend.

"He, um . . . he said he can view the marketplace from his home."

Lines of confusion etched into the guard's face before understanding dawned. He could tell I had no idea where to go.

How could I be such a simpleton? I was the model of a spoiled, out-of-touch foreign princess.

He dipped into a small bow. "Then we start at marketplace."

He murmured something to the older guard, and we set out.

Anxiety crowded out the elation that had made me feel so liberated only moments before. What if we never found him? To fail on my own would be deflating enough, but I'd brought along an entourage to witness my embarrassment.

Victoria practically skipped at my side. She leaned close and touched my arm. "Don't worry, m'lady. No doubt a man as friendly as Sir Colin is well known in these parts. Someone can direct us to him."

I tried to convey my gratitude in my smile. Victoria's optimistic presence was truly one of the greatest blessings on this journey.

The noise of the market reached us before its structures came into view. The older guard led us around a corner, and the view became as chaotic as the surrounding sounds. Clucking chickens, shrieking children, calls strung in words I couldn't understand all coalesced into a stunning and vibrant picture. Striped tents with pointed tops lined the streets and brimmed with kitchen utensils and shining cloths and colorful fruits and elegant pottery.

I stared, my steps faltering. A sea of faces, of language, of life. None of it familiar. Apprehension wrapped around my insides tighter than any belt.

I don't belong here. I'll never belong here.

I looked around, frantic to find the younger guard and ask him to take me back to the palace. By the time I spotted him, he was speaking animatedly with a vendor. If only I could communicate with the older guard, who stood just ahead.

Victoria pressed closer to my side. "Do ye see that material there?" She pointed to a tent displaying fluid fabrics heavily embroidered with silver thread. "Wouldn't those make stunning *etanas*? Especially the light-blue one. I don't know where Alcie gets her materials, but I'll make sure to mention it to her."

I blinked, trying to isolate her words from the surrounding clamor. "Who is Alcie?"

"The palace seamstress assigned to make yer new clothes. I've been tryin' to help, but many of her sewing techniques aren't familiar."

I noted her easy posture, the joy in her expression. She'd accustomed herself so easily to this new life, not even flustered by the necessity of learning new skills and submitting to instruction from a stranger.

She already swam deep in the ocean, navigating the waves with ease, while I'd hardly pressed a toe to the sand.

I faced her. "You really are a marvel, Victoria. It appears I'm aware of only a small fraction of what you do to occupy yourself every day, but I'm so grateful."

She ducked her head, her lips pressed into a sheepish smile. "I—that is, thank you, m'lady."

"And I agree that cloth is lovely."

The younger guard returned, his boots clipping against the gravel. "Your Sir Colin lives on northwest corner."

He indicated a lane leading away from the opposite side of the market.

I clamped my mouth shut before it could hang open. "Oh. Thank you. But how do you know?"

He grinned. "I ask Faustus." He angled his head closer to us. "Nosiest seller in market."

Victoria's giggle bubbled like a cheery spring. "How very clever of you, Egan."

Shame mingled with my gratitude for Egan's discovery. I'd never thought to ask for his name. "Yes, thank you. Please, lead the way." As the guards marched ahead of us, I whispered to Victoria, "What's the older one's name?"

"Tassos." She waggled her eyebrows. "But I much prefer Egan."

We stopped before a one-story circular white house. A tidy path led to the orange front door, lined with rows of well-tended flowers.

Egan turned to me. "I believe this is house he meant, but allow me to approach to be certain."

I nodded my agreement, and he tromped down the path, reaching the door in less than ten strides. I followed at a distance.

A man opened the door, issuing what I assumed was some

kind of Delunian greeting. Egan responded, motioning to me. The man nodded and disappeared.

I kept my posture tall, but everything inside me cringed. What if we had the wrong house? Would the first impression of me among the townsfolk be my unexpected visit to a random gentleman's home? Shame burned my ears. Before Nicholas, I'd been looked up to, respected, admired. Now I was belittled to an exile facing humiliation at every turn.

Yet not as great a punishment as I deserve.

Sir Colin appeared at the door, a warm smile radiating from his face. Relief flooded my veins. At least this outing needn't be added to my lengthy inventory of mistakes. I hurried forward.

Sir Colin extended both hands and clasped mine. "Princess Penelope! What a lovely surprise."

"It is so good to see you, Sir Colin. I feared we may not be able to find your home. I apologize for not giving you advance notice — I wasn't sure how to reach you. But I've so missed our conversations and hope you don't mind a visit."

"Of course, please visit as often as you like. I'm afraid my home is a great deal smaller and less opulent than what you're used to, but I try to keep it tidy." He gestured for me to enter.

Egan stepped aside. "We shall remain at entrance, unless you prefer us to come within?" He peered inside the door, as though trying to spot any potential threats.

"I shall be quite safe in Sir Colin's hospitality, thank you." My gaze moved to Victoria. "Are you comfortable — ?"

"I don't mind stayin' out here. I shall enjoy watchin' the marketplace, and I'm sure these gentlemen will keep me out of trouble." She directed a flirtatious smile toward Egan.

Tassos, at least, would keep her out of trouble.

I followed Sir Colin into a small sitting room interspersed with large wicker chairs boasting overstuffed cushions.

His laugh warmed the space. "I can only imagine the musings going through your mind right now, princess. It will be hard for a Trellan to believe, but this furniture is quite fashionable here in Delunia." He leaned closer and spoke in a mock whisper. "I found it atrocious at first too, but it's actually very comfortable."

I perched on a teal cushion, trying not to smile at how he'd read my thoughts. "Your home is lovely."

This laugh came out almost as a bark. "Spoken like a true gentlewoman. Now, may I offer you any refreshments? I brought back some rhosyn from Trellich, if you'd like."

"Did you?" I couldn't keep the enthusiasm out of my voice "Rhosyn it is."

I scooted farther back in my seat. "Only if you have enough for yourself. I wouldn't want you to run out."

He waved a hand. "I spend part of each year in Trellich and bring a crate filled with the precious cargo on every return journey. You're not the only one in Delunia with a more refined palate."

He winked and popped his head into the adjoining kitchen, murmuring something in Delunian.

I straightened my skirt and studied the room. A wide painting of a sunset shimmering over the ocean adorned one wall above a mahogany writing desk flanked by four orderly bookshelves. Two small tables carved from dark wood and topped with colorful tablecloths sectioned off the seating area. Beneath my feet lay a rug covered in a swirling pattern.

"Here we are." Sir Colin reappeared, carrying a tray with the hard biscuits Delunians called *psomik* and an assortment of cheeses.

"Thank you, but you didn't need to go to all this trouble just for me."

His expression would've looked affronted if not for the twinkle in his eyes. "Just for you? How often does an old man have the opportunity to host royalty in his house?"

The man who'd opened the front door walked across the room and set a teacup on the table beside me. Scents of rose and lemon swirled in the steam wafting from the cup.

"Thank you."

"Princess Penelope, this is my manservant, Niles."

"It's a pleasure to meet you."

Niles stared at me, then glanced to Sir Colin. After a quiet conversation in Delunian, Niles gave me a tight smile and a low bow. He set a matching cup on the other table, then slunk out of the room.

"My apologies, princess. I'm afraid he only speaks Delunian."

"Nothing to apologize for." I curled my fingers around the teacup. The warmth was hardly needed in such a climate, but it felt familiar and comforting.

Sir Colin blew across his tea. "You've been in Delunia what . . . two weeks? How are you finding it?"

"Yes, two weeks yesterday." At least that question had a simple answer. "And I . . . everyone has been very kind."

He chuckled, tea sloshing from his cup. "A safe, acceptable answer. But there's no need to be a diplomat here, princess. Feel free to speak your mind."

I rubbed my forehead with my empty hand. "Everyone truly has been kind. But it's so—different here. Everything is bright and noisy and hot. I can only converse with about five people, and the rest of the time I'm surrounded by conversations I can't understand. Everyone alternately seems to be laughing at or ignoring me, and I don't even know which is worse. I—I miss home."

I blinked against the tears stinging my eyes.

"Ah, Penelope." He snapped open a handkerchief and handed it to me. "I recall feeling the same way. After the quiet respectability of Trellich, especially Glonsel Palace, the bois-terous nature of the Delunian people is bound to be a shock. Nothing is more alienating than living in a sea of people, all of whom can speak to each other but not to you."

I used his handkerchief to cover an unladylike sniffle.

"You may find this hard to believe, but I think it likely the worst is already behind you."

My arm stilled mid-dab as I looked to him.

He raised a hand. "It won't be easy to see from this perspective, and some days will wear you down until you feel worse than ever. But whether you realize it or not, you're already adapting to your new surroundings. I'd wager you're starting to find the sounds not quite as abrasive and flinching a bit less at the vibrancy. Knowing you, clever girl, you're even picking up a Delunian word here and there."

His smile carried patience and wisdom, so like a father.

"It will take time—far more than you'd like—but it will get better. In the meantime, please visit as often as you'd like and drink up my entire store of rhosyn if it helps. We'll get you through this ordeal."

I gave my eyes a final dab, then took a long sip of tea. Heaving a shaky sigh, I leaned my head back. This—a small, circular house with strange furniture and a servant who couldn't communicate with me—was by far the closest I'd felt to home since setting foot on Delunian soil.

Perhaps with Sir Colin's help, I would get through this ordeal.

CHAPTER 13

I traipsed down the now familiar thoroughfare leading to Sir Colin's home at the far end of the marketplace, flanked by Victoria, Egan, and Tassos.

The noise and press of people, even the smell of sweat, fowl, and spices, had ceased to rouse my distaste. Once I crossed the bright-orange threshold, confined in the peace and quiet of Sir Colin's sitting room with rhosyn steaming in my teacup, I'd feel at home.

Niles maintained his usual somber demeanor as he admitted me. Sir Colin appeared in the hall, scowling at a button on his jacket as he struggled to fasten it.

Spotting me, he stopped short. "Princess Penelope. How delightful to see you."

Lowering his hands, he bent into a low bow.

My swallow did little to douse the warmth searing up my neck. "Good afternoon, Sir Colin. I'm so sorry—it seems I've caught you at an inopportune time. I ought to schedule my visits or send a message ahead."

"Nonsense." He straightened his collar with a smile. "I appreciate that you visit as family does, without ceremony.

Like a long-lost daughter. But I'm afraid you caught me on my way out."

"Don't let me detain you. I shall stop by the market instead."

My words spilled out in a rush—a vain attempt to cover my disappointment. Of course the poor man had better things to do than sit around each day, awaiting my visits.

"Perhaps . . ." He steepled his fingers, pressing them to his pursed lips. "Yes, perhaps you might join me. If you wish to, that is. You brought your guards?"

My pulse sped up a notch. Not the quiet afternoon I'd hoped for, but almost anything would be preferable to another hour wandering the palace halls.

"My guards are just outside. Where are you heading?"

He chuckled. "A reasonable question. It's not a typical destination for a young lady of consequence, I must admit, but you might find it interesting. There is a village outside the palace city walls, Leipon. The people there—they live quite differently than what you've seen of Delunia thus far. I'm afraid they are outside the royal family's favor, and thus suffer a life of poverty and ill health."

I tucked my hands behind my skirt so their trembling wouldn't reveal my cowardice. "And what brings you to such a village?"

His mouth opened and closed once in silence. "I try to help where I can. Bring a few supplies, give ideas for medicine and gardening based on my studies. I provide—education, I guess you might say."

"How very kind of you. But you said this village doesn't have a good relationship with the royal family. Do you think my presence would be welcome?"

Though reluctant to admit it, the timid side of me hoped he'd discourage my company on his venture.

"I believe it would, if you're so inclined. The notice of their future empress would give hope to the people of Leipon they haven't experienced in years. The royals must drive by if they exit the city north, of course, but they hide in their enclosed carriages, relying on their glowering guards to keep the villagers at bay."

I winced. Were Vander and his family truly so callous? Perhaps conditions in Leipon weren't as dire as Sir Colin's descriptions. Or perhaps the royal family was unaware of the hardship just beyond their walls.

Then again, both Sister Rochelle and Sister Eleanor had spoken of the rampant poverty in Delunia.

I straightened. "I would like to join you, if it isn't any trouble."

"None at all." He gestured to a chair. "Rest for a few minutes. I'll have Niles inform your guards of the purpose of our outing and gather a few supplies. Then we can be on our way."

Tassos wore a dour frown as Sir Colin closed the door behind us. Even Egan's expression exhibited concern, but he said nothing as we set out toward the north city gate.

Within minutes, sweat trickled down the neckline of my *etana*. My guards' stern countenances only added to the heat's oppressive weight.

Was this outing a bad idea? But Sir Colin would never put me in danger. And besides, as future empress, it was only right I become acquainted with the country I was to rule one day.

Most people ignored our unusual procession as they bustled about their daily lives—hanging linens to dry, tending to gardens or livestock, chasing mischievous children in amusement or anger.

Several called salutations to Sir Colin, which he returned with enthusiasm. Others openly gaped at me. I drew closer to

Victoria, but nothing short of a darker complexion and less elaborate dress could make me inconspicuous.

The North Gate rested beneath a tall stone archway, both beautiful and imposing. Sir Colin grasped the guards' hands in a jovial greeting. One's eyes narrowed at the sight of me and my entourage, and he bent closer to Sir Colin as they conversed.

I pulled back my shoulders and made my gaze direct and confident. Sir Colin wasn't escorting a dainty, timid female through the gates.

At least, I didn't want it to appear so from the outside.

Beyond the gate, the smells of animals and spices gave way to unfamiliar plant and floral scents. Trees lined the road, their large glossy leaves shading us from the sun's incessant heat. Spiny plants and patches of weedy grass spotted the caked dirt, not a home in sight.

I turned to Sir Colin, brows raised.

A hint of sadness dampened his smile. "Leipon is here, I assure you. Over the years, they've been driven farther and farther from the city gates."

Egan and Tassos had stiffened, each with a hand on his sword hilt, but they remained silent as we walked on. Victoria's gaze was questioning as it met mine, but even she didn't utter a word.

Luminate, let Sir Colin be as trustworthy as I've come to believe. The prayer rose unconsciously before I could stop it. The Luminate no longer cared for my safety.

I swiped at a trail of sweat trickling down my cheek. The sides of my slippers pressed into my feet, becoming more painful with every step. Perhaps I should've asked Sir Colin to defer this outing to another day, when I could've worn more appropriate attire or used one of the palace carriages.

We passed through a copse of trees, their trunks thin compared to the trees at home and so tall the lowest leaves floated well above my head. At the other side, my steps faltered. The open expanse seemed to house an entirely different realm. One filled with animal skin–topped piles of sticks for dwellings and stinking of dung and rotting meat.

Victoria swallowed audibly and stumbled back. Egan gently took her arm to steady her. Tassos stepped closer to me, his eyes traversing our new surroundings with suspicion and concern. I caught up with Sir Colin and Niles.

My friend's lips pressed together in a grim line. "Welcome to Leipon, princess."

The people moving about had none of the color or vibrancy the residents of the palace or Ambrus had. Each person's garb was faded to gray or tan, limply hanging over their thin frames. Tired lines etched each face, a stoop curved every back. Even the children had little bounce in their step, their cries lacking exuberance.

An old woman was the first to notice us. Her greeting of "Colin! Colin!" was followed by other words I didn't understand. She stretched out her hands, and he hurried to meet her.

We followed, Tassos sticking close by my side.

Sir Colin turned to us. "Please, allow me to introduce my friend, Madame Yalena."

He spoke to her in Delunian, and her eyes widened.

Facing me, she lowered her head in an unsteady bow. "*Principela*."

My heart galloped under her mystified gaze. In such a setting, my clothing felt too elaborate, my hair too styled, my hands too soft and uncalloused.

She called out. I jumped at the sudden change from her silent perusal. Several others approached, some smiling at Sir Colin, others darting wary glances at the guards. Two children ran ahead, a girl with stringy dark hair and a shorter boy with dirt smudged on his face.

Sir Colin grinned and ruffled the boy's hair. "And this is Basil and his sister Leda."

"It's nice to meet you."

Sir Colin translated for me. The boy—Basil—ran forward and hugged my legs, his rush of words muffled in my skirt. I awkwardly gave his back a pat. Leda kept her distance, regarding me with wide eyes. How lovely she'd be with proper nourishment and attire. If only I had something that would fit her wasted frame . . .

The collection of haggard adults trailing behind the children reached us. Soon a wave of Delunian immersed me, voices melding and crashing over one another.

Sir Colin didn't have an opportunity to translate before the villagers' attention swarmed to me. A woman and man, presumably a couple, stepped closer with their hands clasped in a pleading gesture. Another woman opened her palms to me, and several children tugged at my skirt.

My breath came in gasps, the desperate eyes and unintelligible pleas pressing upon me like a physical force. "Help. Yes, I want to help you."

None of them would understand a word I said, of course, but I couldn't let such supplications go unanswered.

Sir Colin pushed through the small crowd to stand at my side. Whatever his next words, they seemed to have a calming, almost-cheering effect.

The villagers smiled, and Madame Yalena executed another shaky bow. Sir Colin dug in his basket, distributing wrapped bread to one frail man, a bundle of carrots to a young mother with a baby strapped to her chest, and a bowl of some kind of salve to Madame Yalena.

Tassos relaxed his grip on his sword hilt as the crowd dispersed, a few remaining to talk with Sir Colin.

A teenage boy exited a dilapidated tent far to our left and ran in our direction. His bare feet kicked up a cloud of dust as he scrambled to a stop before us. Sir Colin dipped his head and asked something in Delunian. The boy nodded vigorously and pointed back toward his tent. Sir Colin started walking, beckoning for us to follow.

I fell back to join Victoria, who still clung to Egan's arm but no longer trembled. "I apologize, Victoria. I should've thought this through, perhaps offered to join another time when we could've brought more guards or you could've stayed at the palace."

She shrugged. "There's no need to apologize, m'lady. I'll admit to being a bit taken back. I've never seen people in such dire conditions. I had no idea . . ." Her words trailed off as she watched a young woman scrubbing cloth in a murky stream. "But they don't seem to mean us any harm."

"True."

We reached the boy's tent, which emanated puffs of black smoke. I tucked my arms closer to my sides. What could cause so much smoke in such a small space? A fire? An explosion?

Sir Colin ducked inside, but Egan raised a hand to prevent me from following. I gladly obeyed.

"Can you tell what's happening?" I coughed as the fumes entered my lungs.

Egan's brow creased. "The boy says something about spell. It—not working. His mother tried to preserve spoiled meat from deer, but as meat cooks the blaze becomes too hot and makes it"—he gestured, as though searching for the right word —"blow apart."

Victoria twined her fingers together. "Oh my. I hope no one was hurt. And that their tent isn't ruined. I doubt they could easily make a new one."

Egan responded, but I only half listened. My mind had seized on the word *spell*.

Had the boy's mother truly been attempting magic? Black spots danced across my vision. I thought I'd left all traces of sorcery behind in Imperia. The last place I'd expected to encounter it again was a charity call to poverty-stricken peasants. My fingers instinctively clutched my amulet. What had Sister Rochelle said about my needing protection?

Stop it, Penelope. Even if the woman had attempted a spell, she was trying to preserve meat, not injure someone. And perhaps Egan was mistaken or had given an imprecise translation.

Sir Colin emerged, shaking his head. He paused to speak in undertones to Niles, who hurried away.

Steeling myself with a shaky breath, I stepped forward. "Is everything all right? What happened?"

"I'm afraid Ilene is badly burned. Her arm took the brunt of it. Niles is fetching water, and fortunately I brought my basic medical kit so we can clean and bandage the wound."

"Can I help in any way?" The question felt necessary but foolish. My pampered upbringing had taught me nothing of medicine or healing.

"No, princess. But it's good of you to offer." Lines creased his face, making him appear much older. "Bringing you here was a mistake. I apologize. I had hoped . . ." He shook his head. "I appreciate your willingness to come on this fool's errand. I do believe it has given them hope to know at least one of their future rulers hasn't forgotten them."

A wail sounded from inside the tent, and he winced.

"But this could take some time, and there's hardly room for me in the tent, let alone anyone else." He patted my arm. "Let your guards escort you back to the palace. But visit again soon, if you're able."

"Of course."

Relief flowed through me at his instructions, coupled with a hint of guilt that I'd so eagerly abandon my friend and the people he was trying to help.

"I hope she'll recover from her injuries. And I don't regret your bringing me here today. It's difficult to witness their desperate state, but I'll speak with Vander and his family and see if we can be of assistance."

"I fear your words will fall on deaf ears, but it's commendable you at least want to try."

The woman within the tent emitted a low groan.

Sir Colin tensed. "I must tend to her, but you should be safe with your guards. Farewell."

"Farewell."

He spoke in Delunian to Tassos, gesturing to the path leading toward Ambrus. Tassos nodded, and our smaller party made our way back through the village and into the tree cover.

It took all my willpower not to break into a run.

Visions of Leipon haunted me for the remainder of the day.

I flinched as we entered the main hall of the palace. The entire village could fit inside. One gold-filigreed vase could likely feed every one of the townsfolk for twelve lunar cycles.

I wanted to bathe, to cleanse myself of every hint of the stench and filth. Of the memories crowding my head, tainting my enjoyment of the luxuries that surrounded me. But Madame Yalena, Leda, little Basil—their faces cycled through my mind in an endless rotation.

With only a muddy stream for drinking and washing, they'd probably never had a proper bath in their entire lives. Leipon was so much more than just memories they could choose to reflect on or ignore. It was their entire existence.

Fortunately, dinner was a small affair consisting of just the royal family. But even without the ceremony of serving palace guests, the table decor was elaborate, the food decadent.

I pushed small pieces of oyster around my plate, creating a swirling pattern in the spiced sauce. How could I allow myself to enjoy multiple courses of a carefully prepared meal when those frail children were likely gnawing on meat that hadn't been cured properly or attempting to fill their stomachs with a handful of unripe berries?

Vander cleared his throat at my side. I blinked and raised my head. The entire family regarded me with expressions ranging from curiosity to concern.

Nadia waved her fork in my direction. "The oyster *salata* does not please you, Penelope?"

"It does, thank you. I'm just not very hungry."

Tertius pursed his lips. "I hope you are not unwell. Adjusting to a new climate can cause dreadful illnesses, I hear."

I put a generous bite in my mouth and forced myself to chew and swallow. "I appreciate your concern, but I assure you I am quite well."

"Good to hear." The emperor saluted me with his raised goblet. "I did promise your father we would take care of you, after all."

"And you have fulfilled that promise in its entirety."

I mustered a smile, grateful when Nadia changed the subject to gossip surrounding the mysterious death of a young nobleman.

Vander leaned close, his voice in an undertone. "Will you join me for cup of tea in my study following the meal?"

My stomach squirmed. I'd had few tête-à-têtes with Vander since my declaration in the garden, and each had been uncomfortable. Still, I'd promised to speak with him about Leipon.

"Yes, thank you. Though I don't need any tea."

His brows raised, but he merely nodded. "Very well."

After one more course, the meal ended. The emperor and empress watched Vander and me exit with apparent satisfaction, while Dionne's face remained as impassive as ever.

Vander closed the door to his study behind me. The isolation put me on edge, but I shook my head. No doubt we'd be expected to spend many such evenings together once we were married.

Bookshelves covered in an array of mismatched volumes flanked the empty fireplace. I missed the coziness of home, where a fire always glowed within each hearth. But, of course, such warmth was rarely needed here.

Vander pulled out a chair for me on one side of a small table, then settled himself in the chair opposite. "Are you truly well, Penelope? You seem most, hmm, distracted at dinner."

"I am very well, thank you." I filled my chest with a deep breath, wishing it could similarly inflate my confidence. "Only troubled by something I experienced today."

He sat up straighter. "What troubles you?"

"I—" I traced the gold trim edging the table. "How often do you venture beyond the North Gate?"

He leaned back. "We visit northern provinces on occasion, and the Dellis family in Teresi has hosted our family many time. But I need not travel that direction so often. Why is it you ask?"

"Have you ever been to the village of Leipon?"

"This village is beyond road heading north?" His lips pinched to one side. "I've heard it mentioned, but I don't believe I've been there, no."

I tried to keep my voice steady. "Perhaps you ought to consider paying them a visit. It's only a short walk beyond the city gate, but the living conditions are terrible."

The curiosity in his expression darkened to alarm. "You went beyond city walls? Alone?"

"Not alone. With Sir Colin and one of his servants. And my own guards."

I sat up straighter. As the future empress, I shouldn't have to confess my comings and goings like a repentant child.

"I am not familiar with Sir Colin."

"He's a scholar who traveled on the same ship with us to Delunia. When a sailor accosted me on the ship, Sir Colin came to my rescue." I shuddered at the memory. "He also has lived most of his life in Trellich, though now he spends some of the year in a house in Ambrus."

"I see." He took a slow sip of tea. "And why did this Colin think it wise to put his princess in danger?"

"He had no desire to put me in danger. I happened to visit when he was on his way to Leipon. He tries to help the people there with medicine and supplies. He allowed me to accompany him."

"It seems this man is quite generous."

Could Vander be moved to such generosity as well? "He is. The villagers look up to and respect him. He stayed behind to help bandage a woman's injured arm."

Vander tipped his chair back, rubbing his thumb along his chin.

I pressed on before I could lose my nerve. "The people there are starving. Their clothes are tattered, their houses look like they're about to fall down, and Sir Colin said they don't have proper medicines. How could an entire village so near *Palati del Chrysos* be allowed to fall into such poverty?"

He drummed his fingers against the table. "My father had to increase the taxes some years ago as our navy expands. Perhaps these poor areas are more affected than we realize."

"They're being taxed? How could they be expected to pay anything to increase the royal family's wealth when they already have nothing?"

His jaw set tighter than I'd ever seen it. "Your family lives in moderation, *rei*? You share your wealth with all people so no one will be poor?"

"I . . ."

No doubt people lived in similarly dismal conditions in Trellich. Had I ever given a thought to the commission of a new dress fashioned from the most elegant material, another lavish banquet to impress our court?

"No. At least, not as much as we should. I regret now that I didn't investigate the conditions of our people, didn't find out whether Trellan children were starving." I swallowed, steeling my resolve. "But this is happening right outside your doors. Can you really ignore it in good conscience?"

"You forget I am not yet Emperor of Delunia."

"But you will be! And the emperor is your father. You must have some influence with him."

The hard glint in his eyes softened. "It does disturb me to hear of such suffering so close by. Perhaps another time we might pay a visit together. But please, never again travel beyond the gates on your own."

"Of course." My smile crept forth, timid but hopeful. "And thank you."

"Problems with deep roots, the solutions are not so simple." He gave my hand the briefest pat. "But I do appreciate your concern for our people, Penelope."

Our people. My heart didn't rear against the phrase nearly as much as I would've expected.

CHAPTER 14

$\mathcal{I}$ filled my plate with eggs, fruit, and a trigonis. Guilt nudged the corners of my mind as I settled at the table. My light dinner the night before was enough to stir my hunger this morning. In fact, I was the first of the royal family to arrive to breakfast. How must it feel for the people of Leipon to eat so little every day?

Vander entered, his footsteps resonating more loudly than usual on the marble floor.

"Good morning." I nodded to him, but my greeting went unheeded.

I returned my gaze to my meal, replaying the prior evening's events in my mind. Our conversation had been tense in a few moments, but we'd parted on friendly terms.

Hadn't we?

A servant approached Vander with a pot of tea, but he barked what I could only assume was a refusal.

My hand wobbled as I brought my fork to my mouth. I'd never seen him deal with a servant so harshly, not even following the revelation of my intentions for our marriage.

He sat at the far end of the table, not sparing me a glance.

I sucked in a breath. "Good morning, Vander."

His jaw tensed. "I trust you slept well, princess." His words seemed edged with irony.

Princess. The term buzzed in my ear like a mosquito. "Reasonably well, I thank you. Did you — ?"

"My preference would be to eat in peace. My thanks."

"Of — of course." I shrank into my chair as heat inflamed my cheeks.

We ate in silence, aside from the sharp clanging of his cutlery as he sawed his sausage and the clap of his glass against the table each time he slammed it down. Never before had I been so eager for the company of his parents, his sister. Even a visiting nobleman or diplomat would be a welcome break in the palpable tension.

Appetite soon forgotten, I set my plate aside and rose. My mouth opened by force of habit, but no words came. What could I say, when he gave no indication of what upset him?

I made my way to the door but paused as I reached for the handle. "Enjoy your breakfast."

I slipped away before he could growl a response.

Vander failed to appear at luncheon.

At my hesitant inquiry, Tertius mentioned an impromptu outing on horseback. "But do not fret, Penelope. I have no doubt my son will be back at your side by the evening meal."

He concluded with an expressive nod, apparently unaware or unconcerned about his son's foul temper that morning.

Only Dionne's glower gave any indication Vander might've confided his woes to someone. And that they might've been related to me.

At dinner, Vander strode in just after we'd sat down, clean-shaven and smelling of soap. He took the seat at my left, his posture stiff. The emperor asked him a question about the stables, to which his response was polite but brief.

I forced a light smile. "Did you enjoy your excursion this afternoon?"

"*Rei*. Yes." His eyes met mine, but their hard edge made

them seem unfamiliar. "I do enjoy occasional outing, though not so many as you."

I flinched back. "Is there any reason I shouldn't go on outings?" I leaned closer, glancing toward his parents to make sure they were still engaged in their own conversation. "I already promised not to venture beyond the gates again without your consent."

A vein pulsed in his neck. "Perhaps beyond gates isn't where problem lies, after all."

"What—?"

Nadia interrupted me. "Penelope, dear. Perhaps you can resolve our question." She brandished her fork. "Does Imperian king have one brother or two?"

My mind scrambled to make sense of her inquiry. "Three, I believe."

"Is it so many?" Tertius raised his brows.

Nadia shook her head. "I knew answer was more than one. Another example why you defer to me on these matters." She directed a wink at me. "Keep in mind for your marriage too, Vander. Wife is always right."

He cleared his throat but offered no further response.

My mind churned for the remainder of the meal. I had to do something. I hadn't realized how much I relied on Vander's quiet good nature, his steady dependability, until he'd thrown it off to become someone else entirely. Someone who lost his temper with people he usually treated with respect, who shut out those closest to him.

"Vander." His name escaped before I'd fully thought through what I planned to say.

He darted a glance in my direction but didn't speak.

I licked my lips. "Remember when you said I must learn to play *zappas*?"

Apparently, it was a popular Delunian strategy game involving dice. His assent came in the form of a grunt.

"Would you teach me this evening?"

His goblet paused on its way back to the table, then he shook his head. "This evening is not—"

"Please. It would be a welcome distraction after . . . the events that were so upsetting to me yesterday."

Guilt tugged at me for playing on his emotions, but I had to access the kind, gentle side of him. The side that seemed to still care for me, despite the many ways in which I'd proven to be a disappointment.

His goblet slammed to the table. "Certainly there are other distractions you might prefer?"

The same bitter tone. The same accusation. What could've lowered his opinion of me so much in such a short time?

A knot lodged in my chest. Had he learned about Nicholas?

Perhaps it was inevitable he'd discover the truth at some point. But no matter my past, I'd hardly spoken to another man since my arrival in Delunia. I'd just have to earn back his trust.

I smoothed my skirt. "None at all. I appreciated being able to talk so openly with you yesterday, and I hoped we could continue the conversation."

He ran a hand through his hair, then raised his head to view his parents watching our interaction with curiosity. His breath released in a huff. "*Rei.* Yes."

"Thank you."

Tension gripped my limbs as I struggled to finish my meal with a relaxed air. Either I'd convince Vander to admit what was wrong, or I'd just volunteered for the most painful night of my life.

∾

Vander made his way to the parlor, apparently assuming I'd follow. I traipsed along behind him, tripping over my skirts in my attempt to match his longer stride. He entered, almost letting the door close behind him before I could catch it.

Indignation seethed in my veins. Regardless of how he felt about me, I was a princess, deserving of respect. Grasping the door, I took one, two, three steadying breaths.

I'd never get any revelations out of him if I approached the discussion with anything other than humility. *Luminate knows I have plenty to be humble about.*

Inside the parlor, I glanced around, ensuring no servants lingered. The room was empty, lights flickering eerily in the sconces lining the walls.

Vander stood just inside the doorway, as though unsure how to proceed.

Steeling my resolve, I stepped to his side and touched his arm. "Is everything all right?"

He flinched away, putting several paces between us. "Why should it not?"

I hastily drew my hand back but suppressed my desire to cower. The changes I'd noted in him throughout the day weren't just my imagination.

"This morning you scolded a servant, you hardly spoke a word to your parents at dinner, and you've been slamming everything in sight."

"My faults, they are many." He clenched his jaw.

"Not usually." I ached to draw near again, but my feet stayed rooted in place. "You're not acting like yourself. I'm — I'm worried about you."

His laugh conveyed anything but mirth. "Why do you bother to concern yourself with me? A man you cannot love. A man you have no wish to marry."

"Vander, I thought we'd been through all this. I regret more than I can express that I can't give you what you want in a wife, but we agreed to move forward with our alliance."

My mind spun in circles, searching for an explanation for his altered behavior.

"I'm sorry if I was too harsh last evening. I was so over-whelmed by what I'd seen in Leipon. But that doesn't under-mine my commitment to our future marriage."

"Commitment." Another hollow chuckle. "Yes, we would hate for that to be undermined."

He walked to a table and leaned down to open a drawer. Withdrawing a small box, he set out four dice and a number of colored game pieces.

The indignation burned to fury, bubbling to the surface. "What are you doing?"

He closed his eyes for a long moment. "You want to learn to play *zappas*, *rei*?"

"Yes, but you walked away in the middle of our discussion." My exhale agitated the curls dangling at my cheeks. "You're speaking in riddles. You still haven't told me what's wrong."

His chest rose and fell with several shaky breaths. "Penelope."

I shrank back at the intensity of his gaze. "Yes?"

"If it truly matters so much to you, I will explain. Though I think it should come as no surprise."

"It does matter. And I don't—"

He raised a hand to cut me off. Replacing the game pieces in the box, he stepped away from the table. "Perhaps we will save *zappas* for other time." He faced me, his eyes wary.

Our relative postures set me further on edge: poised in a standoff as though preparing for combat. But to take a seat would feel more vulnerable somehow. It seemed safer to remain on my feet, able to dart away should the need arise.

Vander looked down to where his feet shifted beneath him. "I try hard to respect your wishes. I keep distance, not make you endure my—affection."

Swallowing, I nodded.

"But I shall not abide being such a distant fiancé, such a distant husband, if I must witness your heart given to another."

"Another?" Air escaped my lungs with a painful pinch. It must be about Nicholas. But how had he found out? What could press Victoria into making such a disclosure? Or—

"I spoke with your guards last night, to ensure they would never again be so careless to take you beyond city gates into danger. They inform me . . ."

His brow creased, as though he were in physical pain.

"I do not express myself so well in Sandrinian, and I have no practice in ways of courtship. But I am not blind nor slow in my wits, Penelope. They say you visit this Sir Colin nearly every day. You spend hours within his home. You readily follow him to Leipon only because he asks. Just yesterday you spoke of his heroic rescue."

He crossed his arms and angled away.

Tension drained from my shoulders. "Sir Colin? That's what this is about? He's old enough to be my father."

His head tilted toward me. "It seems some women do not mind such, hmm, stateliness."

I swallowed a giggle. "Perhaps, but I'm not among their number. At least, not in any romantic way."

"No?" His arms dropped, his body poised in indecision. "But then . . ."

"Sir Colin has been a mentor to me. Almost like a father. I seek his company because he reminds me of home, yet he knows enough of Delunia to teach me the customs here. I never dreamed you might become jealous of him."

He faced me again, eyes narrowed. After a moment, his posture slumped. "Then I must make apologies for my accusation." He collapsed into the nearest armchair. "I understand you cannot love me, and I have no wish to cause you discomfort with efforts to persuade you otherwise. You say you would not love any man, yet you are young and beautiful. I fear your affection will be won by another, making our marriage more of the fraud."

"Oh, Vander."

I knelt beside his chair, sorrow and anger warring in my chest. Nicholas had stolen so much from both of us.

"I truly intend to be finished with romance entirely. I would've made the same resolution no matter whom my father chose. Please be assured I have no interest in looking for love elsewhere. I cannot offer you my love, but you do have my loyalty."

He searched my face, his expression softer than it'd been all day. "This is good to hear you say. Though with such a face, few men shall be willing to keep distance."

I wrapped my fingers around his arm. "Then I'll count on you to protect me from them."

A hint of red flushed his cheeks, accompanied by the faintest of smiles.

I loosened my grip but kept my hand in place. "And I so appreciate your willingness to give me the distance I've requested. You are certainly correct that many men would not do the same." I lowered my gaze. "I apologize for causing you so much pain. You are in no way deserving of it, and I . . ."

He patted my hand. "No apology is necessary. It is not what I would wish, but I would rather the honesty than pretending in such matter. My greatest shame would be to force affections on a young lady who prefers not to receive them."

"You are a perfect gentleman, and I'm grateful." I stood carefully, my knees already stiff.

"But Penelope"—he rose, his expression guarded—"I shall not continue to pain you with such subject, but should your mind change about your desire for romance, please . . ."

I held my breath as he tucked a stray curl into its hairpin.

"I would wish to be given first opportunity."

I bobbed my head in a quick nod, my returning breaths still shallow. Giving a slight bow, he pressed my hand and strode from the room.

CHAPTER 15

I idly tapped the keys of the pianoforte in the music room.

Grateful the air had been cleared with Vander and reluctant to cause any additional suspicion, I'd avoided going into town for the past week. Instead, I'd wandered the gardens, perused the few books in the palace library written in Sandrinian, composed letters to my family, and even sat with Victoria for several games of spades.

But my lack of acquaintances and meaningful employment made the time pass slowly. Leaning my chin on one hand, I trilled a little air with the other. How much of my existence would plod along in such boredom, such uselessness?

The door creaked, and my hand bumped the ivory keys in surprise, producing a dissonant chord.

Vander strode in with a chuckle. "I apologize for the startle, Penelope. I would almost think to ask my parents to find you music tutor."

I rose and flexed my fingers. "I've had enough tutors to last me a lifetime. In recent years, my father seemed of the opinion that he could make up in lessons what my sisters and I lacked in mothering."

His humor faded. "I'm sure a father in such position can never feel he's done enough for his daughters." He shifted his weight between his feet. "Now that ambassador from Turkanov has departed, my father has no need of me this afternoon. I noticed you take no outings after . . ."

He rubbed the back of his neck.

"Would you be willing to accompany me to town? I'd very much like to give you a tour of Ambrus; it is a thing I should have considered weeks ago. If we travel by carriage, we may see all sights without lateness for dinner."

My heart lightened at the prospect of venturing outside the palace grounds.

I gave him a warm smile. "Yes, I would enjoy that."

The roof of the carriage jutted out beyond us to the seat on which the driver perched, shading us all from the sun's unrelenting heat. The open sides made me feel exposed compared to the sturdy walls of our carriages back home, but they allowed a breeze and added to the air of novelty.

Vander kept a respectable distance between us on the seat, eagerly pointing out homes of various noble families, sites of historic or political importance, and decorative fountains and murals. Our path through the marketplace to Sir Colin's home had never taken us through this wealthier portion of the city.

Delunians seemed to view the world as their canvas.

The exuberance of color and paint inundated me at first, but as I paused to take in each individual scene, the artistry struck me with more meaning. Entire walls were painted with a landscape rather than one solid color. Gardens overflowed with wild assortments of blossoms, no more organized than a field of wildflowers. Even walkways were paved with a mosaic of colorful tiles instead of practical gravel.

We turned onto a main thoroughfare, and I winced against

the increased noise and crush of additional carriages, wagons, and buggies. A cart careened past us, narrowly avoiding the protruding axle of our front wheel.

My breath choked in my throat as I clutched the armrest. I glanced to Vander. Would he reprimand such careless driving? Especially when it endangered a member of the royal family?

Vander's face betrayed no hint that he'd even noticed the near miss. He smiled into the sunshine, giving a wave or nod here and there to brightly dressed lords and ladies we passed.

Annoyance mingled with my relief. While I didn't relish the thought of making a spectacle of ourselves by stopping the cart driver and scolding him for his recklessness, didn't Vander care that we'd nearly been jostled off the road?

I ducked toward him as a chaise rocked around a turn, briefly leaning onto one wheel before righting itself. I squared my shoulders, trying to resume a somewhat regal posture instead of the timid stance of a frightened schoolgirl.

Perhaps Delunia contained far too many reckless drivers to reprimand them all.

I winced, watching a guard on horseback dodge a brisk wagon. *Thank heavens no one in Sir Colin's neighborhood has the means to own a carriage.*

"Is there something going on in town today?" I asked.

Vander swiveled his head to me with a quizzical lift to his brow. "The town always has plenty of activity."

"Everyone seems to be in such a hurry. As though each carriage is trying to outpace the others."

"Ah, that." He thrummed his fingers on one knee. "We do not mind a more—exciting ride. There is nothing wrong with speed when one stays out of others' way."

"Oh." I deflated against the cushion. Such chaos was the norm, then. "But the royal carriages take a slower pace?"

At least that was a small blessing.

Vander's cough bordered on a chuckle. "Yes. At least, when I instruct Filip to drive at camel speed."

My frown provoked a more obvious laugh.

"You are not used to our ways, Penelope. I have knowledge of this. I do not desire to frighten you." He leaned near, almost brushing my shoulder before backing away with a creased brow. "One day we introduce you to the fun of a bumpy ride."

Fun? I resisted the urge to cross my arms. No use pouting like a spoiled child, especially when he'd been considerate enough to tell his driver to go slower on my account. But how a faster journey could possibly be worth the risk of . . .

A chorus of shouts dislodged the thought.

Had a collision between carriages finally occurred, or some kind of riot? I angled my head to peer beyond the driver and our team of dark horses.

A group of people surrounded a fountain, pausing from drawing water and conversations to stare at us. But their expressions held joy, anticipation—not anger. Another cry rose up, almost a cheer. A word, repeated over and over.

Kise? I turned to Vander. "What does—" The apology in his eyes and the red in his cheeks gave me pause. "What's wrong?"

He glanced to the crowd, then back at me. His chest rose and fell with a heavy breath. Throat bobbing, he reached a hand to my face and leaned close.

I edged back as subtly as I could. "Vander, I—"

Something about the look in his eyes begged me to stay still, his fingers holding my jaw. I flinched as his breath warmed my cheek. Feather light, his lips brushed my skin.

He reeled back, pink tinting even the tips of his ears.

What had come over him?

The crowd clapped with more hollers but less enthusiasm than before. A few passersby patted the side of our carriage or shook Vander's hand as we circled the far end of the fountain.

I straightened my skirt to precision, keeping my eyes fixed on the detailed embroidery. If Vander's tanned skin could take on such a pink hue, what shade of crimson must've invaded my own?

We reached a quieter stretch of road, and a bit of the tension left my shoulders.

Vander shifted at my side. "My apologies for this."

Making him clarify would only increase the awkwardness, so I stilled my hands and stayed silent.

"The people are jubilant to have future empress." He linked and unlinked his fingers. "Such event has been anticipated ever since my coming of age."

"So they felt the need to shout at us?" I lowered my tone to a less shrill register. "What does *kise* mean? Is that what they were saying?"

"The word, it is not so different from your language. It was invitation to—"

"Oh." My stomach churned. "But why would they want to embarrass their prince by demanding such affection in public? We're not even married yet. It's indecent."

"Not in Delunia, Penelope."

The combination of sadness and patience in his voice caught my attention. I finally dared to meet his gaze.

"Here, to show such affection brings no shame. Even before formal engagement."

I couldn't completely stifle my huff. "But still, to demand it of others . . ."

He chafed his palms against the smooth material of his trousers. "Marriages here, they are not for gain. Not for money or connection. People enter such a union for love." He waved a hand to the crowd we'd left behind. "They have no under-standing of couple who would not want to kiss. To celebrate such love."

Love again. Apparently, I'd come to the wrong place to distance myself from romance. "But after all that, they seemed disappointed. I still don't understand."

Despite my best efforts, it came out as a grumble.

Vander gave me a sidelong glance. "Kiss on cheek does not quite match their hopes."

Fire heated my face once again as I took in his meaning.

"Please understand, Penelope. They know little of Trellan ways, and no disrespect is intended. Although royal family may marry for the peace, the connections of politics, they still hope for us to have happiness in our unions."

"Of course." I fiddled with the beads on the edge of my sleeve. "Thank you for once again taking my wishes into account, although they go against Delunian ways." My head drooped lower. "I apologize you aren't getting the romantic marriage they wish for you."

He laid a hand on my arm. "A marriage without such passion is not of necessity unhappy."

I nodded. "I suppose that's true."

I'd cling to that hope with all my heart.

CHAPTER 16

A knock sounded at my door. I winced.

Although several days had passed since my excursion through town with Vander, I wasn't ready to repeat the experience. It had been a pleasant-enough ride on the whole, but my cheeks burned every time I recalled the crowd, cheering for us to kiss as though we were in a play. A spectacle for their amusement.

Shaking myself, I set aside my book and hurried to the door. I was greeted not by Vander, but by a thin servant with deep creases lining his face. I smiled, then hesitated. Was it worth even trying to communicate with him?

Before I could resolve my dilemma, he extended his arm. On his silver tray sat a thick envelope. A thrill of expectation soared within me.

"For me?" I placed a hand on my chest.

He nodded. *"Rei."*

Mail, at last! Until the prospect of news from home—seeing my father's and sisters' handwriting again—loomed right before me, I hadn't realized how desperate I was for a connection to them. *Any* connection to Trellich.

I struggled to wait the endless seconds before the porter

placed the letters in my hand rather than snatch them from his grasp. "Thank you."

He nodded with a tight smile.

"I mean, *efcharis te*."

I'd heard the phrase spoken often enough, but the odd combination of consonants stuck in my mouth like the creamy spread the palace cook made from *vasak* nuts.

His smile widened. "*Te parakal*."

I closed the door as he turned away, then sank against it. So much effort for the exchange of four words. How would I ever learn to converse with these people?

Finally releasing the sigh I'd kept at bay, I straightened and retreated into my sitting room. Snatching my letter opener, I sank onto the divan.

The thick envelope promised at least three letters. My hands quavered as I removed the first folded sheet of parchment and tried to straighten it. Papa's thick, boxy script covered the page from edge to edge.

My lips curled into a tentative smile, even as a sheen of moisture dampened my eyes.

He was well. All continued much the same in Trellich. He'd had to dispatch guards to a northern province, but the new cook made the best apple tarts he'd ever had. Imperia had finally signed the trade agreement after weeks of negotiation.

My family missed me.

Oh, Papa, you've no idea . . . I brushed away the droplets gathering on my lower lashes before they could smudge the ink.

Sniffling, I set his letter carefully aside and withdrew the next. Vivienne. I giggled through her accounts of boring history lessons, horseback riding adventures gone awry, and gowns that always turned out an inch too short just weeks after they'd been commissioned.

My heavy exhale fluttered the paper. She'd be a woman the next time I saw her. Accomplished, refined—at least, if her tutors had anything to say about it—and probably dwarfing me in stature. Why did Delunia have to be so terribly far? I unclenched my fingers to avoid crinkling the parchment.

Now for Sophia. Her cramped, dainty handwriting filled two entire pages, front and back. I nestled farther into my pillow. Jealousies between other young ladies at court. Lavish accounts of every new gown and item of jewelry, down to the last detail. Ruminations on dancing lessons and who should be invited to the next ball.

I bit my lip, resisting the temptation to roll my eyes. She meant well, and I could hardly fault a sixteen-year-old girl for taking an interest in balls and dresses.

Her narrative began to wrap up, with many wishes for my happiness and entreaties for descriptions of Vander and my new dresses. Odd. I glanced to the back of the page, where she'd continued to write another three paragraphs. Had she forgotten something?

I skimmed the words more quickly.

Then the paper nearly fell from my grasp.

Oh, Penelope, thank goodness I haven't posted this letter yet, for I just received the most wonderful news! Papa has arranged a match between myself and Prince Gael of Lower Flynn, and Gael wrote the sweetest letter with his proposal! Can you believe it? Me—engaged at last! I do hope we can be married in the spring, but Papa says not this year yet. Wouldn't dearest Gael look splendid with a springtide rose on his lapel? And I must have lilies of the sunrise, of course. I wish you had come with me to see the Lower Flynnite palace; the gardens are magnificent. Soon it will be my home! How shall I ever write a proper response? I can hardly . . .

My tumultuous mind couldn't keep up with Sophia's jumble of thoughts regarding her upcoming marriage. She was engaged. My little sister.

I could just imagine how she must be drifting through the

halls, squealing with every aristocrat and servant who'd humor her excited ramblings.

And I wasn't there. I was missing all of it.

A tear coursed to my chin before I realized it'd fallen.

Setting the letter aside, I fumbled for my handkerchief. It wasn't as though the news came as a surprise—Sophia had spoken of little else for months before my departure.

But that her life could take such a significant turn, completely without me . . .

My door thudded with a soft rap.

"Come in." The instinctive reply left my lips before I gave it conscious thought. I swallowed and swiped at my eyes, trying to erase evidence of tears.

Vander nudged the door open just wide enough to step inside. "Good afternoon, Penelope. I hoped you might—" His words cut off the same instant his formal demeanor softened to concern. "Something upsets you."

Smoothing my skirt, I made a pathetic attempt at shaking my head.

He hurried to my side, glancing to the abandoned letter on the adjoining cushion. "Your family—someone is unwell?"

"No, everyone is quite well. There's no cause for concern."

His narrowed eyes remained fixed on my face.

I blew out a breath. "It is a letter from my family, but it contains good news. My sister is to be married."

"Ah." His heavy brows raised a notch. "But you do not approve the match." His gaze moved to the ground. "Or perhaps is to a gentleman you would rather—"

"No, nothing like that." I hurriedly folded the letter and replaced it in the envelope, my fingers unsteady. "I'm very happy for her. It will be a good match and a strong alliance for our country. It's only that I—I'm not there."

"Of course." He perched on the spot vacated by the letter. "A moment of such importance for one you love, and you cannot share it with her."

"Yes." I sniffled as a new round of tears threatened.

He squeezed my arm. My instinct was to recoil, but the touch was so gentle, so comforting—without a hint of romance or expectation—I posed no objection.

I stifled a hiccup. "I'm sorry. It's not that I'm unhappy to be here, it's just—"

"It is natural for you to miss family. I would think the less of you if you did not." His hand tightened, then let go. "Does she say when wedding shall be held?"

I blinked, curling my fingers around my handkerchief. "I don't believe a date has been set. She mentioned something about spring, but not until next year."

My mind seemed to be trudging uphill against a foot of snow in its struggle to recall any details.

"Then perhaps we might attend."

My head snapped toward him. "What?"

He reddened at the sudden attention. "I believe our wedding will take place before so much time has passed. And what better time to plan a visit?"

The prospect of our marriage didn't make me shudder the way it usually did in light of this prospect of home. Seeing my family. A significant event I wouldn't miss.

Before considering what I was doing, I grasped his hand. "Thank you."

"Certainly, Penelope." He inclined his head, his expression a mixture of confusion and hope. "I do wish to make you happy."

"I know." Experience had taught me no man could ever be acting solely for my good, but the sentiment seemed in earnest. "And I appreciate it more than I can say."

Empress Nadia took a sip from her goblet and faced me. "I understand your sister shall marry a Flynnite prince."

I glanced to Vander, who lifted his shoulders in a barely perceptible shrug. "Yes, she is. I just received the news in her letter today."

Thanks to Victoria's cream, my eyes didn't show the effects of my turmoil earlier in the afternoon. But I wasn't sure I could trust myself to have a lengthy discussion of the subject yet.

"How lovely. Do you have acquaintance with this prince?"

"Only a little." A smile crept to my face. "His family visited Trellich on several occasions, but my sister commandeered so much of his attention the rest of us hardly had a chance to speak with him."

"A match of affection, then. The most happy kind."

Her eyes sought her husband, while I studied the swirling blue and gold pattern on the edge of my plate.

She gasped and turned her attention back to me. "This gives reminder. Vander has discussed with you about the ball we plan?"

Vander jumped in before I could respond. "No, Mother. You're doing the planning, so it's right for you to share the news."

"But the idea was from you! And what a good one it was." The empress patted my hand. "It is time we give you formal introduction to our people, Penelope. You should have the opportunity to develop friendships in addition to our small family."

"Hear, hear!" Tertius pounded his fist on the table, making the plates clink. "This engagement is something to be celebrated."

I slowly lowered the fork that had hung suspended over my plate ever since the word *ball*. "Thank you, that is very kind. But I'm afraid I don't know any of your traditional dances."

Nadia's musical laughter floated over us. "They are not so very different. You have much grace, and Vander will be excellent partner to lead you." She gave her son a meaningful smile before turning her attention to Dionne. "You must wear the tiara from your grandmother. It will be expected, so close to her birthday."

Dionne wrinkled her nose but nodded.

At my other side, Vander avoided my gaze, his cheeks flaming red. Had he truly suggested the ball, or were his parents simply trying to give him credit? He'd never struck me as the type who would enjoy dancing.

"This was your idea?" I asked him.

"Yes. You were so sad this afternoon, you have such a longing for your family, I thought perhaps we might make you feel more welcome." His cautious eyes met mine, and he lowered his voice. "My apologies. If you are displeased, I will speak to Mother and—"

"I'm not displeased. I would like to meet more of the people here, though being on display in front of a large crowd makes me nervous."

The confession startled me, both for its vulnerability and its truth. As a girl, I'd enjoyed parading my wealth and beauty before the aristocrats of Trellich. But now, as the subject of scandal . . .

"Then I shall request Mother to make guest list not so large, though I cannot promise she listens." He scrunched one corner of his mouth in a comical expression. "But you—you have nothing to fear. You shall be admired by all."

Visions of my last function in Trellich taunted me. Stares ranging from accusing to mocking, whispered conversation wherever I went, not even bothering to pause as I passed.

I shook my head. To my knowledge, nothing of my disgrace involving Nicholas was known in Delunia. That's why I was here—my chance for a fresh start.

Time to start feigning some enthusiasm for it.

"Yer first ball in Delunia! What could be more exciting?" Despite the language barrier, Victoria always seemed to have a grasp on the news around the palace.

I sank onto the edge of my cushioned mattress. "Yes, I suppose it's a nice gesture. But to be introduced to the people as Vander's fiancée . . . makes it all feel more official somehow. As though any possibility of escape is closed off forever."

"Escape?" She perched at my side. "Have you a wish to escape, m'lady? Has the prince been unkind to you? He is not so very handsome as, well . . . but I thought—"

"No, he's been very kind. A perfect gentleman."

Her brow scrunched. "But ye still wish to go back?"

Did I? I lowered my forehead into my palms. "I hardly know. I long to be back in Trellich, where everything is familiar and no one needs to translate for me."

But I'd been isolated there too. In a way, the distance created by my shame had been more palpable than a barrier of language or culture, a wall between myself and my former peers, erected from intention rather than circumstance.

I shook myself from my reverie, regaining awareness of Victoria at my side.

I tossed my hand in a careless gesture. "But goodness knows what my father would've done with me back in Trellich anyway. In many ways I'm better off here."

The truth of the statement weighed on my chest. With or without a ball, there'd never been any hope of escape for me.

"Now cheer up, m'lady." The momentary gloom in Victoria's voice had already vanished. "The Delunian people can't help but adore ye, especially when they see ye in the dress the palace seamstresses and I are designing."

I raised my head. "You've already started on my dress?"

"O' course!" She looked as though I should've had her banished for treason if she hadn't. "I visited the seamstresses straightaway the moment I heard the news."

Thank heavens I had Victoria to think of these things. "What kind of attire do Delunians wear on such occasions?"

"A bit like an *etana*, with some gathering in the bodice and a sleeve over one shoulder, but in a silky material overlaid with chiffon and a flowing skirt." Her bouncing shook the bed as she gestured, trying to illustrate. "With your hair flowing over your other shoulder and your finest tiara, you'll catch the eye of every guest in the palace."

I swallowed back a sigh. When had I lost enthusiasm for the prospect of being the most beautiful woman in a room? Now I'd rather hide among the draperies and avoid notice altogether. But no need to mar Victoria's excitement.

"I hope you'll be able to enjoy the festivities as well."

"Oh, yes." She clasped her hands. "They said the servants enjoy the music from an adjoining room when we aren't needed. We'll even do some dancing."

At least one of us was looking forward to the evening. "I'm sure you'll be a favorite among the staff of *Palati del Chrysos* in no time."

She hopped up and crossed to my vanity, a twinkle in her eye. "I believe I already am."

CHAPTER 17

Three dress fittings and a handful of food and decoration consults later, the day for the ball arrived. The flurry of activity produced a corresponding flutter within my chest, but more of anxiety than excitement.

Victoria sat me down hours before the guests were to arrive to get my hair and accessories perfected to her satisfaction.

I passed my hands over the smooth material of my skirt, trying not to fidget. "You really did a wonder with this dress, Victoria."

The shimmering fabric hugged my chest and waist to an extent that was flattering but not gaudy, and the skirt fell in a ripple of delicate folds. The ruching of the bodice and thick strap covering one shoulder somehow gave a more regal impression than all the stiff layers and underskirts of my gowns in Trellich.

Her gaze met mine in the mirror. A grin crinkled the corners of her eyes. "The seamstresses did much of the work. But I believe my supervision was invaluable."

"I'm certain it was. Have you seen any of the other dresses? For the empress or Princess Dionne?"

"Yes, they've been workin' on a number of ballgowns ever

since the event was announced. Theirs are a similar style, but much bolder colors." She tugged a curl into place at the base of my neck. "I hope ye don't mind—I thought ye'd prefer this lighter shade."

She knew me well. The vibrant colors of Delunian clothing still struck me as flashy and overdone. In contrast, the muted coral of my dress was elegantly understated.

"I don't mind at all. You chose well."

Victoria lifted the cover off the decorative box housing my silver tiara. She placed it atop my hair, holding it steady with one hand while the other deftly inserted pins.

"Almost ready."

She slid a smaller box forward and removed a length of silver chain adorned with pink-tinted diamonds. My stomach tightened. These jewels were once my mother's, gifted to me by my father. A welcome reminder of home, yet jarring in this strange place, paired with this unusual dress and hairstyle.

She fastened the clasp, then patted my shoulders. "And with that, m'lady, ye're all set to be the toast o' the ball."

I rose and leaned closer to the mirror. As promised, curls spilled down my otherwise bare shoulder in a dark cascade. Smaller diamonds were embedded throughout, giving a subtle sparkle no matter how I turned my head.

"Thank you, Victoria. I look every bit a princess." A *Delunian* princess, my reflection screamed. I kept the smile pasted on my face. "Now, I must wait for Vander to escort me downstairs, but you go ahead and get yourself ready."

"If you insist, m'lady." She curtsied with a giggle, then traipsed to her own room.

I shifted my chair so it no longer faced the mirror, regretting that I'd sent Victoria away so quickly. The silence pressed on me, forcing me to think, to feel. To remember.

My maids had made a hauntingly similar proclamation the day I was presented in Imperia as Prince Raphael's future bride. I'd been so pleased with my appearance, so ready to face my new life. The subterfuge had excited me. I'd been intrigued by the challenge of playing the part of Raphael's devoted fiancée while keeping clandestine meetings with Nicholas.

My face burned with shame. What a vain, thoughtless coquette I'd been, flirting with danger and deceit as though I were invincible, above reproach.

Of course Papa had to send me away.

I clutched for the amulet, but of course the diamond necklace had taken its place for such a formal occasion. How silly to feel bereft without it, as though it actually would provide me some level of protection. And yet . . .

I lifted it from where it lay pooled on my vanity and tucked it into the small reticule I'd attached to the belted waistline of my dress. I'd take all the extra security I could get.

A rap at my door startled me. Victoria appeared, now wearing a light-blue dress.

I rose, fiddling with the overlay of my skirt. "You ought to make an *etana* for yourself, Victoria. I'm sure the high waist would be very flattering on you."

"Perhaps I will, in time, but I don't mind standing out a bit." She paused before the door and flashed me a grin. "Ready, m'lady?"

Closing my eyes, I inhaled deeply. "I'm ready." *As ready as I'll ever be.*

She pulled the door open with a little squeal. "Greetings, Yer Highness."

She lowered into a deep curtsy, then stepped back.

Vander dipped his head to her. He straightened, and his gaze landed on me. "Penelope! You . . . I mean . . ." He swallowed and muttered something in Delunian. "You look lovely this evening. Are you prepared for departing?"

"Yes, thank you."

I approached him, wishing I could roll my eyes at Victoria's undisguised pleasure at his reaction.

His jacket and trousers were fashioned from a thick ivory material with a slight sheen. The deep green of his shirt complemented his tanned skin and the emerald in the center of his crown.

Vander's posture remained stiff as we made our way down the corridor, but I felt his eyes on me more than once.

Perhaps I should've discouraged Victoria from putting any special effort into my appearance. After all, I was hardly trying to impress anyone here—at least in that way—and gaining more admiration from Vander would only torment the poor man.

I kept my gaze forward, focusing on walking in this new style of skirt without tangling my legs.

We slowed at the top of the stairs, and Vander took an audible breath. "Shall we go down and meet your future subjects?"

My heart rate hurtled into a gallop like a spurred horse, ignoring all my attempts to quiet it. My future subjects. What a strange, jarring thought.

"Yes. That is, of course we may go down." The tremor in my voice lit a blaze beneath my cheeks.

Vander patted my hand resting on his arm. "They will treasure you."

His whisper tousled the hair at my ear. I didn't dare meet his gaze. "I'm not so sure, but thank you for saying so."

Releasing my hand, Vander angled to stand before me. "You have traveled for many days, left your home and your people, all to become their princess, one day their empress. You are beautiful, elegant, and kind. How could they not embrace such a woman?"

His statement startled my eyes into seeking his. "I've hardly been kind to you."

"Just because our wishes are different doesn't make you unkind."

"Thank you, Vander. Truly." I gripped his arm. "I—"

A fanfare from some variety of horns sounded below. The din of murmurs rose to an excited pitch.

Vander resumed his place at my side. "They have opened the ballroom. We had best join them."

I nodded and clung to him as we made our way down the winding staircase. His arm trembled under my grasp. I glanced at him. His smile was broad but shy. He had a right to be nervous too, after all. This was his first and only time introducing his future bride to his people.

Hopefully.

I pulled back my shoulders, lifted my chin, and smiled graciously at the throng of upturned faces. Regardless of my feelings for Vander, he deserved for this event to go well, and the least I could do was support him.

Our entrance met with a sea of wide, curious eyes. Some smiled, some frowned, but all studied our every move.

I allowed instinct and training to take charge — inclining my head to those we passed, keeping my smile steady, not letting my gaze rest on any one person.

I dipped into a curtsy each time Vander bowed and allowed my hand to be kissed by each gentleman who took it. The words uttered with each greeting weren't what I was accustomed to — weren't anything I could even understand — but the intentions behind them seemed exactly the same.

We reached the ballroom, and I allowed myself a relieved exhale.

Here the lighting was much dimmer. Candles peeked from the tops of flower arrangements dotting each table and suspended from the ceiling, bathing the room in an ethereal glow. We'd likely draw attention throughout the evening, but here the scrutiny would feel less harsh than under the bright radiance of the entrance hall.

Vander did his best to translate for me as we met each noble family, but their names and faces and compliments all swam together with the musicians' lively tunes.

"Welcome to our fine country."

"What a handsome couple you make."

"Our prince has been snatched up by a foreigner, has he? At least she's a pretty one."

"We hope you'll visit our estate someday."

I nodded and smiled until my head felt heavy and my facial muscles taut.

Vander steered us to a table laden with heaping trays of food. "Let us take pause for some refreshment."

He bent his head closer so I could hear him over the music and surrounding chatter.

"It is not a necessity you meet each one this night. There will be plenty of the time."

My shoulders sagged in relief.

"The servants, they will assemble a plate for your food." He mumbled something to the nearest footman. "I shall find a beverage."

"Thank you."

I sank into the chair he indicated, gratefully accepting the plate a servant delivered with a bow. Nibbling at a flaky roll, I took in the scene before me. As Victoria had indicated, most of the young ladies wore dresses in a similar style to mine but in brighter colors.

The dancers formed circles, meeting in the center, retreating to the edge, and back again. In the muted candle-light, the vibrancy appeared less gaudy.

Almost like a mysterious rainbow formed under the moon's gentle illumination.

A set of three ladies approached the table. Catching one's gaze, I gave a tight smile. She frowned and nudged her companions, who glowered at me. Abandoning the food, all three raised their heads and stalked off. My trembling fingers clinked my nails against my plate.

Could they know? Had news of my past indiscretions followed me to Delunia after all?

Vander returned and handed me a goblet. I gratefully took a drink, the liquid both sweet and a little tart on my tongue.

A couple danced past as Vander settled at my side. The gentleman watched us with wide-eyed curiosity; the woman smiled at Vander before darting a glare at me. I glanced at him, but he ignored the couple, instead visiting with the servant who handed him a plate of food.

If only I could find out whether my humiliation in Imperia was known among the Delunian public. But such an inquiry could hardly be made amid a crowd.

I ate the berries from my plate, asking Vander about the various types to avoid the gazes of other passersby. When I'd had all the food I could stomach, another footman relieved me of my plate and cup.

Vander patted his hands on his lap. "Penelope, I know you . . ." He pursed his lips, then began again. "I believe they shall have the expectation we dance together this evening, if you don't have objection."

The small meal I'd just consumed churned in my stomach. "I don't know any of these dances, but I'm willing to try."

Vander's uncertain expression turned to a smile. "This is all I ask."

The other dancers made space for us as Vander led me to the center of the room. The musicians had paused, as though waiting for us.

Please, don't be waiting for us. Don't draw any unnecessary attention our way.

Vander turned toward me, and they struck up a new song. A bit slower than the previous tune, with a lilt reminiscent of a waltz.

I followed the steps with surprising ease. The dance involved more swaying and sliding than our more formal equivalent, but I only misstepped on a few occasions. Vander's hand was warm at my back, his eyes darting away from my face every time I caught his gaze.

I tried for an easy conversation. "I'm surprised your dances are so similar. Not quite what I'm used to, but only a few of the step patterns are altered. Even the songs sound familiar."

"*Rei.* Yes. My father has many reasons for to seek this, hmm, bond." He squinted one eye. "Alliance. He has great admiration of the culture of Trellich, of all of Sandrin. He seeks to mimic such sophistication in our own culture."

Fascinating. Just when I was beginning to find the less structured society of Delunia refreshing. "The pageantry can be impressive, I suppose, but also stifling."

"True. Perhaps you and I can find balance?"

I attempted a smile as he released one of my hands and spun me in a circle. Disconcerting as the thought was, perhaps he had a point. A partnership blending two backgrounds and distinct cultures might bring forth the best of both worlds.

A young woman narrowed her eyes as she glided past.

Or might only serve to highlight the differences and widen the gap.

"You do not enjoy the party?" Dionne stepped to my side, the gems in her hair sparkling in the candlelight.

My hand jerked, nearly spilling the contents of my goblet.

After several dances, Vander had wandered off to mingle with more nobles, and I'd resumed my seat near the refreshments. Several people had approached and attempted to communicate with me, but it seemed Sandrinian was not understood by many outside the royal family.

I attempted a smile in the face of her harsh look. "The party is lovely. I am so grateful to your mother for planning it."

Hopefully, the statement came across as genuine. I was grateful for all the effort that had gone into the ball.

But I would also be grateful when it was over.

Dionne swept her voluminous skirt into one hand and

perched in the chair beside mine. "But this answers different question, eh? Just because party is lovely does not mean you enjoy."

My eyes widened. Dionne was always so quiet and demure in family settings, never voicing a strong opinion. In truth, hardly speaking at all. But I'd rarely had the opportunity to speak with her outside the watchful gazes of her parents.

Perhaps there was more spunk to this girl than I'd originally thought.

"I am enjoying the party," I said evenly.

Her brows raised.

"Aspects of it, at least." Politeness and truth walked such a narrow line sometimes. "Not everyone seems eager to welcome me into your royal family."

A middle-aged woman spotted us, then turned to whisper to her companion. The two pointedly glowered at me and stalked off, the perfect illustration of my remark.

Dionne shrugged. "Can they be blamed?"

My face couldn't have heated faster if I'd stuck it in an oven. "I—"

She waved a hand. "I mean none of the offense. But Vander is prince, *rei*? These maidens hope to marry him, these parents hope to wed him to their daughters. Then pretty foreigner comes to snatch him away."

My mouth opened and closed without a word. I'd never thought of it that way—of all the hopes and romantic fantasies that might've been crushed by my father's agreement with Emperor Tertius.

"Was there anyone in particular who—?"

"No, no, no. But no matter your opinion, my brother is considered excellent match. Strong, kind, powerful, rich." The corners of her lips twitched upward. "What more could mother want for child, eh? What more could maiden want?" She directed a meaningful look at me before turning to watch the dancers. "Unless she is *principela* with other ideas."

Apparently this girl had much more to say than she let on in front of her parents. Not necessarily in a good way.

I tried for a diplomatic response. "I do realize how fortunate I am to have Vander as my fiancé. I could've done much worse."

The accuracy of the statement struck me in the chest. He wasn't cruel or simpleminded or old enough to be my father. He respected my wishes, acted with honor and loyalty, made me laugh and think, and cared deeply about his people.

Even if I could never fall in love with him, perhaps it was time I learned to appreciate him.

"Hmm." Dionne pursed her lips, clearly not convinced.

I hurried to redirect our discussion. "Some people have been very kind, but I find it challenging to be able to talk with so few people. To be surrounded by conversations I can't understand."

"Ah, *rei*." She nodded vigorously. "I imagine such would be difficult. Then we must teach you to understand, eh?"

Teach me to understand? To learn Delunian, of course.

Why hadn't that occurred to me before? I was to live here, one day to be a ruler of these people. It would only make sense to learn their language.

Yet the idea brought with it a certain finality. To embrace their language felt like accepting I would never return to Trellich. That I was becoming more of a Delunian at the expense of becoming less of a Trellan.

I blinked against the sudden moisture crowding my vision. "You're right. It would be beneficial to learn your language. If you know of a tutor who could be spared, or perhaps I should speak with your parents —"

"No, no, no." She clicked her tongue. "No need for tutor when I can teach."

"You? But surely you have other duties and lessons to attend to. I couldn't ask you to —"

She interrupted me again. "You do not ask. I offer. I

surrounded by servants and tutors all the day. Mother and Father expect the meekness, the obedience. There are few girls with which I talk, and now, here you are." She gestured toward me. "I take break from studies to teach. And such is good for improvement of my Sandrinian, eh?"

I hardly knew whether to feel sorry for her or concerned about the kinds of subjects she might desire to speak of with a fellow young lady. I gnawed the inside of my cheek.

Princess Dionne was only a year younger than Sophia. Surely her confidences—gushing about gentlemen, dresses, whatever might spark her interest—couldn't be worse than Sophia's ramblings.

Suddenly, thankfulness filled me at her overture of friendship. "Yes, I'm sure it would be. Your offer to teach me is very generous, thank you."

A young gentleman in a loose silk shirt and vest approached. Bowing before Dionne, he extended a hand. As usual, I had no idea what he said to her.

Her smile turned soft and beguiling, her curtsy executed to perfection. She responded in Delunian, then followed with "Yes, I would be pleased to dance with you."

She turned to waggle her brows at me before following him to the edge of the circle of dancers.

Such a small gesture, but her translation meant so much. One less conversation among so many in which I didn't have to be left in confusion. It was like a tiny window had been carved out of the thick barrier separating me from the Delunian people.

Unpredictable as she was, I was disappointed to lose her company.

More music played, more dancers swirled past, and more food and drink disappeared from the table. The experience felt more like watching a play than participating in an event.

A figure blocked my view. I blinked as Vander bowed before me.

"My great apologies, Penelope. I do not intend to be away so long, but there are many who wish to congratulate on our engagement."

I shook my head. "I don't mind. Of course you want to mingle among your people."

I didn't bother to correct myself to *our* people.

He held out a hand. "The musicians prepare for final song of the evening. Will you dance it with me?"

"Certainly." I grasped his fingers, clutching my skirt with my other hand.

Once again, we headed for the center of the room, a place of honor on the dance floor. The musicians struck up the song, lively and jubilant. My feet could hardly keep up with the rhythm and Vander's nimble steps.

I apologized for my first several mistakes, but Vander chuckled more animatedly each time until I was laughing too. We completed the dance with smiles and heaving breaths.

The musicians concluded with a flourish, and everyone in the crowd applauded. One word seemed to rise above the cheering. I frowned. Something in Delunian, and yet familiar . . .

Vander rubbed his forehead. "My apologies, Penelope. I suspected this might occur . . . I should have given you warning."

Warning? I closed my eyes, focusing on the cheer.

"*Kise! Kise!*" My groan vanished beneath the crowd's growing uproar.

My eyes sought Vander's, alarm biting into my words. "They want us to kiss at a ball? I thought that was just a tradition among the peasants."

He blew out a breath. "I regret it is not. The entire people of Delunia savor a story of love."

Beads of sweat tickled my neck as I glanced around. Some of the young ladies glowered at us, refusing to join the chant.

But the rest of the crowd beamed, raising their hands as though in a toast without beverages.

Dionne, who had rejoined her parents on the dais, caught my eye. Only a slight eyebrow raise marred her demure expression.

If I had to marry, I was fortunate it was to Vander. Everyone in the room thought so, and I couldn't disagree.

Forcing my bewilderment aside to make way for a smile, I tipped my head up toward Vander. Rising to my toes, I placed a gentle kiss on the corner of his lips.

The crowd erupted into cheers. I laughed, catching the comical mix of surprise and pleasure lighting Vander's face.

He gripped my arms and lowered his head to murmur in my ear. "*Efcharis te*, Penelope. Thank you."

CHAPTER 18

*D*ionne leveled a smug look my way. "This day, we start work on the greetings."

I barely managed to curb my grin. Greetings.

Dionne had given me lessons in Delunian nearly every day since the ball, insisting I recite my numbers until I could practically say them backward.

Counting to ten should never have been so humiliating.

"That sounds lovely," I managed.

She narrowed her eyes. "They are the words, not the pictures."

I swallowed a groan. "What I meant is . . . never mind."

"To greet in morning, we say *Tuena ma*. I wish you pleasant day."

"*Tuena ma*."

She nodded emphatically. "*Rei*, yes. In afternoon, we say *Tuena osso*."

"*Tuena osso*."

"*Osso*." She drew out the "o."

"*Osso*."

"Is better." Her fingers tapped the table. "But for nighttime, is different. *Poloi ipa asteria.* Is—eh—sleep under blanket of stars."

The corners of my mouth tipped up. "That's beautiful."

Dionne's brows pinched together. "But none of the picture."

"It sounds beautiful." Apparently, I needed to find new ways to describe words before Dionne and I drove each other mad. "*Poloi ipa* . . ."

"*Asteria.*"

"*Poloi ipa asteria.*"

"*Rei*, yes. But for friend, for family, we not so formal. We say *Antes*. For both the greeting and goodbye."

"*Antes.*" Maybe I had a hope of getting a knack for this language after all, now that we'd passed numbers.

She folded her hands before her. "Time for practice. You see me in morning at the breakfast, so you say . . ."

"*Antes.*" I wouldn't let her fool me with her reference to the morning.

"No, no, no." She tipped her head back, as though the ceiling would commiserate with her. "Too informal for speak with your *principela.*"

"But you said—" Heat flared in my cheeks. "I assumed you would want me to address you as family."

"Not family yet, eh?" She pursed her lips. "Perhaps never family?"

"What?" I gripped the edge of the table.

They couldn't be planning to send me home, could they? My mind raced through my recent interactions with Vander.

Ever since the ball, we'd reached a new degree of camaraderie. And they'd just introduced me to the aristocracy barely a week before. As much as I longed for home, to be sent back under the shame of another failed engagement . . .

She waved her hands. "You have no care for my brother."

My thoughts fled under her blunt statement, relief blurring with confusion. "I—"

"Is clear to all. You do not wish to marry."

How could I argue against that? I could speak to my affection for Vander as a friend, but she was right. I had no desire to marry. Him, or anyone.

I struggled to speak. "I wish to fulfill my promise to my family and yours."

She coughed out a laugh. "Vander is the fortunate groom."

"I will be kind to Vander and respect our marriage vows. But it's true I don't care for him in a romantic sense." What concern was it of hers, anyway?

She fixed me with a hard stare, then shrugged. "Not so bad. Perhaps my son will be emperor one day."

The heat in my face blazed to an inferno. How dare she imply that—?

My elbow slid off the table, nearly sending the rest of my arm with it. I'd never thought through the implications of inheritance regarding my marriage arrangement. Vander's odd comment about consulting laws finally clicked into place.

The poor man had to suffer not only the disappointment of a loveless marriage, but the loss of any hope of producing an heir as well. But that was a worry for another day, and certainly no business of hers.

I smoothed my skirt. "Does this mean our Delunian lesson is done for today?"

"No, no, no. You must give correct greeting for princess at breakfast." Her eyes crinkled with mirth. "But such lessons of love might be more for the benefit, eh?"

My nails clawed at my chair. "*Tuena ma, Principela* Dionne."

≈

"Penelope."

I glanced back at Vander, who hurried to catch up with me from the end of the hall. We had just completed a round of spades against his parents. We'd lost three times in a row.

I feigned a pout. "You still want to speak with your miserable gaming partner?"

He chuckled. "Our cards will have more good fortune the next time." He fell into step by my side. "And my parents, they like you for teaching them this game and allowing them to take wins."

"Ah, so perhaps we ought to continue losing on purpose?"

He narrowed his eyes, but a grin played at the corners of his mouth. "It is my belief they like you plenty already."

We continued on in companionable silence past a guard, who lowered into a deep bow.

After we nodded to him, Vander asked, "You have another lesson with my sister today? How do you progress?"

I almost laughed, recalling Dionne's gruff corrections and snide remarks. "So far we've covered basic numbers and greetings. It's a lot to learn, but I'm eager to understand more of what's being said around me every day."

"It is much to learn, yes." He gave me a sidelong glance. "I hope she is gentle teacher?"

"Well, she—" How could I answer such a question honestly? "It is very kind of her to take the time to instruct me, of course."

Vander's laugh echoed down the marble hall. "You would make impressive ambassador. All the schoolmasters your father hired, you give them pride. I know Dionne is perhaps not as, hmm, meek as she might appear."

The tension gripping my shoulders eased. "I'll admit she's taken me by surprise. But I've enjoyed getting to know her better."

"She enjoys this time with you as well. Life in royal family can be lonely for her, especially with none of the sisters to talk to. My parents do not allow her much company."

I nodded. Life as a princess certainly did create a distinct sense of isolation, with a limited number of companions deemed acceptable. If only I'd appreciated my sisters more when they were near.

Vander watched me, his brows creased.

"I do hope we can be friends." I adjusted my skirt, hoping to hide my discomfort under his scrutiny.

"You are lonely as well." It was an observation, not a question.

I laced my fingers behind my back. "I miss my family, of course. Hopefully another set of letters will arrive soon. And once I've learned enough Delunian, I should be able to—"

His sigh cut through my chatter. "You miss your friend. Colin."

I didn't realize I'd stopped until he turned around to rejoin me. "I—I haven't seen him since before the ball. I know how upset my visits made you."

I willed my expression not to pucker into a wince.

"And now you miss him."

I tried to give my shrug a casual air. "He was a nice reminder of home, and my acquaintances here are few. But I shall make more over time."

Vander hung his head. "My great apologies that I let my anger, my jealousy, cause you sorrow. I have no wish to make you unhappy."

His gaze met mine, the resolve in his eyes flickering with a hint of uncertainty.

"You may resume your visits with no objection from myself. I will trust your assurance that he is more father than"—he glanced down, his cheeks reddening—"rival."

"Truly?" My heart leapt at the prospect of resuming my friendship with Sir Colin. Of a cup of rhosyn tea and reminiscences of Trellich. "Thank you, Vander." I clasped his arm with both hands. "I will not betray that trust."

We paused at the juncture in which the royal family's chambers lay in one direction, the guest rooms in the other.

Vander caught one of my hands before I could remove it. "I do want you to be content, Penelope."

"I know. Thank you."

The glow of the hall lanterns softened his dark eyes. His smile held a glimmer of mischief. "*Poloi ipa asteria, principela.*"

Sleep under a blanket of stars. I pressed his fingers before letting my hand fall to my side. "*Poloi ipa asteria.*"

"Princess Penelope!" The width of Sir Colin's smile rivaled my own. "How delightful to see you. I'd despaired my lapse in judgment had cost me the pleasure of your company for good."

"It is wonderful to see you as well." I grasped his outstretched hand. "I'm afraid Vander was a bit—distressed when he heard of our eventful outing."

No need to taint our friendship with mention of Vander's other objection.

"But just last night he gave me his blessing to resume my visits."

"Marvelous." Sir Colin led me inside.

The familiarity of his sitting room warmed me in a way the sunshine and humidity couldn't touch.

I added, "He'd prefer we not venture back to Leipon, though. At least not without more guards."

Sir Colin nodded. "I couldn't agree more. I can't tell you how much I regret my thoughtlessness that day. To think that I put the future empress of Delunia in such unwarranted danger . . ."

"Please, think nothing more of it." I touched his arm. "The villagers were curious, not hostile, and it was beneficial to see the living conditions outside the walls of Ambrus."

"It is most generous of you to view my blunder in such a light." He gestured to my favorite chair. "But please, take a seat. Make yourself at home. I believe my neglected sitting room has missed your presence."

Some time later, Niles handed me a second cup of rhosyn.

Sir Colin told me of his latest business venture, a local festival at the market, and his butler's amusing struggles to eradicate a family of mice trying to settle in a kitchen corner.

I listened with enjoyment and told him of the ball and my lessons in Delunian. But questions whirred in the back of my mind, casting a shadow upon the pleasantries.

With a bow, Niles exited the front door, carrying a basket.

Sir Colin answered my unspoken question, though I tried to keep it from my face.

"He's gone to fetch a few items at the market. We men tend to have little foresight when it comes to things like what we'll eat for dinner." He stretched his hands behind his head.

"Sir Colin."

He straightened, brows raised. "Yes?"

"I keep thinking about that woman in Leipon. The one who was burned. What . . . whatever happened to her?"

"Ah." His chair creaked as he shifted. "Our timing that day was especially poor. I would not have subjected you to such an upsetting event." He blew out a breath. "Ilene is all right, though she may never regain the use of her arm. We fashioned a sling for her and reduced the pain, but as of my last visit to Leipon, she had little sensation in her forearm."

"She can't use her arm? But that must be devastating. How will she cook and care for her children?"

"It is a significant loss, yes." His throat tensed as he swallowed. "Others will certainly help her, but her life will never be the same."

"What happened in their tent to cause such a thing? Egan tried to translate when Ilene's son came to fetch you. He said something about a spell"—I struggled to contain my shiver —"but I'm sure that can't be right." *Please, don't let it be right.*

His nod was slow and solemn. "It indeed was a spell, or at

least an attempt at one." He regarded me with narrowed eyes, as though making an assessment.

I had to know more. The sound of Ilene's agonized cries had haunted me in the weeks since our visit to Leipon. "But how would someone like Ilene know anything of magic? And why would she try to use it?"

"You saw the state of their village, princess. Poverty, disease, filth, malnourishment. If you lived in such conditions, desperate and ignored by the rulers who should care for you, wouldn't you do anything you could to produce more food or keep your children healthy?"

"I suppose." Basil and Leda's wan faces appeared in my mind. How frantic their mother must be to give them a better future. "But why magic? How would one even—access—such power?"

Wrinkles creased Sir Colin's forehead. "Typically, only a sorcerer can wield such magic. But so close to the Delunian palace . . ." He shook his head.

"What's wrong with the Delunian palace?" A vision of Lord Lessox, curled in a ball and muttering, sent a chill through my shoulders.

He glanced toward the door, as though ensuring no one else had entered. "Perhaps I ought not tell you this, but . . . you deserve to know the truth." He ran a hand through his hair, making it stand on end. "Sorcerers were once quite welcome in Delunia. Embraced, even. The royal family worked closely with them."

Nausea tightened my stomach. Vander had said something similar but made no connection to the present. Was my new home to be just as tainted by sorcery as my time in Imperia? I nodded for him to continue.

"Sorcerers working together was a rarity in the rest of the world, but it became commonplace in Delunia. The royal family offered to support them as much as possible, in exchange for the occasional magical favor, of course."

He gave a wry laugh. "An idea arose from this partnership that was too intriguing to ignore. They wanted to . . ." He scratched his chin. "My apologies, princess. I must go further back than that. Of course you aren't familiar with the inner workings of sorcery."

I settled my hands in my lap, clenching my fingers in my skirt.

"Every sorcerer must derive his power from a puissance — the essence of a spirit contained within some kind of bottle and worn on his person. 'Demon vials' they're called by those who disapprove."

He quirked a corner of his mouth into a half-smile. "But these sorcerers, goaded by the emperor, wondered whether such power might be combined. Whether they might take the spirit within each puissance and direct it into a larger vessel, strong enough to hold many spirits from which they could all draw power.

"Such an amalgamation, so the theory went, would allow even those without access to a spirit to perform basic sorcery.

"The emperor, the father of our own Tertius, funded the creation of a stele — hollow on the inside, thick and ornate on the outside, with one sliver of stone that could be removed and replaced to accommodate the transfer of spirits."

"Did it work?" I'd unintentionally shifted forward in my seat as he spoke. Striving too late to regain my composure, I straightened my back.

"To a degree, yes." His eyes took on a distant expression. "The combining of spirits produced unmatched power, magic the likes of which they'd never seen. But it was wild, unpredictable. The royal family began to distance themselves from the project following several mishaps. Explosions instead of displays of fire. Murders instead of warnings. Delunia was soliciting more positive relations with Sandrin around the time Imperia outlawed magic altogether.

"The sorcerers were sent away, left to practice their art

with whatever dregs of power they could glean from the stele. No recompense for losing access to their individual spirits."

He leaned his elbows on the table, his gaze returning to mine. "As for the stele? It was hidden deep within the palace. No one but the royal family knows its precise location. But its magic continues to seep out, ready to be snatched by those desperate for its power."

Dread wormed its way through my chest. The stele was hidden within the palace? Nowhere near my chambers, presumably, and it was a large structure, but still . . .

I shuddered to think of such a collection of dark magic—of these so-called "spirits"—residing within the same palace I now called home.

"How strange that they would keep it rather than destroy it or let the sorcerers retrieve what they'd contributed."

"Perhaps. Perhaps not." He spread his fingers on the table. "Some say the royal family still uses the magic and prefers to hoard it for themselves."

I drew back so quickly, my head hit the top rail of my chair. *Could it be true?*

My heart rose into my throat, threatening to choke me. Tertius, Nadia, Dionne. I bore no great love for them as yet, but they'd been kind and welcoming.

And Vander.

The layer of ice in my chest that had so recently begun to thaw froze itself anew.

Was he keeping this from me? Did he use this borrowed— stolen, really—dark magic for his own ends? Put his own people at risk just so he could have more power?

Sadness laced through my chest like the intertwining strands of a necklace.

Vander may be no more trustworthy than Nicholas.

CHAPTER 19

"*Carda.*"

"*Carda.*" I drew out the vowel this time, trying to match Dionne's tone.

"*Rei,* yes. Now word for cheese. *Vello.*"

"*Vello.*"

She nodded, avoiding my gaze. I squinted at her. Something was different today, her demeanor more subdued than usual as she taught me words for basic foods. She hadn't made a single snide comment about describing words as pictures or her rank as a princess.

"Next, milk." Her voice was flat, no hint of its usual animation. "*Talmi.* Like how you say—"

I couldn't concentrate on the pronunciation. "Is something wrong?"

"*Quel?*" She shook her head. "What? Nothing wrong."

"But there must be. You seem sad about something."

"No, no, no." Her eyes finally met mine. "I am not one who is sad."

My brows pulled together. "What gives you the impression *I'm* sad?"

Her lips pressed into a thin line. "Not everything about you. Vander, he . . . he mourns you."

I struggled to keep a rigid posture despite my sinking chest. Mourns. Almost as though I were dead. The word came from her formal training in Sandrinian, of course, but it felt appropriate. I wasn't dead, but his dreams of a happy marriage were.

Especially after I'd reestablished a veneer of cold formality over our friendship following my conversation with Sir Colin.

In a way, I mourned it too. The bond we'd started to form, the ways in which we'd begun to understand and appreciate one another.

But I couldn't afford to let my guard down around anyone who'd even consider toying with sorcery. I knew where that road led, and I had no intention of traveling it again.

She took my silence as an invitation to continue. "He is good man, you know. Not so handsome as some, but good."

Before I could scold her for interfering in my personal matters, my sisters' faces came to mind. Would I want Sophia's Flynnite prince to disappoint her with such coldness? Could I bear it if Vivienne were stuck in a loveless marriage?

My breath ruffled the curl at my cheek. "Vander does seem to be a good man."

Part of me still clung to the hope that Sir Colin was mistaken, or that Vander remained untainted by his predecessors' meddling in sorcery.

"It's nothing he's done," I continued. "I didn't wish to marry at all, but my father made the choice for me."

Much as Dionne's parents would likely do for her. Perhaps someday she'd understand.

She propped her chin on her fist, studying me anew. "But if one must marry, the kissing—it is meant to be pleasant, eh?"

I coughed into the crook of my elbow, heat blazing up my neck. This girl had less reservations on the subject of courtship than Sophia.

Unbidden, unwelcome memories flooded through me. Nicholas's hands on my waist, his lips coaxing against mine.

Pleasant, certainly. Far too pleasant, to the point of numbing my mind and allowing his ambitions to overcome my own values and judgment.

Dionne still regarded me, brows raised.

"Yes, it is meant to be pleasant." I swallowed, hoping the red in my face was starting to recede. "But it's more complicated than that. Loving someone can be painful, can cause you to change without realizing it. I'd prefer to keep some distance. I hope Vander can learn to be happy that way, too."

"Change not all bad." She shrugged. "Sad to miss joy only to escape the pain." The usual mischief returned to her eyes. "But what do I know, eh? Except for the balls and parties, Mother and Father not let me speak to the boys. No kisses for me." She blew a kiss into the air. "Next, we learn word for plate."

"What do you think, Dionne?" I surveyed the game board before me, striving for a casual air.

She turned to stare at me, eyes wide. "What do you mean?"

"The party is to celebrate your birthday, is it not? Shouldn't you have a say in the guest list?"

I hadn't been able to get Dionne's words off my mind following our lesson in Delunian. Her parents wouldn't let her speak to young men. She hardly spoke to anyone in her parents' presence, despite having plenty to say when they weren't around.

Throughout our dinner with the Grovenese ambassadors, she'd sat with her hands folded in her lap, her eyes directed at her food.

Was it because the emperor and empress wouldn't allow her to speak to anyone at all, or because she chose not to?

Now that the ambassadors had retired for the night and only Nadia, Dionne, Vander, and I remained to play *zappas*, I intended to find out.

Dionne was about to turn fifteen. Plenty old enough to start having her own voice in the family. And the planning of her birthday celebration seemed the perfect opportunity to encourage her to express her opinion.

Nadia rolled the dice with a dismissive laugh. "Even birthday celebrations are matters of state for a princess, Penelope. Surely Trellich is not so different."

"True. But even so, I'm sure there would be room on the guest list for Dionne's close friends or a young gentleman she'd like to know better. Perhaps the tall one you danced with at the ball? I don't think I caught his name."

I slid a mischievous glance to Dionne before returning to my scrutiny of the board. Thus far, the proper strategy for *zappas* had completely eluded me, no matter how many times the empress invited me to play.

Dionne squirmed in her seat. "His name was Savan, but I don't—"

Nadia set her game piece down more forcefully than necessary. "A girl of Dionne's age has none of the interest in suitors, if such you seek to imply."

I sat back. Dionne's face had turned a deep shade of crimson. Perhaps I'd gone too far. But was the empress truly indulging in such willful ignorance?

I fought to keep my tone light. "You might be surprised. My sister had her eye on the Flynnite prince she's now engaged to since she was fourteen. And surely it wouldn't be considered inappropriate here in Delunia. When I've ventured into town, I've seen many maidens interacting with young men without any hint of scandal."

Nadia's smile tucked in at the corners, giving her a smug air. "Perhaps, but such ladies are not held to the equal standard as royalty. A princess must have decorum and restraint always.

Her wisdom and strength are shown by a quiet presence, not forceful words."

She gave a small nod, as though pleased with the delivery of her speech.

I took my turn in silence, my lack of concentration sending my piece straight into Vander's clutches. His smile was more sympathetic than triumphant.

No wonder Dionne refused to speak in public, if this was what her mother impressed upon her day in and day out.

I blew out a breath. If I couldn't change the empress's strict notions, I'd have to request as many lessons in Delunian as possible to at least give Dionne an outlet in which she could speak freely.

I flinched at the prospect, recalling her earlier assessment of my relationship with Vander. But for her sake, I'd continue listening to whatever opinions she wanted to express that she couldn't air at other times.

No matter how little I wanted to hear them.

"Penelope." Vander's hesitant call slowed my departure from the breakfast room. "Would you be so kind to accompany me to my study?"

I traced the toe of my slipper along the marble floor. "I thought your father asked you to join him with the Grovenese ambassadors."

The hurt in his eyes wounded me each time I spurned an opportunity to renew our friendship. Unfortunate, but necessary.

"I need not keep you long." He glanced down the hall, then stepped closer. "I wish to speak with you about something without overhearing."

"I see." I tried for a pleasant smile. "In that case, lead the way."

We traversed the passages in silence. Keeping up with Vander's quick strides gave me little opportunity to ponder what this meeting could be about. My foot caught on my skirt. I stumbled a little, but I righted myself before he noticed.

If he inquired about the cause of my increasingly reserved behavior, what excuse could I give?

We reached his study, and he waited for me to enter before closing the door behind us. Never before had he insisted on such secrecy.

"Is something the matter?" Only the slightest quaver betrayed itself in my voice.

Vander paced a few steps away. "My apologies for the rushing, the mystery. I have no wish to give you concern. Nothing is the matter, no." He linked his fingers behind his back. "Is only . . . Dionne values time with you, more than she will likely admit. I hope you will continue friendship with her. She needs so much to have this opportunity."

"Of course. I enjoy my visits with her." Usually.

"Yes, good." He bobbed his head in an ongoing nod. "But I see what you try to do for Dionne last evening. You want to help, and I give you my thanks. But in the past, when we interfere to give Dionne more opportunities to speak for herself . . . it has effect with Mother that is opposite of our intentions. You see? Her determination to turn Dionne into quiet, proper lady increases all the more."

I gaped at him in dismay. With Dionne already so silent in front of her family, was it possible to make it even worse?

"But why? Your mother doesn't stay silent and let the men do all the talking. Why must Dionne?"

"You must understand. No matter how mistaken, Mother does what she thinks is best to ensure Dionne's future." He pressed a finger to his temple. "Her mother, my, hmm, grandmother, was stern woman. She insists my mother will catch the eye of heir to the throne. My father. She expects nothing less than perfect for Mother's behavior."

His shrug spoke of sad resignation. "Plan works, as you see. Mother is married to emperor, and the union is happy. So she thinks she must do the same for Dionne. Produce marriage to a great man, making Dionne happy and provided for."

But at such a cost to her relationship with her daughter, to her daughter's entire childhood.

I nodded slowly. "My mother, she . . . she always insisted on proper behavior in front of guests and at public events. But when it was just our family, we could speak our minds. We would run and laugh and—"

An ache for Mama tore through me, so painful I could hardly stand.

Vander reached to put an arm around me, then let it drop. He indicated a chair. "You miss her very much."

"Yes." I sat, hardly taking in my surroundings as memories washed over me.

She'd been such a soothing, loving presence in our family. An open ear to all my childhood and adolescent dreams and fears. An example of graceful strength. Now enclosed in a coffin, buried beneath a decorative slab of rock.

Oh, Mama, if only we'd had more time.

But Vander was speaking. I followed his voice back to the present—the soft leather chair, the smell of ink and mahogany.

". . . wish you did not have this pain. Children should never have to lose a mother so young." He crouched before me. "I know it could never be the same, but perhaps my own mother might one day be like mother to you as well."

A laugh broke through, coarsened by a hard edge. "That's a nice thought, but I don't think I could ever live up to your mother's expectations of a proper princess."

And although she'd been kind to me, she could never replace Mama.

His warm smile eased a bit of the ache in my chest. "No, no, no. Mother likes you very much. For you, is different. You have already secured husband." His lips twitched into a playful smirk. "Future emperor, no less."

I grinned in spite of myself. "True."

He offered his hands, and I let him help me from my chair.

"I suppose by her standards, then, I have no further need for instruction in decorum."

Yet I couldn't help wondering how much she, too, would despise me if she knew the full extent of my past indiscretions.

CHAPTER 20

*V*ictoria hummed as she pinned curls atop my head, where they wouldn't bathe my neck in heat and sweat. I studied her in the mirror as she worked.

An extra flush darkened her cheeks, and a secretive smile tilted her lips. Even the usual bounce in her steps seemed exaggerated.

I sifted through my recent interactions with my lady's maid. She'd been taking more pains with her appearance in the weeks following the ball, and she'd seemed a bit more distracted. Almost like she was always keeping her eye out for something.

Or someone . . .

She turned to pull the curling iron out from the fire, but I laid a hand on her arm. "Victoria, you've always been cheerful, but today you're positively giddy. Has something happened?"

I tried to keep my expression open and inquisitive, but a pebble of foreboding sank into my stomach.

Indecision warred in her eyes before a grin lit her face. "Oh, m'lady, it's just . . . isn't Egan the most handsome man ye've ever seen?"

My hand left her arm and hovered mid-air. "Egan? The guard? I suppose he is handsome, yes." Caution laced my tone.

She practically floated back to me with the curling iron. "So sweet and kind. And last night, he implied, well . . ." She hugged an arm around her waist. "I think he wants to marry me."

"Last night? Marry you?" Shock made me incapable of more than parroting her words.

She grasped the edge of the vanity. "'Twas was nothing improper. We talked while you and the family were at dinner. He said I was more beautiful and more intriguing than all the girls in Delunia combined." Her chest rose and fell in a dramatic sigh. "Wasn't that romantic?"

I hated to quash her joy, but I had to put a stop to this before she got hurt. "That was a very romantic thing to say. But Victoria, I'm afraid men say many romantic things they don't truly mean. Just because he complimented you on this one occasion —"

"It wasn't just this once." She still bobbed on her toes. "We speak every opportunity we can. Ever since that first day ye visited Sir Colin. The night of yer ball, he didn't dance with anyone but me." She did a little twirl.

My first visit to Sir Colin? My eyes widened. Nearly two months ago.

I rose, and she took a surprised step back. "I'm sorry this will disappoint you, but I must request to have Egan reassigned. This has clearly gone on far too long already."

"M'lady?" She set down the curling iron with shaking hands. "Why would he need to be reassigned? He's done nothin' wrong. *We've* done nothin' wrong."

The pain etched in her wary eyes and trembling jaw made me wince. "Not a punishment, a precaution. Egan may appear as a kind friend now, but I'm worried he may take advantage of you. You're so young, and —"

"Only a year younger than you! And ye're to be married

soon. Ye were my age when you and the duke . . ." She shook her head, averting her gaze. "Why shouldn't I be married?"

I raised a hand to placate her. "Of course you're welcome to marry, someday. But you can't just trust the first man who gives you a compliment."

My voice lowered almost to a whisper. "I was too young to be playing with love when Nicholas courted me. I see that now. It showed in every poor decision I made. And I want to prevent you from making the same mistakes."

"I'm not you! And Egan is nothin' like the duke. He's a good, kind man. He would take good care o' me."

I frowned. Nicholas had certainly turned out to be anything but kind and good, but Victoria had been charmed by him too when he'd first arrived in Trellich. Everyone had been taken in, almost mesmerized, by his false allure. Hadn't they?

I had to make her understand. "Just because a man is handsome doesn't make him good, Victoria. You don't have any family here, no one else to watch over you. I feel responsible for you, and I just want you to be cautious. Not rush into—"

"No." She slashed her hand through the air. "Ye can squander as many of yer own opportunities for a happy marriage as ye want, but I won't let ye ruin mine."

Her words stung like riversnake venom. Was that how she saw me? Throwing away perfectly good opportunities for happiness? I sank back into the chair.

Was she right?

Victoria bit her lip. "I apologize, m'lady. I should not've said that. It's just . . . have ye had any complaints of my performance? Have I neglected any of my duties?"

"No, you've served me well, as always. But—"

She leaned forward to interrupt. "Then don't request a change for Egan. At least, not yet. I promise to make my service to ye my highest priority and to avoid any inappropriate behavior." She clasped her fingers. "But I can't lose

Egan's friendship. The chance to possibly gain his love. Please."

The gathering resolve hardened in my chest. Victoria had voluntarily given up her entire life in Trellich without a word of complaint. For me. I hated to deny her this one request, but I'd meant what I said. It was my duty to protect her.

"I'm sorry, Victoria, but I must. I can't allow you to suffer a broken heart, possibly a ruined reputation, when there's something I can do about it."

A cry escaped her throat. "But—"

"I know it will be hard at first, but one day you'll thank me."

Her glare could've heated the curling iron without the need for a fire. "If I may say so, *m'lady*, a heart can be broken just as easily from an excess of caution as it can from foolhardiness."

The words felt like a slap. My spine stiffened. "That will be all, Victoria."

Dropping the iron onto the vanity, she fled the room.

"This guard. He is new, eh?" Dionne narrowed her eyes as I entered the parlor where we conducted our language lessons.

I dismissed Victoria's pleading expression from my mind. Tertius had acted quickly and without question when I'd asked him to give Egan an assignment elsewhere in the palace.

"Yes, he is. Petri."

Petri was rotund, with a large nose and beady eyes. The kind of man who was in no danger of catching my lady's maid's eye.

"He is none so nice to view as last guard."

Nor did he speak any Sandrinian. But Victoria's long-term peace of mind was worth the sacrifice. "True. But in this case, that's probably just as well."

"You do not like to see handsome man? You Trellans, you

have the odd ways." Dionne splayed a hand on the square table of painted wood we usually used for games. "But perhaps this change pleases my brother."

I gritted my teeth. These days I could be trusted around any man, handsome or otherwise. "I don't believe Vander had any objection to him, but I was concerned my lady's maid was developing an attachment."

She tipped her head. "Your maid, she is allowed no attachment? Much like one of your Sandrinian nuns, eh?"

My laugh came out as an unladylike snort. Victoria and Sister Rochelle were about as opposite as two women could be. "No, she certainly doesn't need to live like a nun. But I would've hated to see her heart get broken."

"You fear the heartbreak, so she must fear it too?" She drummed her fingers. "This is why you treat Vander as foreign diplomat rather than fiancé?"

Heat surged into my face. "This has nothing to do with Vander. I was merely trying to protect my lady's maid, as she has no one else here to look out for her."

"Hmm. But to protect from love is a little sad, eh?" She shook her head. "Perhaps you spend too much of the time with Mother."

My breath fled my lungs in a huff. The comparison stung more than I allowed myself to acknowledge.

"As we speak of Mother, I must give my thanks. Savan, he has been extended invitation to the birthday celebration."

"Truly?" Perhaps I hadn't made things worse after all. "I'm glad to hear that."

"Ah, but will you make allowance for us to dance, or must I too be protected from this fearsome love?" Her smirk was playful, but a challenge glinted in her eyes.

I swallowed before I could say something I'd regret. "I'd hate to see you get your heart broken, but I certainly wouldn't interfere if you were merely dancing with Savan."

"Hmm." She wrinkled her nose. "Today, I think we learn how to say, 'Please direct me to nearest chamber pot.'"

My choking cough left me spluttering. "Excuse me?"

"Is most helpful phrase, eh? Especially for visiting the new places."

The fire reddening my face increased threefold. "But I . . . it's —"

Her smile was that of a predator toying with its prey. "Unless you prefer to return to the counting? We have not yet reached one hundred . . ."

I shook my head. Chamber pots it was.

My slippers slapped against the corridor's marble floor. I relished each hard *thwack* reverberating along the walls. Hopefully, Victoria could hear them from my chambers.

The nerve of that ungrateful little . . .

For the third day in a row, she hadn't spoken a word to me aside from "Yes, m'lady," or "This *etana*, m'lady?"

My agitated steps faltered. I missed her company, her easy laugh. And I supposed I could hardly call her ungrateful when she'd been the one —

No. I'd only been trying to help her. To protect her. She had no right to turn on me so completely.

Footsteps echoed from an adjoining hall. I pushed my legs faster. I was in no mood for company. Not that whomever it was could likely speak my language anyway.

"Penelope!" Vander's voice chased me from behind.

My stomach clenched. *Not now.* Fisting my hands in my skirt, I forced myself to slow down.

He caught up, venturing a timid smile. "Allow me to escort you to dinner."

"Certainly." I pushed the word through my clamped jaw.

"And after, I hope you will join me for a walk in the gardens." He kept his head down, wringing his hands.

I took a deep breath before responding. "I appreciate the invitation, but I'm really too tired for an excursion tonight."

"I have something I should like to show you."

"Vander, I—"

"Please, Penelope?" In several long strides he was before me, blocking my path. "I know you have little wish to spend the time with me, but I cannot ignore your recent sorrow. I think this might be cheering for you."

My mouth opened, then closed again. He'd noticed I was upset? And wanted to cheer me? A hint of warmth wound through my chest, melting anger in its wake.

"I suppose I could, if it won't take too long. Thank you."

He nodded and stepped aside, gesturing for me to continue down the hall. I gratefully accepted his arm, weariness flooding my limbs as my fury subsided.

Tertius and Nadia beamed at us as we entered the dining hall. Tertius leaned forward as we neared the head of the table, his voice a conspiratorial whisper. "You treat your betrothed well, son. It does us good to see it."

I avoided Vander's gaze as I released his arm and took my seat. Visitors from some northern province filed in, providing a fortunate distraction.

I'd agreed to marry their son—couldn't Vander's parents be content to leave it at that?

The meal passed in a slow drone of what I assumed to be pleasantries exchanged around me in Delunian. On occasion, a familiar word or phrase caught my attention, but listening closely enough to follow the conversation would've required energy I couldn't muster.

Dionne sat across from me, her head lowered, her hands dainty and precise as she sampled her food. I caught her darting glances at the visiting nobleman's handsome son and suppressed a smirk.

No interest in suitors, my slipper.

The servants cleared the last of the dishes, and we rose from the table. I curtsied to the visitors, then turned toward the door. Maybe if Vander wasn't ready to depart yet, I could sneak back up . . .

"Are you prepared for our walk, Penelope?" Vander stepped to my side, extending his arm.

So much for sneaking away. "Yes, thank you."

I touched my fingers to his arm as lightly as I could, conscious of his parents' watchful gazes. Dionne, at least, was distracted studying the movements of her attractive guest.

We exited to the gardens, and my chest heaved an involuntary deep breath. Perhaps this *would* be good for me.

Soft moonlight bathed the surrounding plants in an ethereal glow, and freed from the sun's heat, the moisture in the air felt more like a soothing dew.

"Have you been to the gardens of late?" Vander paused to regard me in the dim light.

"No." I found the gardens stifling during the day, and most of my excursions were into town. "Not since the last lunar cycle, I believe."

"Good." He patted my arm and sped up our pace.

Among the disorderly clusters of bushes and blossoms in the Delunian gardens, without the palace in view, I could almost imagine we weren't in a royal enclosure at all. That we'd wandered to some distant, remote field of wildflowers, free from the inquiring or disdainful stares of strangers. Free from the expectancy surrounding my every interaction with Vander. Free from a past that would never break its hold . . .

"Do you think you might now tell me?" Vander's soft question startled me from my reverie.

"Tell you what?"

"What it is that bothers you."

Ah, that. "I, well . . . it's silly, I suppose. A simple disagreement with my maid."

"I see." He lowered his brows. "Shall we find new maiden to serve you? Not many of our young ladies speak Sandrinian, but if we make the adequate inquiries, I am certain —"

"No, thank you." My chest constricted painfully at the thought of being separated from Victoria, my last piece of home. "I'm sure we'll sort it out." If only that could be true.

A question lingered in his expression.

"It's just . . ." How could I explain without raising the touchy subject of romance? "Victoria is my friend as much as she is my maid, so it pains me to be at odds with her."

He nodded. "My great apologies we do not provide more of the friends for you. Hopefully, in time . . ."

We reached a small clearing, the wider path beyond leading to a different section of the garden.

"But here we are. I cannot fix the troubles with your maid, but I do hope this shall bring some good cheer."

Vander's face hadn't lit with such hopeful excitement since I'd first arrived in Delunia. He stood before me and grasped both my hands, drawing me forward.

In spite of myself, my pulse jumped in rhythm with our hasty steps. What could be in these gardens to produce such anticipation?

"Would you please oblige me and close your eyes?"

My feet faltered. Close my eyes? *Calm down, Penelope.*

I willed my heart to settle back into my chest. Vander had yet to show any signs of an interest in sorcery, and he was unlikely to perform a spell in the middle of the gardens with no provocation.

"All right."

I winced at the non-regal tremor in my voice. I closed my eyes, allowing Vander's hands to lead me.

"Just a little farther."

I couldn't help smiling at Vander's excitement, like Dominick when he wanted to show me a leaf or rock he'd found on one of his walks with his nurse.

Vander came to a halt. "There."

I slowed my steps until I'd stopped what I hoped was a respectable distance away. The vulnerability of being alone with him, unable to see where I was going, left me breathless.

His feet shifted on the dirt. "Your eyes can now open."

I blinked, trying to establish our new location among the gardens' many winding paths.

"Do you see anything familiar?" He watched me, expectation lighting his eyes.

"Umm . . ." My eyes roved my surroundings. What was I supposed to recognize? "These flowers are all lovely, but I don't—"

My words disappeared in a gasp. Lilies of the sunrise bloomed on a square patch of dirt that looked recently cleared. Their stems were feeble compared with the ones at home, their purples and pinks less vibrant, but the shape was unmistakable.

I approached them cautiously, extending my fingers to brush a soft petal. "They're beautiful. I didn't realize you had such flowers here."

Vander stopped trying to contain his grin. "We did not, until just lately. I discussed with our gardener which of your Trellan flowers had the most likeliness to thrive in such a climate."

"You planted these for me?" Thank heavens the dim light wouldn't reveal the tears pooling in my eyes. "Not that you'd be the one to plant them, of course, but—"

"Not in the entire, no. But I did help." I'd never seen his chest puffed out so far.

Vander had worked here in the garden, likely digging in the dirt on his hands and knees, for *me*.

"You—you did a wonderful job. I would've never guessed how much it'd mean to see . . . thank you. This will be my favorite part of the gardens from now on."

I tore my gaze from the captivating familiarity of the

flowers to look at him. His eyes radiated something new, something perilous and invigorating, as they held mine.

Sudden awareness washed over me of our close proximity, my hands still encased in his.

Before I could step back, he brought my fingers to his lips. "I am glad to have done well."

With one longing glance at the lilies, I straightened and took a step back. "It must be getting late. We should return."

He released my hands, and I almost wished he hadn't. "Yes. But you are cheered?"

I smiled, taking his arm before he had a chance to offer it. No one was around to scrutinize my every move, and I was too tired to do it to myself.

"*Rei.* I am very much cheered."

CHAPTER 21

A smile stretched across my face as I woke. How lovely
to get a good night's sleep, to see the sun's bright rays
threatening to burst through the edges of the thick curtains
covering my windows.

Had I truly been moping just last evening? Now the world
seemed welcoming, full of possibilities.

Something fluttered within my chest, pleasant but a bit
frantic. Almost like . . .

I sat up, tossing my blankets aside. *No, no, no.*

Recognition washed over me, sharp and chiding. Memories
of lying abed, daydreaming about Nicholas—the way his eyes
sparkled when he made a secretive comment just for me, the
way his touch sent tingles up my arm—mocked me.

Vander was attentive. Thoughtful, even. But that was no
reason to start acting like a ninny. I could appreciate his kind
gestures without thinking of him unnecessarily. Without
wondering when I'd get to see him again.

Stomping to my wardrobe, I plucked the nearest *etana*
from a shelf. It was time I learned to wrap myself in the
ridiculous garments. I pulled the material over my head,
then swiveled and tugged until it was mostly in place, letting

the activity drive every last thought of Vander from my mind.

Victoria knocked from her adjoining room, then entered. She raised a hand to cover a yawn but stilled when her gaze landed on me.

"I—I'm sorry, m'lady." She scooped up my discarded night-dress and laid it across the end of my bed. "I didn't realize ye were so eager to get dressed. Ye should've woken me."

Apparently, her surprise at my unusual behavior had temporarily eclipsed her anger.

"No need to apologize. I'd like to take my breakfast in my room, please. Something light—I'm not very hungry."

"O' course, m'lady. But allow me to help ye dress first."

I took a deep breath. I'd have preferred to be left alone, but my agitation could quickly undo this small amount of progress toward reconciliation.

"I think I have a handle on it. While I appreciate your assistance, I'm sure you'd agree it's important I be able to dress myself when necessary."

"Certainly, but . . ." She bit her lip. "Ye're doing well, m'lady, but I'm afraid ye're a bit twisted in the back."

"Am I?" Fire blazed in my cheeks. No wonder it'd been so tight around the waist.

Her laughter bubbled over like a fountain bringing forth water after a drought. "I'm afraid so. At least three times over."

My laugh joined hers, chipping away at the thick layer of ice that had grown between us. "It seems I need more help than I thought."

"Ye'll get the hang of it, m'lady. I'm just glad ye didn't leave yer room dressed like that."

Our laughter mingled again, and I let her assist me.

Following breakfast, I paced my room like a caged leopard until mid-morning. I peered into the hall. No sign of Vander. Hopefully, his father had closeted him away with a stack of budgets or reports.

I stepped back into my sitting room. Victoria sat mending a skirt's hem, her cold demeanor firmly back in place after encountering Petri on her way to get my breakfast. Gloom covered her cheerful disposition like a cloud blocking the sun.

"I'm going out for the morning. You needn't accompany me." No doubt she wouldn't want to anyway, now that Egan wouldn't be along.

She glanced up, a storm stirring in her eyes. Straightening, she returned to her work. "Very good, m'lady."

I marched to the door without giving her a second glance. My feet led me out of the palace and toward Sir Colin's before my mind even registered an intended destination. If the boots clattering in my wake were any indication, Tassos and Petri followed close behind.

My weakening resolve toward Vander was a mere matter of loneliness. Being homesick. Surely a visit with my Trellan friend would make an end of it.

Or at least bolster my spirits enough to face Vander by dinnertime, my polite reserve in place once more.

Sir Colin greeted me with his usual affability, but deep purple shaded the skin beneath his eyes.

I straightened my now correctly wrapped *etana* before perching on my usual chair. "Are you well, Sir Colin?"

"What?" He paused on his way across the room to blink at me.

"You seem a bit—tired—this morning."

"Ah, yes. I did get to bed rather late last evening." He pressed his fingers to his forehead. "More excitement in the village, I'm afraid."

My chest constricted. "In Leipon? What kind of excitement?"

"Foolish, foolish man." He rubbed a hand across his face. "I don't believe you met Raimo the day you visited. He is a stern, proud fellow. Desperate to take his family away from the village to a better life. He found a rusty ax in the woods and thought with enough power he could . . ." He raised his hands in a helpless gesture. "I believe his goal was to turn it to gold or some such nonsense."

"Could magic do such a thing?" I couldn't help a bit of morbid curiosity.

"Only the most powerful. In Raimo's case, inserting a spell into the ax gave it an energy of its own. He couldn't contain it with his bare hands, at least not without injury." He shuffled to a seat and sank into it. "The cut on his palm is deep. I fear infection."

"How dreadful."

My memories of Leipon seemed shrouded in haze, as though I'd visited a different world instead of an impoverished village only miles away.

"But I don't understand. After witnessing such horrible results in their neighbors, why do these families keep trying to use magic?"

He leaned back, exhaling a sigh. "The consequences aren't always bad, of course. Only the spells gone wrong require my attention. Some use magic successfully. I've heard of gardens growing at unnatural speeds, healings, tax collectors wandering away with empty hands, confused about why they came." He reached for a teacup that wasn't there. "To many, the benefit of a successful spell is greater than the risk of a negative outcome."

"So even warning them—educating them—won't solve the problem? Then how can we stop it?"

His shoulders slumped. "I've spent years pondering the same question with no resolution. Obviously, if their poverty didn't make them so desperate, they wouldn't feel such a need for the outside help of magic."

I rubbed my palms over the arms of my chair. "True. I could try speaking to Vander on the subject."

"Would he listen, do you think?"

My cheeks warmed at the unspoken question in his eyes.

"Though there is no great affection between us, he is a good man. I like to think if he knew more about the plight of his people, he might be persuaded to help."

"Perhaps." Sir Colin shrugged. "Even so, I fear any hope of significant help might remain far in the future. Prince Vander might be moved by the people's desperation, but I doubt Emperor Tertius will feel the same way."

Emperor Tertius seemed like a reasonable man as well, but Sir Colin had decades more experience learning Delunian ways than I did. And just because a man seemed good and kind was no guarantee of his true character.

I forced myself to speak again before my thoughts could ramble too far down the path of regret they so often traversed.

"Vander might be able to help without his father's full approval."

"It certainly would be worth a try." His thoughtful expression transformed into a smile. "It does this old heart good to know the Delunians will one day have an empress who cares so much for their welfare."

He waved over Niles, who'd emerged from the kitchen carrying a tray laden with teacups and scones.

"If only we could remove the temptation in the meantime."

"What do you mean?" I accepted a cup of tea and blew into it, watching ripples skim across the surface.

"Well, if we could remove the source of dark magic, the people would have nothing to access."

"Oh, of course." I took a tentative sip. "You said the stele was hidden somewhere deep within the palace?"

"Not in a location I could access, that's for certain." His gaze fixed on me, his eyes narrowed. "You, on the other hand . . ." He pursed his lips, then sighed. "No. No, I couldn't possibly ask it of you. To take on that kind of danger, jeopardize your place within the royal family . . . there must be another way."

"Ask what of me?" My thoughts wavered as tumultuously

as the ripples in my tea. "Oh—" *I* had access to the palace. I lived within its walls, had free roam of its corridors. "You mean I could try to find the stele."

He shook his head with slow determination. "Please, princess. Forget the thought ever crossed my mind."

In seconds, he turned the conversation to town gossip surrounding an attachment between the baker's daughter and the blacksmith. But though I smiled and responded at appropriate intervals, my mind roamed the palace.

Was it possible I could find the stele?

I eagerly watched the door of my sitting room, willing Vander to appear in response to my summons.

So much for resuming my stony indifference.

But this was different. I was anxious to see him to discuss my ideas for Leipon, not for my own sake.

At least, not entirely.

I'd rearranged my wardrobe, stared at the pages of my book, and counted the carved flowers edging the large mirror above my vanity when a knock sounded at the door. Victoria had been out all afternoon, so after forcing myself to pause for a breath, I hurried to greet my visitor.

"Penelope." Vander's gaze held a confused mix of pleasure and concern. "I was surprised to receive your note. My apologies for the delay—I took my horse a different direction than is common. Nothing is the matter, I hope?"

"No. That is, I am well, but there's something I'd like to discuss with you. If it's no trouble." My pulse sped too fast. *No need to be nervous, this is just Vander.*

"Not a trouble at all." He straightened his shoulders, as though proud I would come to him with a concern.

"Please, come sit down." Leaving the door open a crack to

appease any concerns of impropriety, I sank into the nearest chair. Perhaps sitting would ease my lightheadedness.

Vander took the seat across from me, leaning forward with his hands on his knees. "Your chambers suit you well?"

"What?" I glanced around. "Oh, yes. They are very comfortable."

He nodded, his brows raised in expectation.

I'd been so eager to approach him on this subject, but now every well-rehearsed explanation and plea fled my mind.

"I called you here because . . . that is, do you remember when I spoke with you about Leipon? The impoverished village outside the city gates?"

His lips pressed in a firm line. "You visited your friend today." It wasn't a question.

"Yes. You should be aware that some of the people have become so desperate, they're turning to dark magic to try to solve their problems. The day I first visited, a woman burned her arm beyond repair trying to use a spell to cure spoiled meat. Now another villager has injured himself with an attempt at magic. This time, he—"

Vander bolted upright, rattling his chair. "He took you to Leipon again? After—"

"No. Sir Colin was there late last night, but he only told me of this occurrence. I haven't ventured beyond Ambrus since we last discussed this subject."

His posture drooped with a sigh. "I am glad to hear it, and I apologize for my interruption. What happened with this man?"

"He tried to turn metal into gold and ended up with a cut from a rusty ax. They have very little medicine in the village, so he can't afford for the injury to get infected."

"Why would he think ax could turn to gold? Or did magic produce this ax?" Lines of confusion creased his forehead.

Either he truly knew nothing of sorcery, or he was a better actor than I would've given him credit for. "I agree it doesn't seem logical, but I understand little of what effects spells can produce."

And yet, still more than I'd like. Prince Raphael's face had gone so blank when under the control of Lord Lessox. He'd become so easy to manipulate . . .

I shook my head. "It merely demonstrates how desperate these people are. They have next to nothing, and no way to improve their situations. The irrational draw of dark magic is the only hope they have."

Vander ran his fingers across his jaw. "So what do you suggest?" His tone seemed open, genuinely curious.

"Couldn't we help them with some material goods? Food, clothing, medicine? Surely the palace has something to spare."

His hesitation seemed an eternity as he drummed his fingers on the arm of his chair. "We could put together some baskets, I believe. Yes." He blushed under my giddy smile, then looked away. "But unless we are satisfied to bring basket after basket, a few additions are needed. Seeds, maybe herbs. We may inquire whether a few chickens can be spared. Or tools for hunting and fishing?"

I clamped shut my gaping jaw. "You would do all that?"

He picked at a chip in the tabletop at his side. "It seems this project is most important to you. And you are correct, we are fortunate to have more than enough." He raised his eyes to meet mine. "We seek to put a final end to dark magic in Delunia, and our people should not stoop to use such measures if there is something we might do."

I couldn't seem to break away from his lingering gaze. Seconds, possibly minutes, later, he blinked and stood.

"I must discuss these plans with the steward and cook. Unless you had something more —?"

"No, this is more than enough. Thank you, Vander. Truly."

Before I could think it through, I found myself clutching his arm. He patted my hand, his expression pleased but guarded.

"It is my hope we can work on many more projects together over time." He searched my face, then winced and stepped back. "Enjoy your afternoon, Penelope. I shall see you at dinner."

"Yes. Thank you again."

Elation soared in my chest. Such a simple but significant victory. We were going to help, and my fiancé had shown thoughtfulness and concern even beyond what I'd hoped for.

If only he hadn't had to leave so soon . . .

I batted the thought away before it could fully form. I would not sit around and mope all afternoon, missing the man I had no intention of falling in love with.

Perhaps I'd visit the gardens instead to get a better look at those lilies of the sunrise.

CHAPTER 22

$\mathcal{M}$y heart was lighter than it'd felt in weeks as I traipsed through the streets of Ambrus. People called out greetings, and thanks to Dionne, I could respond with some accuracy.

The air had released some of its moisture, sending a cool, refreshing breeze to disperse the heat. The vibrant colors that'd once made the shops and homes seem gaudy now looked bright and festive. I even caught Tassos whistling a lively tune.

I knocked on Sir Colin's door, inclining my head to a girl playing in the yard of a neighboring home, who curtsied to me.

The door opened, revealing Sir Colin in a trim riding jacket. I smiled. While I had a growing appreciation for Delunian fashion, his reminders of home always brought a certain comfort.

"Good morning, princess. What an honor, to host my sovereign two days in a row."

He placed a kiss on the back of my hand in his customary greeting, a twinkle animating his tired eyes.

"*Tuena ma*, Sir Colin."

He dropped my hand, surprise lighting his face. "You've been dutiful in your studies. I'm impressed."

"Thank you." Pride widened my smile. I'd worked hard, and it was refreshing to share it with someone who could appreciate my efforts. "You need only host in location today. We brought tea and pastries."

I gestured for Tassos and Petri to precede me with their baskets. The palace kitchens had been my first stop this morning.

"How wonderful. I'm forever hearing tales of the surpassing delights of the palace kitchens. It makes me envious at times."

He helped the guards arrange breakfast as I poured tea. At our urging, Tassos and Petri each took a plate with buttered rolls and berry-filled tarts to their station outside Sir Colin's door.

The cook's trigonis were especially crisp today. After savoring a few bites, I set the remainder on my plate.

"I do hope my frequent calls aren't becoming a nuisance."

"No inconvenience at all. It is always a pleasure to see you, princess. And the bounty of the palace kitchens is every bit as delicious as I anticipated." He raised his roll into the air to admire it from all angles. "But I must confess, I'm curious if there's a particular reason prompting a return visit so soon."

I crossed my legs to prevent myself from doing something so unladylike as bouncing in my seat.

"Vander and I spoke after I returned to the palace yesterday. I told him more about Leipon, about their dangerous use of dark magic, and he wants to help. He's already begun talking with palace staff about assembling baskets filled with clothes, food, basic herbs, and medicines. We hope to have them ready to distribute next week."

Sir Colin's responding smile failed to dispel the weariness in his eyes. "That's wonderful news. It seems you're already having a positive influence on the royal family. Your baskets will truly be a blessing to the people. Thank you for your efforts."

A bit of the joy that had bolstered me throughout the morning deflated. "I'm happy to help. But you fear it won't be enough?"

He chuckled. "How very astute you are. I can't hide a thing from that perceptive gaze." He sighed, rubbing his hands together. "I believe your baskets will do a great deal to alleviate their suffering. However, old ways of life are not so easily altered, and even a week can . . . well, it will still be a beneficial, welcome change."

I narrowed my eyes. "What aren't you telling me?"

He took a long drink of tea before responding. "It happened again last night."

This time joy was forced from my chest, like a compressed bagpipe. "Last night? Already?"

"Indeed." The last traces of his smile faded. "A little boy, six years old. His foot had been seriously injured when he fell out of a tree. His mother was desperate to heal him, but . . ." A swallow tensed his throat.

"What happened to him?" My voice came out in hushed, almost reverent tones. "He didn't . . . he couldn't have —"

I couldn't bring myself to finish the statement.

Sir Colin hung his head. "I'm afraid so."

I clasped my shaking hands. A six-year-old boy, dead. Because the royal family—or at least the emperor—was too greedy or arrogant to give up their source of dark magic.

A fire burned in my chest, painful but invigorating. "If destroying the stele is the only way to keep this dark magic out of the people's hands, then it must be done. In addition to the provisions. But how?"

He leaned back in his chair. "I think I've done enough research to have a fair chance of managing it if we could just get it out of the palace."

"But the palace is enormous. Where could I even begin to search?" I toyed with one of the curls Victoria had left to hang beside my cheek. "It could take me weeks—*months* to find it."

"Unless you had help."

"You want me to bring you to the palace?"

He might have a better method of searching, but how — ?

"No. That would appear far too suspicious. Recall that Emperor Tertius is invested in keeping the stele hidden." He rested his hands on his knees. "But there is someone within the palace who might help you."

"You know one of the guards? Or a servant?"

His lips tugged upward. "Someone *you* know, princess. He happens to be your betrothed."

"Oh." A clamp tightened around my chest at the wrongness of his statement. "I don't think I dare ask Vander. He may be willing to help with these baskets, but I doubt his motivation goes far enough to betray his family."

I looked away under Sir Colin's intense scrutiny.

"If I may say so, Your Highness, I think you grossly underestimate your ability to influence the prince."

"I've told you before, there is no affection — "

"On your side." His tone was gentle but firm. "But perhaps you are not aware of the great deal of affection the prince seems to hold for you."

I shook my head, but he raised a hand to stop me.

"Your modesty does you credit, princess, but servants, visitors — they observe, and they talk. It's common knowledge among the people how smitten our prince is with his new fiancé. The way he watches your every move. You need but say the word, and he would shower you with all the affection your heart could possibly desire."

I gaped at him, every bit of poise and etiquette training deserting my mind. Was it possible? I'd done nothing but push Vander away, reject him at every turn. Perhaps he admired me, but surely nothing more.

I clamped down the ridiculous flutter interrupting the pace of my normal heartbeat. I didn't desire the admiration of

Vander or of any man. Such vanity would only lead down a path I had no intention of revisiting.

I fought the warmth invading my cheeks until I could safely meet Sir Colin's gaze. "Even if that were accurate, how could it impact our search for the stele?"

"Ah, princess." He barely swallowed down a chuckle. "I tend to underestimate the naiveté of youth."

I frowned, but he pressed on.

"I'll say outright what I apparently failed to imply. Prince Vander's feelings for you might make it possible to persuade him to reveal the stele's location. Apply enough of your feminine charms, and he may lead you straight to it himself."

The heat in my face flared, as though someone had added kindling to a fire. Feign affection? Use my feminine charms to distract, to persuade him? Disgust wormed through my veins, almost a physical presence.

Flattery. Fraud. Betrayal.

In my mind, I was back at the Imperian palace, smiling at Prince Raphael, complimenting his mother, acting the part of a dutiful bride-to-be.

Not again. My relationship with Vander lacked affection, but at least I'd been honest.

Concern lined Sir Colin's face; my inner turmoil must've shown in my expression. He blinked, shaking his head.

"I'm weary from last night's events. Forgive me. I shouldn't dare suggest a course of action that would cause you to deceive and jeopardize your alliance with the Delunian prince, simply to accomplish my own goals. I only . . ." He rubbed his forehead, his face constricting in pain. "That boy last night. Seeing his lifeless form, hearing his mother's wails. It ought to have been a nightmare, not reality."

I rubbed my arms against the sudden chill coursing through my body. A child had died. I hadn't been there to see him, yet his shadowy image haunted my mind.

Was my desire for honesty, for distance from Vander, more

important than a human life? Than the lives of children like him I might be in time to save?

"I understand. You needn't apologize. If there's any way to prevent such tragedies, then we must try. I'll"—the words caught in my throat—"I'll see what headway I can make with Vander."

～

Vander's expression brightened when I entered the dining hall, lit with the same hope that'd filled me just that morning. The lack of enthusiasm in my responding smile caused his brows to furrow.

Emperor Tertius kept his son's attention throughout the meal. They conducted the conversation in what, on another day, might've been an amusing blend of Sandrinian and Delunian.

I caught snatches of discussion regarding budgeting, the selection of a new ambassador, and the health woes of an elderly relative. Nadia seemed intent on quizzing Dionne regarding the titles and land holdings of a noble family who would be visiting from an eastern province, so I was left to stew in my own gloomy thoughts.

More than once, my gaze collided with Vander's searching eyes. He did care for me; it wouldn't be fair to deny that, even to myself. But in a romantic way?

Memories jostled through my mind, like a swarm of young children seeking attention.

The look on Vander's face when I was first escorted into the throne room. The warmth of his touch after I read Sophia's letter. The embarrassment flushing his face after the crowd's demands prompted him to kiss my cheek.

A corresponding heat threatened my own face. Perhaps Sir Colin's surmises weren't as absurd as I'd wanted to think. How could I use such affection to trick Vander into revealing his family's secrets?

But if more lives were at stake, how could I not?

I pushed the salmon and beans around my plate until a servant cleared the large dinner platters, replacing them with small bowls brimming with sweet cream topped by a berry compote. If only I could tuck mine aside for the day my appetite would return — assuming such a day would come to pass.

I watched the last drop of tea drain from Nadia's cup before I folded my cloth napkin on the table and rose. Before I could utter an excuse to retreat to my chambers for the evening, Vander appeared at my side.

"The moon is full of beauty this evening. Will you walk with me?"

I'd never tire of the unique way he phrased his statements, putting a fresh veneer on the language I knew so well. But time alone with him sounded exhausting in my current state.

"Thank you, but I think it best if I — "

"You didn't even eat your dessert." He shook his head in mock disapproval. "Do not try to tell me you have headache or tiredness. Something is wrong."

His hand gripped my arm — gentle but unwavering — and steered me toward the door. My mouth failed to form any semblance of denial or excuse. Something *was* wrong. To deny it could be nothing but a falsehood. And despite my reservations, it might be a relief to share my sorrow.

We made our way to the garden, his hand still on my arm as though he feared I might try to get away. I felt his gaze on me over and over again, but I stayed facing forward.

Finally, he released my arm and stepped in front of me. "You visit Sir Colin again this day, yes?"

I winced at the venom that still laced his tone whenever he spoke of Sir Colin. "Yes, I stopped by his home this morning."

He tilted his head. "Did he have displeasure with our plan

to make baskets? Or with my interference? Perhaps he prefers to help village alone, raised up as sole hero?"

"That's not fair." He at least had the decency to flinch under my glower. "Of course he wants them to receive as much help as possible. He's very appreciative of your involvement and our plan to bring supplies." The fire faded from my voice. "But he had bad news."

Vander ducked to look into my face, his expression softening. "What news?"

"Last night, before they could even receive the good tidings that more aid is on its way . . ."

I swallowed against the vile lump in my throat, as though every bite I'd managed to choke down had congealed into a mass halfway to my stomach. Hearing the words had been painful enough—to speak them felt impossible.

Vander led me to a nearby bench, gently cradling my hands in his. I didn't have the strength to pull away.

"A mother tried to heal her son after he was injured. She drew on the dark magic, and it . . . he didn't make it."

Tears streamed down my face, blurring my mental image of a boy on a bedroll. His pale lifeless face transformed into that of my mother. Lying across her silken sheets, a hint of a smile trying to trick me into believing all would be well. But how could it, when no breath escaped her lips? When no pulse carried blood through her veins? Dominick's wail belied her form's tranquility, as though even in his first hour of life, he knew he'd been deprived of a mother.

I was sobbing now, the carefully tucked-away grief bursting from the dam I'd closeted it behind, mixing with fresh sadness in a powerful torrent.

Vander's arms surrounded me, pulling me against the warm firmness of his chest. I nestled against him, embracing the opportunity to let someone else share the weight of my sorrow, if only for a moment. He held me for long minutes as I wept and wept, missing Mama and home and a little boy I'd never even met.

As my tears dried up, embarrassment crept in to replace some of my sadness. I'd exposed something to Vander I'd meant to keep hidden, shown him a vulnerability I couldn't take back.

I tried to convince myself that was why I hesitated to leave his embrace—I simply sought to avoid his gaze. But even a surface-level evaluation of my feeble heart warned it was more than that.

The feeling of his fingers gently stroking my back roused a familiar longing. Safety, warmth, affection. The tingling in my nerves tried to convince me this man's love could provide it all, if I would just give in.

But it wouldn't provide the security it promised. I knew that well.

So I stiffened my spine, dismissed the falsely pleasant sensations, and sat back. "I apologize. I don't know what came over me."

"Sadness, it would seem." His lips quirked into a hint of a smile. "Nothing to have shame for, responding to the death of an innocent child in such a way. Did you . . . you did not see this body?"

The body. I quelled a shiver. "No, but somehow just hearing about it reminded me of my mother. I don't understand why I keep thinking of her lately."

"You have adjusted to much in recent months. Much to upset you, much to make you wish for the comfort and guidance of a good mother. And the grief, it comes not in one wave but many." He reached for my hand.

I rose. "Yes, thank you. But I feel quite recovered now. Shall we continue walking?"

He stood at my side, his eyes never leaving my face. "As you like."

Sweet, sometimes tangy scents drifted to us on the evening

breeze. I breathed deeply, letting the refreshing air calm my agitation. Vander seemed to relax at my side, similarly lulled by the effects of the moonlit flowerbeds.

My pulse hitched. I'd never find a better time to ask about the stele. But how should I begin? How much could I reveal of what I already knew without putting him on edge?

I swallowed, suddenly wishing I'd at least consumed my goblet of water at dinner. "Vander?"

His responding "Yes" held an unnerving intimacy in its quiet resonance.

"This dark magic the peasants draw on . . . do you know where it comes from?"

If the question bothered him, nothing in his posture or gait betrayed it. "Delunia has unfortunate history with dark magic. Once it was embraced, given the admiration. When such forces get a hold of people, they do not easily consent to let go."

I bumped into his shoulder and quickly sidestepped. "But even then, I'd imagine the magic must have something to latch on to. It doesn't just exist in the air, does it?"

Distaste bubbled under my skin at playing this part of a wide-eyed innocent trying to extract information I already knew. But if his family truly was hiding the stele, a direct reference to it might put him on guard and cost my chance to find out more.

"True. My grandfather made mistake of playing with magic like a toy, with testing and experiments. Sorcerers were his friends, and together they created a fixture"—he gestured, struggling for the right Sandrinian words—"a container for much magic. Too much magic." A shudder shook his shoulders.

"How dangerous." I took an exaggerated pause, as though thinking. "Do you know what happened to this container full of magic? Was it destroyed?"

"I regret, no. When my grandfather came to his senses, realized his mistakes, he could not turn over such power to sorcerers. Such an act could destroy our family. Destroy our country. But neither did he know how to drive such magic away."

Exhilaration and guilt spiraled in my chest. I was so close; it'd almost been too easy. "What did he do with it, then?"

My voice held just the right tinge of frightened awe.

He shrugged. "He hid it away, out of reach of the sorcerers. His descendants must guard the magic, protect our people from its effects."

"Hid it away?" *Eyes wide. Act surprised.* "You mean, in the palace somewhere?"

Vander exhaled a light chuckle. "Somewhere, yes. Where it cannot cause any harm to a lovely *principela*. Nothing to worry about."

He lifted a hand as though to touch my hair, then let it drop. In the quiet garden, the moon softening the angles of his face, I almost wished he hadn't stopped himself.

I shook my head. *Time to return to the palace.*

I turned, and he followed my unspoken request.

"But the magic is affecting your people."

He spread his palms in a helpless gesture. "You are correct. I do not know if the effect of the magic is worsening, or if we were not aware of earlier troubles. But container doesn't keep all magic in, this much is clear."

"Isn't there something we can do?"

"I wish I knew, Penelope. The slow, hmm"—he pinched his fingers against his thumb—"leak has more safety than releasing all magic at once, yes?"

I twined my fingers into my skirt's silky fabric. "But what if we found someone who could destroy it?"

Vander paused, tipping his head as he regarded me. "If someone were to make such a claim, I would be cautious to believe him."

hy can't Vander just trust Sir Colin?

   I paced my room, taking an extra-long step to avoid snagging my toe on the rug.

Though I'd placated his initial jealousy of my friend, it felt like a lack of trust in *me*. I refused to dwell on why that thought stung with such intensity. They were my two closest allies in this strange country I was trying to accept as my home. Couldn't they make an effort to get along?

I was trying to help. Sir Colin was trying to help. Vander had shared with me so openly at first, but then . . . did he secretly not want the dark magic destroyed? Or did he truly believe it wasn't possible?

Rain spattered against my window, smearing the colors of the sunrise until they blurred like an artist mixing paints. A perfect day to stay indoors. A perfect day to locate the stele.

My footsteps tread faster, swishing my nightdress against my legs. Simple curiosity hadn't been enough to pry the secret from Vander. Today, I'd have to employ any tactics at my disposal. Including my feminine charms.

A delightful, treacherous flutter ran down my spine as I recalled Vander's embrace the evening before, the anticipation of his hand reaching for my hair. Somehow, without even real-izing it, I'd set out on a dangerous course.

The breathless excitement, the rush of nerves and sensation and longing felt all too familiar. And yet different with Vander. Less frantic, less demanding—more safe and tender.

But still not to be trusted.

Heaving a sigh, I peeked out the window once more. I'd continue down this path as long as it took to ensure the stele was destroyed, then I'd rebuild the walls around my heart.

Victoria entered from her adjoining chamber. I started, turning and pressing my back to the wall.

"Good morning, m'lady. Sorry to scare ye."

A trace of amusement lit her face before it settled back into the frown she'd worn around me of late. Another of my few allies in Delunia slipping from my grasp.

I splashed water on my face and wiped it dry with a cloth as she rifled through my collection of *etanas*. She withdrew a pink dress highlighted with red beads.

I swiped at my chin once more before refolding the cloth. "No, I'd like to wear the purple one today."

Victoria raised her brows and turned back to the wardrobe. "Certainly, m'lady."

I pressed my cold palms to my cheeks before they could display the heat simmering in my veins. She had a right to be suspicious. This was the first I'd shown any notable interest in my appearance since arriving in Delunia.

But the royal family seemed to favor purple, and the cut of this *etana* was especially flattering through my shoulders and waist.

So much for forestalling my blush.

Victoria helped drape the rich cloth around me so it settled gracefully over my frame. I blinked at myself in the large mirror. Aside from the lighter hue of my skin, I fully fit the part of a Delunian princess.

Unnerved, I let Victoria lead me to the cushioned chair in

front of my vanity. I pivoted my head, watching my curls fall against my arms.

"Let's leave my hair mostly down today." I hurried to continue. "There's no point in taking the time to pin it up if I won't be stepping foot outdoors. And there are no visitors at the palace at present." I squinted at my image in the mirror. "But could you find that headpiece with the amethyst? I think it would complement this dress nicely."

"It certainly would, m'lady." She strode to my jewelry box atop a dresser.

Her formality grated on me. I'd hoped by now she'd understand I'd been trying to protect her, not hurt her. I rubbed my forehead. And now, here I was, flagrantly disregarding my own advice.

Victoria returned with the headpiece and began twisting locks of my hair to gently sweep up on one side of my face. I studied her reflection.

I missed the excitement that used to sparkle in her eyes when she could tell I was making an effort to impress a gentleman. To impress Nicholas—I'd never worked so hard to catch any other man's eye.

Now bitterness took its place, as though she resented me for caring about my appearance when I'd insisted she had no reason to care about her own.

The simple hairstyle was soon completed, and after draping a string of glossy pearls around my neck, I quickly set out into the corridor. Victoria was welcome to pout at my belongings all she wanted—at least I was free to escape the tension swarming the room.

Vander nodded a greeting as I entered the breakfast parlor, then blinked and gave me a longer appraisal. His fork remained poised over his plate until I'd crossed the room. At least I hadn't roused Victoria's suspicions for nothing.

The pleasure forcing a smile to my lips stemmed solely from the success of the initial step in my plan. Nothing more.

Scents of eggs, cooked fish, and herbs roused my stomach as I approached the table. Although spicier than what I'd been accustomed to in Trellich, they were enticing nonetheless.

I took my time filling my plate and selecting colorful fruit before settling beside Vander.

"Good morning." I folded my hands in my lap. *Thank you, Luminate, for this food and this new day. Amen.*

Though still not accustomed to sending up the morning prayer in silence rather than as a chorus with my family, I couldn't convince myself to abandon the practice entirely.

Vander waited in respectful silence, but he smiled the moment I opened my eyes and turned to him.

"Good morning, Penelope. You look lovely today. Like sunshine to push back the rain."

"Thank you." I demurely looked to my plate, taking up my knife and fork. "Though I have no wish to drive the rain away. I rather enjoy an occasional gloomy day."

"I cannot share this enthusiasm, but the rain will benefit the plants." He drained his glass, which contained a red juice I didn't recognize. "You sleep well?"

I exaggerated a yawn. "I'm afraid not. I couldn't help but be haunted by"—I glanced around the table, lowering my voice—"thoughts of dark magic right here in the palace."

"Ah." He pursed his lips, releasing a breath. "I apologize our conversation disturbed you."

"It's not your fault. I'm grateful you told me." I curled my fingers around his arm.

His eyes widened, then brightened at my touch. I fended off my rising guilt with a surge of determination. This was my time to move forward. The gentle, apologetic retreat would have to come later.

I leaned closer. "I just wish—" I glanced to his face, then to my hand on his arm. "I think if I knew where it was, it wouldn't frighten me so. I'd know which part of the palace to avoid and not feel as though it's coming at me from all sides."

He nodded slowly, indecision pinching the lines of his forehead.

Please, Luminate. Please, let this work.

Vander glanced to his parents, who sat at the opposite end of the table, then back to me. His whisper tickled my cheek with warm breath. "Join me in the library following this meal so we may discuss."

The excitement bubbling in my chest deflated a bit, but at least he hadn't completely denied my request. "Of course. Thank you."

I gave him my most vivid smile and squeezed his arm before removing my hand. Warning bells rang through my mind as I hastened to finish my breakfast.

These gestures and flirtations felt too easy, too natural. If I wasn't careful, they could quickly become our accustomed manner of interacting, undoing all my vigilant coolness and distance.

A traitorous thrill ran through me. *But for today, maybe I'll let myself enjoy it.*

Vander rose and exchanged a few pleasant words and laughs with his parents. The familiar ache for my family tugged at my chest. He paused at the doorway and let his gaze linger on me once more. I gave him a hint of a nod. The cautious hopefulness in his returning smile made my heart ache.

What was I doing to this man? To myself?

The library was the most subdued room in the palace, the deep browns of the bookcases muting the colorful paint on the walls.

I paused in the doorframe, allowing the scents of wood and ink and paper to wash over me. If I closed my eyes, I could almost pretend I was home, visiting Papa in his study full of shelves brimming with books.

Letting the familiarity buoy my spirits, I entered and closed the door behind me. Vander emerged from a reading alcove on my right and beckoned. I joined him, tucking my legs beneath me in a large chair.

He took a seat at my side. "I perform a quick tour. Servants and visitors, they are permitted access to our family's library as well. But it seems we have the space to ourselves this morning."

My pulse quickened. We could easily be meeting here as a couple seeking a private rendezvous, just as Nicholas and I had . . . any hint of excitement fled, leaving only nervousness in its wake.

The sooner we got this over with, the better.

"Thank you for taking the time to discuss this further with me. I must seem such a ninny, frightened by nightmares of dark magic."

I brushed my hair off my shoulder in what I hoped was a self-conscious gesture.

He leaned forward, resting his forearms on his knees. "Not at all. Being away from home, in an unfamiliar place, must lead to an abundance of anxiety on its own. Add to this such news—the death of a young boy and a fount of dark magic hiding nearby. It is enough to unsettle the sleep of any person, *rei*?"

I nodded my grateful acknowledgment, clasping my hands in my lap. "So will you show it to me, then? I suppose it sounds absurd, but—"

Vander sighed and relaxed into his chair. "Not absurd, no. But, Penelope, this vessel—it is nowhere someone might stumble upon it by chance. Nowhere it could do you harm. Can you trust that this is true?"

The earnest set of his jaw threatened to melt my resolve. If only I could say, *Yes, I trust you*, and leave him be. But though such an explanation was sufficient for me, it wasn't sufficient for the peasants.

The ones who, at this very moment, might be feeling a

desperation strong enough to make them reach out to the dark magic leaking into the atmosphere.

"I do trust you, but . . . I'm sorry to admit I don't feel any safer. I sense it all around me, perhaps behind that wall, or underneath the floorboards . . ." I sent a wave of distress into my voice.

He cradled his forehead with his palms. "This is my fault. It was foolish for me to tell about this dark magic receptacle — this stele — at all. My great apologies. I should know such a disclosure would frighten you."

"Not at all. I appreciate your honesty. It means more than I can express that you trust me." I placed my fingers on his knee.

His head snapped up, and I timidly pulled my hand away. While my arm was still extended, he clasped my hand in his.

Our hands hung there, suspended between us.

"You do have my trust. Most completely." He traced his thumb along my palm. "But I would not put you in danger. This stele . . . I fear some wish to locate it for purposes of their own. To access the powerful magic within. If you knew the precise hiding place, they might use you, threaten you, to gain such knowledge."

A shiver prickled my skin. I certainly knew what it felt like to be used for nefarious purposes. But if I could get the stele to Sir Colin so he could destroy it, the danger would be lessened for us all.

The temptation to reveal our plan nearly won out. I could be honest with him, maintain his trust. He could even help in our endeavor.

But while he might trust me, he'd made it clear he did not trust Sir Colin. The mere mention of his name would likely be enough to close our conversation on this subject forever.

Trying to ignore the pleasant tingle running up my arm, I pressed on. "No more danger than you or the rest of your family. Besides, guards accompany me wherever I go."

He shook his head. "Not entire family. We have not made

such information known to Dionne. And guards can be compromised."

My pulse drummed in my ears. They hadn't even told Dionne? How could I possibly convince him to tell me?

I tugged my hand back, letting my fingers fidget with my handkerchief. "I hate to think of you in danger you won't allow me to share."

He quirked a brow as though wanting to make a retort, likely noting the hypocrisy of my statement. Based on previous discussions, I planned to share very little with him, even once we were married. Thankfully, he held his tongue.

"But I do appreciate your concern for me." My shoulders rose and fell with my sigh. "I guess — I suppose I must try my hardest to put it from my mind."

"That would be best, yes." The indecision in his eyes belied the certainty of his statement.

He might not be ready to reveal the stele's location today, but I wouldn't give up hope just yet.

CHAPTER 24

a knock startled my gaze from the pianoforte, where my fingers had rested for who knew how long without playing a note. "Yes?"

A tall, clean-shaven guard hovered in the doorframe. "*Principela.*" He lowered into a stiff bow. "There is—hmm . . ."

He shuffled his boots on the marble floor.

I gave him an encouraging smile. Most of the guards knew little to no Sandrinian, so delivering messages to me must've been a highly unpopular task.

"Guest." His eyes lit with pride. "Guest . . . for you."

A guest for me? Surely, the poor man had gotten his translation wrong. Unless Sir Colin . . .

I hopped up from the dainty pianoforte bench and joined him at the door. "Thank you. I'll follow you there."

I motioned for him to lead. He nodded, clearly grateful I required no further explanation.

I followed the guard through winding corridors, paying little heed to where he led. What would I tell Sir Colin?

Despite my lengthy discussions with Vander, I hadn't yet learned anything about the stele Sir Colin didn't already know.

I'd only seen Vander in passing since our rendezvous in the library the day before.

A recollection of his warm smile from breakfast sent my heart racing faster than it had a right to, considering the moderate pace set by my escort.

The guard stopped at a small sitting room near the palace front entrance. "She is here, *principela*."

She? I squinted into the room but could see only windows from my vantage point. "Thank . . . that is, *efcharis te*."

"*Te parakal.*" A smile accompanied his bow as he took his leave.

I lingered outside the door. A strange sense of unease mingled with my curiosity. Who had come to visit me—and why? I drew back my shoulders. Whoever it was, the guard clearly perceived no threat, and no one would be foolish enough to harm me within the palace in broad daylight.

Tugging the folds of my *etana* into place, I strode into the room.

"Princess Penelope! I can't express how pleased I am to see you well." Sister Rochelle rose from a chair near the hearth and hurried forward.

I blinked at her, my open mouth failing to form any sound. "Sister Rochelle, I—"

She grasped my hands, her expression equally relieved and troubled.

I forced a smile. "It's lovely to see you, of course, but I thought you had traveled south. Is something wrong?"

Perhaps she'd received news from Imperia. Or Trellich.

Gooseflesh rose on my skin.

"I am well, and yes, I have been in the southern regions for the past months. But I had to assure myself everything is well here."

Mystics had such a knack for unnerving me. "I believe all is well—is there any reason it shouldn't be?"

"Perhaps not." She searched my face, as though it could reveal the answers to her unspoken questions.

Every muscle in my body ached to squirm under her scrutiny. "We are all in excellent health, and I'm getting on well with the royal family. Including Prince Vander." Heat invaded my cheeks. *Maybe a bit too well.*

"I'm glad to hear it."

I waited for her to continue, but she merely smiled in her uncanny way and resumed her seat.

I shook myself out of my surprise at seeing her and into the role of hostess. "Might I offer you some refreshments? Shall we make up a room for you?"

As much as I didn't relish the thought of hosting her, I could hardly allow the poor woman to be exposed to the elements when she'd come all this way to see me.

"Oh, no, my dear. Thank you for the offer, but I don't need anything. I've settled at an inn—*Danthos del Mila*—for the present."

"I see." Then what under the heavens *did* she want? I perched on the chair across from her. "Could I interest you in a tour of the palace? Or perhaps the gardens, if the rain lets up? They're very different from what I'm used to back home, but quite pretty."

"Thank you, princess, but I don't need to take up so much of your time. It's only . . ." She folded her hands in her lap. "My visions lately all seem to center around the royal city. A darkness is gathering, begging to be released. Do you have any idea what might be producing such a disturbance?"

Her earnest gaze bored into me, as though she already knew the answer but wanted to see if I would confide in her.

"I—it is my understanding that an object created by sorcery is stored somewhere within the palace, but I don't know the specifics. Of course, they don't involve me in such matters, but I hope one day it will be destroyed."

"Indeed. That does sound like the best outcome, but you

must be on your guard, princess. Some would place great value on an object of such power, and not everyone can be trusted. Doing wrong is never the best way to produce a right."

Did mystics receive training in speaking riddles? "I appreciate your concern and will try to be cautious."

"Very good." She tilted her head, making the black cloth of her headdress slide across her cheek. "But has anything been troubling you? Is there something you wish to discuss?"

Not with you. Despite her kind intentions, Sister Rochelle's unsolicited advice set my every nerve on edge. What good would it do to discuss my predicament with her anyway? Of course the stele's power could prove a temptation, and I knew better than most the dangers of trusting the wrong person.

I tried to give my shrug a lighthearted air. "No. As I said, I've been fortunate to receive a warm welcome from the Delunian royal family. It has been an adjustment, but I feel more at home every day, and letters from home are such a consolation. The princess has even offered to teach me Delunian."

She studied me a moment more, then nodded. "It is comforting to hear such a positive report. If all is going well, then I needn't inconvenience you further." She rose and brushed off her skirt. "But I shall stay at *Danthos del Mila* at least through the end of the week. Please, don't hesitate to seek me out if you need guidance or a listening ear."

"You are very kind." I stood, snuffing out the guilt flaring in my chest. It wasn't as though I'd asked her to come or owed her any admissions. "I hope you enjoy your stay in Ambrus."

"I'm sure I will. It is a beautiful city." She turned abruptly as she reached the door. "You do still wear the amulet?"

My hand automatically strayed to the thin chain encircling my neck. "Yes."

Her chest deflated with a sigh. "Good. Remember the Luminate is always there to guide you. All you have to do is ask."

What do they do with all these rooms?

I pressed forward, my slippers dragging against the gray-streaked marble with every step.

Another corridor loomed to my left, just as pristine and deserted as the one I currently traveled, as though they kept this wing of the palace as a spare, in case something happened to a section actually in use.

I paused, closing my eyes and stretching my mind out for . . . what? An aura? A sense of foreboding?

Torn between the urges to laugh or to cry at my feeble attempts, I turned left and set out down the new passageway. The echo of my footsteps was oddly comforting, as though I had a band of explorers and not just my own useless self.

Increased guilt and foreboding had been my constant companions ever since Sister Rochelle's visit two days before. I'd tried to banish her words from my mind, but one phrase continued to haunt me: *Doing wrong is never the best way to produce a right.*

Somehow, I couldn't bring myself to broach the subject of the stele with Vander again. Too much cajoling and manipulating already plagued my goaded conscience.

Instead, I'd spent the past few days wandering the halls of *Palati del Chrysos*, opening a random selection of doors and squinting into dark corners and high rafters. If only I could find the stele myself, I could help Sir Colin without betraying Vander after all.

A container filled to bursting with dark magic. What would such a thing look like? What would such a thing *feel* like? And where in all of Sandrin—or in this case, Delunia—would they put it?

All traces of magic had drained from Lord Lessox before I'd ever met him. Prince Raphael and his parents had been put under a spell, but . . . they'd been markedly different under the influence of dark magic. Devoid of personality, of any true willpower. Speaking with them was like interacting with a ghost or a shell. A convulsion shook my shoulders.

But even then, nothing about the magic had been detectable from a distance. There'd been nothing palpable to latch on to.

I chose a room partway down the passage and tried the handle. Locked. No doubt if I ever managed to draw anywhere near the stele, it would lie behind one of these locked chambers anyway.

I pounded my fist against the door, pressing my forehead to the smooth painted wood. *What else can I do?*

The hope and anticipation lighting Vander's eyes in recent days haunted my dreams. Pleasant at first, when I imagined those hopes coming to fruition. His thumb caressing my hand, the tension of possibilities growing between us . . .

But they always turned nightmarish at the recollection that it wasn't what I wanted. That it had only been produced by my attempts to sway him, not from true strides forward in our relationship.

He'd seemed to want to tell me that day in the library, yet . . . I shook my head. I couldn't bring myself to plant more false hope than I already had, to push this charade even further just to get him to reveal information he wished to keep secret.

But neither could I live with myself if another person were injured—killed—by the effects of this stele while I stood by and did nothing.

I pushed myself to start moving again. Apparently, I was doomed to wander these halls like a shadow in a silent vigil until a better option presented itself.

My fingers toyed with the amulet dangling just below the nape of my neck. *Love surrounds you. My love will protect you.*

The sentiment should've brought reassurance, but instead it rang false. Flitting through the halls, aimless, no clear path to my destined goal—all symptoms of being abandoned, not protected. And where was that surrounding, protective love for the little boy in Leipon?

I let the charm drop, stopping short of ripping it from my neck and tossing it aside. Sister Rochelle had meant well, and she still seemed to place importance on the small token. I couldn't bring myself to show such disregard for her gift, no matter how ineffectual it was proving to be.

Hours later—at least, it felt like hours—I faced another long corridor, doorways along each side. Hadn't I already walked this way? The hallways were starting to blend together, a labyrinth of marble, wood, paint, and plaster.

Being lost didn't bring the sense of dread or panic I would've expected. Merely resignation, my senses deadened by weariness and the fruitless nature of my search.

Had I missed dinner? My mental shrug didn't reach my tired shoulders. I'd need to eat at some point, but avoiding the inquiring gazes of Tertius and Nadia, Dionne's knack for seeing behind my outer facade, the tempting pull of Vander's quiet devotion . . . it was just as well.

Occasional candles lit the otherwise uninhabited corridor, and little dust shrouded the floors and sconces. Presumably a servant or two would be sent to this section of the palace eventually. Or perhaps a guard would—

"Penelope? At last!"

Before I had time to wonder whether Vander's voice was hallucination or reality, he grasped my hands, stopping short of pulling me into a hug.

He peered into my face, brows drawn. "You are well—unhurt? I have looked for you all over the palace. No one has seen you in gardens, at the stables. Your lady's maid, even your guards, know nothing of your location. I began to fear you vanished."

His concern and pressure on my hands gently drew me back from my dreamlike ramblings to reality.

"I apologize—I never meant to cause any concern. I

promised my guards they didn't need to follow me because I wouldn't leave the palace. And I haven't. But these halls all seem to circle back on each other. I'm afraid I've become quite lost."

"It is good to see you safe and well." He tucked my arm around his and led me back the way he'd come. "This wing of the palace saw use some decades ago, when the court was large and many noble families lived within *Palati del Chrysos*. But recent generations, they prefer more privacy and separation, and so the nobility built their own homes in Ambrus. These rooms are now deserted."

I coughed out a wry laugh. "I noticed."

"But what could bring you here?"

My breath hitched. I'd never prepared an explanation for my search. The servants and guards always gave me a wide berth, unable to communicate with any hope of reaching an understanding. It hadn't occurred to me I might be caught by a member of the royal family.

"I was just exploring, trying to better discern the layout of the palace. But as I said, I got lost and — "

"Penelope." Vander stepped in front of me, dipping his head to look directly into my face.

His dark eyes were so fathomless, such a perfect representation of his wells of inner strength and compassion. His breath fanned against my mouth, smelling of mandarins and a hint of rosemary. Inviting me to lean closer . . .

I blinked and edged away. "Yes?"

I winced against the breathlessness of my whisper.

"Your eyes are tired. It is as if your smile has disappeared." His fingers grazed my cheek with the delicacy of a lacefly's wing. "Does this have relation to the stele? Does it truly haunt you so?"

I couldn't lie faced with such a direct question. Not this close to him, this . . .

I didn't allow myself to complete the thought. "Yes. I'm

sorry to go against your wishes, Vander. I know you want me to forget it ever existed, but I—"

"I do understand. Its presence is an upset to me as well. And you agreed to live here with no knowledge such a cursed object would blight your new home."

His throat constricted on a swallow, indecision warring in his eyes as his gaze swept the hall.

Was he about to tell me? I clenched my jaw, willing my features to betray no hint of my elevated pulse.

He stepped closer and placed a hand on my back. "I hope it may bring you comfort to discover the stele does not truly reside within our palace at all."

"It doesn't? But I thought you said . . ."

A hint of a smile twitched the corners of his lips. "The horses have more to fear than yourself."

The horses . . . it was in the stables. I'd noted the wide spread of the buildings, the large number of stable hands present almost any time of day. What a perfect place to hide an object free from the eyes of prying servants and visiting emissaries.

My shoulders sagged, in part from relief, in part from something akin to resignation. My futile search was over, and now Sir Colin would have an opportunity to destroy the stele forever. But although I'd stopped pressing him for it, the information had come from Vander. To communicate it would require a betrayal of his trust.

I glanced up to find him watching me, lines creasing his forehead.

"To know this . . . it does not bring comfort?"

"It does, thank you." Before I could think better of it, I placed my hand on the smooth material of his shirt, just over his heart. "I truly appreciate your willingness to confide in me. Your desire to make me feel better."

His gaze darted to my mouth before he looked away. My own breaths struggled to stay steady. I started to remove my hand, but he caught it in his.

"It is a pleasure to share with you. I want you to feel like a true member of our family. A true partner, equal, in my life."

"I'd like that too."

There was that draw toward him again. All the more enticing because he made no conscious effort to create it.

I took a slow step back and extracted my hand. "Have I missed dinner?"

The yearning in his eyes cleared after several blinks. His smile returned, genuine but a little stiff. "Not if we hurry."

I nodded, preparing to set a brisk pace.

His grip on my arm halted me. "But, Penelope, do be careful." His eyes held a strange pleading, as though he knew what I planned to do with this revelation. "No one outside our family can be trusted with this information. Not even friends or someone claiming to help."

"Of course."

A fist clamped around my heart, stilting its beats. *Traitor, traitor, traitor* seemed to ring in my ears.

But it wasn't really a betrayal when I meant him no harm, was it? Not like last time. If he knew Sir Colin like I did, if he could just learn to appreciate my friend, then he would understand I was doing the entire country a favor.

I could only pray that when the demise of the stele was discovered, he'd be grateful.

Not angry enough to turn me out on the street.

CHAPTER 25

The orange door of Sir Colin's house came into view.
My limbs shook with the desire to break into a run,
but I kept my measured pace just ahead of my guards.

The sights and sounds of the marketplace proved no
distraction today. I saw only the path in front of me, heard only
the drumming in my ears.

In the stable. In the stable.

I'd waited three agonizing days before allowing myself to
visit Sir Colin. To run straight to him with the revelation
would've only heightened Vander's suspicions. Three days I'd
spent fully on edge—every noise amplified, every conversation
analyzed for hidden meaning.

Vander's gaze seemed to trail me more than ever, as though
he could tell his disclosure had produced further disquiet
instead of calm appreciation. Thankfully, he hadn't raised the
subject again.

Now, at last, I was minutes away from revealing the information that threatened to burst from inside me.

But then what? I'd pondered the layout of the stable yard
again and again but was no closer to devising a strategy to

retrieve the stele. I hoped my ideas combined with Sir Colin's wisdom and levelheadedness would produce . . . something.

Niles ushered me into the house as usual. Victoria had accompanied us today, but she didn't spare me a glance as she took a seat on the porch, keeping her distance from Tassos and Petri. The loss of her company made the days crawl by that much more slowly.

At least here I would encounter a friendly face.

Sir Colin strode into the room, pausing to give me a deep bow. "Wonderful to see you, princess."

Did his smile hold an extra sense of anticipation, or was I merely imagining a reflection of my own?

"And you, Sir Colin." I dipped into a tremulous curtsy.

"Your usual rhosyn, I presume?"

"No, thank you." My shaking hands would only deposit the beverage onto his meticulously clean floor.

His brows rose. "Is there anything else I can tempt you with?"

"Not today, but as always I appreciate your hospitality."

Fighting the compulsion to pace the room, I lowered into a chair.

"Very well." He turned to Niles.

Following their brief exchange, the servant nodded and exited the front door.

I straightened the ruffle on my skirt for the fourth time. "I hope you didn't send him away on my account."

"Not at all." Sir Colin sank into the chair nearest mine and angled to face me. "I had a few errands for him to run, and I thought, perhaps, today's conversation might require an additional level of discretion."

Only the slight narrowing of his eyes hinted at his deeper meaning, the question underlying his statement.

I bounced on my seat, the news begging for release. "Oh, Sir Colin, he told me where the stele is. He didn't want to disclose it at first because it might put me at risk, so I searched for it myself. Of course I couldn't find it, but once he realized how much it meant to me, he finally gave in."

Sir Colin leaned forward, trying to follow the jumble of words clamoring to rush from my mouth. "I'm assuming you mean Prince Vander?"

"Yes." My initial outburst left my chest hollow, deflated. "I asked him just as you suggested."

He smiled and tweaked my arm. "Clever girl. I knew you could do it if you took the right approach. And what response did he give?"

His posture remained casual, but a new eagerness lit his eyes.

"He said . . ."

The declaration itself faltered in my throat. This was the last moment in which I could turn back, not breach Vander's confidence.

Sister Rochelle's voice drifted through the back of my mind. *Not everyone can be trusted.*

But Sir Colin had been my faithful friend all these months. He'd proven himself a gentleman from the moment we met. Cared more about Leipon than all the other residents of Ambrus combined. I had to see this through.

"It's not in the palace at all. They hid it somewhere in the stables."

He slapped the arm of his chair. "Well done, princess, well done. The stables, you say? What an odd choice."

"I thought so too, at first. But the more I considered it, the more I'm convinced of the wisdom of the decision. Anyone wanting to find it would naturally look within *Palati del Chrysos*, not the palace grounds. Guests don't have as much access there, and the stables are always teeming with servants caring for horses. Even at night, the horses act as guardians since they would likely make a commotion if a stranger approached."

He ran his fingers along his jaw. "Perhaps you're right. Emperor Tertius, or his father—it's hard to say whether the location has changed over the years—has put more thought into this than I would've given him credit for."

"But the ideal protection of the hiding place is precisely what leads to our next problem." I rubbed my hands together, as though I could shed the odd feeling of self-reproach lodging in my chest. "Vander told me three days ago, but I didn't want to rouse his suspicion by telling you right away."

Sir Colin nodded in acknowledgment.

"Ever since, I've tried to come up with a way I might access the stables, but with no luck." My shoulders slumped with my sigh. "I typically go riding several times a week, and I fear drawing attention to myself if my interest were to suddenly increase. As I said, between all the animals and stable hands, I don't know how I could ever search undetected."

"Of course, of course." He shook his head emphatically. "You have accomplished what I never could in determining the stele's location. Allow me to take it from here. If it had been in the palace where you had access, perhaps . . . but it is not worth risking your relationship with the royal family, even less your safety, to infiltrate the stables. How I will manage such a thing, I haven't the faintest idea."

He chuckled and ran a hand through his hair. "But I hope you realize what a gift you've given me, princess." He grasped my arm. "What a gift you've given the people of Leipon. Of Delunia. For generations, this dark magic has rotted away within the palace grounds, touching who knows how many lives. Finally, thanks to you, we have a chance to do something about it. To put a stop to the injuries and failed spells."

Joy flowed through my veins, carrying away my guilt and uncertainty. I'd done something right for once. Something important. I'd taken this journey I had no desire to go on and turned it into something beneficial.

Perhaps, despite so many previous mistakes, I had the makings of a true leader after all.

I hurried down the narrow road, my guards' boots crunching gravel as they followed. Any moment now, the marketplace would come into view. Any moment now, I'd find out if Sir Colin had retrieved the stele. If he'd managed to destroy it.

Only four days had passed since I'd disclosed its location to Sir Colin.

But at breakfast, Tertius had spoken of a mysterious disturbance in the stables during the night. Guards who'd wandered off, unable to recall anything about their watch. Horses that were difficult to wake and unusually sluggish. The furtive glances exchanged between him, Nadia, and Vander seemed to confirm my suspicions.

The stele had gone missing.

Vander's gaze had then slid to me—hesitant, questioning. My stomach coiled in on itself. No doubt he regretted telling me. My departure to visit Sir Colin the moment he and Tertius had set out to investigate the stables would only confirm his misgivings.

But the sooner I spoke with Sir Colin, the sooner I could be certain the stele was destroyed—the sooner I could beg Vander's forgiveness and assure him the stele was gone for good. That I'd done what was best for his family, for the entire country.

Nervous energy churned through me, propelling me to the far side of the market. I plunged ahead to knock on Sir Colin's door before Tassos and Petri had even reached the footpath to the house.

No answer.

I forced my heaving breaths to pause so I could listen. The usual chatter rose from the marketplace, but not a sound stirred within Sir Colin's home. I pounded on the door more forcefully. Where was he?

Likely visiting a colleague or running an errand.

But my pulse raced ever faster, ignoring logic. Avoiding the concerned stares of my guards, I stepped off the front stoop to the nearest window. I shaded my eyes and peered inside.

All was quiet within. But what about . . . there. I craned my neck far enough to see the peg where he hung the basket he used to take supplies to Leipon. Empty.

My feet carried me beyond his house to the path we'd taken to the northern city gate.

"*Principela!*" Tassos's low baritone followed me.

My guards. They weren't supposed to let me beyond the city gates.

But anxiety clawed my chest, sharp and raw, refusing to be denied. I had to know what was happening with the stele. Pacing around waiting for Sir Colin to return wasn't an option.

I turned to find Tassos and Petri hurtling forward to catch up with me.

"I'm sorry. I have no desire to get you into trouble, but I must venture outside of Ambrus today. There's no time to lose. Feel free to tell the emperor or prince or whomever you have to answer to that I ran away. I take full responsibility for my actions."

They exchanged a glance. Had they understood anything I'd said? It hardly mattered; I couldn't take the time to try to convey my meaning in a clumsy mixture of gestures and my scant Delunian vocabulary.

I pivoted and marched ahead once more. Moments later, their clomping boots fell into step behind me.

What had Sir Colin—or Niles or another accomplice— done to the horses and guards to produce such effects? Some kind of sleeping draft? I longed to check on Omorphia to ensure whatever they'd done hadn't caused lasting harm. At least the horses had woken at all. But the guards' confusion almost sounded like . . .

I stopped in my tracks.

It couldn't be. Sir Colin was trying to eradicate dark magic, not use it for his own ends.

Perhaps he'd already destroyed the stele and was sharing the good news with the villagers. Perhaps he'd simply gone in response to a summons or sought a place to hide the stele while he determined the best way to subdue the evil spirits within.

I felt my guards drawing nearer and rushed ahead.

No matter how many explanations I invented, I couldn't shake the feeling something wasn't right.

Once I'd passed far beyond the North Gate, I scanned the underbrush to the left of the road. Where had we — ?

Ahead, a path of trampled grass led toward a familiar copse of trees. I increased my pace, studying the tracks as I went. Two parallel trails outlined a set of hoofprints in the caked dirt, as though someone had come through with a horse-drawn cart.

Beyond the trees, Leipon came into view. My relieved exhale halted in my throat at the sight of villagers gathered into a throng.

On the far side of the cluster of tents and huts, Sir Colin stood near the crest of a grassy hillock. Beside him, mounted on a flat wooden cart he must've hired, sat a cube of stone about the height of my leather-embossed storage chest.

Deep carvings decorated every surface, swirls and symbols made menacing in the way their shadows deepened the stone's gray hue.

The stele.

He hadn't destroyed it. He'd stolen it.

CHAPTER 26

*S*urely I was mistaken.

Sir Colin spoke animatedly in Delunian, smiling and gesturing to his enraptured audience.

Did he plan to destroy the stele in front of the villagers? Such an act could send a strong message but hardly seemed worth the unnecessary danger if something went awry. And would the very people who sought to use dark magic to better their lives look so pleased to hear he was about to demolish its source?

I broke into a run. "Sir Colin, Sir Colin!"

He froze, his eyes wide and surprised—panicked, even?— before his expression eased into a tight smile. Raising a hand in a quelling motion, he spoke again to the crowd.

I recognized the words "wait" and "please."

I made my way around the gathered villagers, who regarded me with a mixture of suspicion and curiosity. Sir Colin crossed in front of the stele to meet me.

"Princess, what a delightful surprise. As I'm sure your keen eyes have already detected, your information proved correct. Let me again congratulate you on a job well done." His words came too fast, strain pitching his voice higher than usual. "I didn't think your fiancé would approve of your returning to Leipon, or I would've certainly invited you to accompany me."

Huffs gave my words a harsh, staccato cadence. "I heard about the odd behavior of the horses and stable guards this morning and thought it must've been due to your retrieving the stele. Vander will likely be furious with me, but I had to know what's happening."

I indicated the gathered villagers, whose chatter rose in a restless hum. "Why did you bring it here? And what do you want with all these people? Are you certain you'll be able to destroy it without putting them in danger?"

"Oh princess, if only there were more time to explain." His softened gaze spoke of sorrow, regret. "You need to trust me just a little longer, and in time I'm sure you'll understand."

"What do you mean? Understand what?" Spots danced in the outer reaches of my vision. "What are you about to do?"

His shoulders tensed, then sagged. "I couldn't expect you to appreciate the truth of the situation, given our home country's prejudice against sorcery. But believe me when I say the real problem isn't the presence of magic, it's the weakness of it. Any of those failed spells would've been guaranteed to work with a proper source to draw from. I'm about to provide that source."

I can't be hearing this. It was as though a different person entirely had taken on my friend's voice and visage.

"No. No! You were going to destroy it. That's why I discovered its location for you. That's the goal we were working toward. So no one would be hurt by magic again. We had plans to provide for them in a safer way. The baskets of supplies are almost ready . . ."

Sir Colin angled himself in front of me, likely to block my rage from the crowd's notice.

"We are still working toward the same goals, princess. Don't you see how this solution is better? The royal family has had plenty of chances to provide aid and have done nothing."

His eyes lit with frenzied energy. "Now the people of Leipon will be able to help themselves! Just think what they can achieve with access to such power. Far beyond basic necessities. And if the spells are allowed to function as they're intended, no one will be hurt."

"But how can you be sure — ?" I choked on the question, the answer slapping me across the face. The drowsy horses, the confused guards . . . "You taught them those spells."

"I did." He hurried on before I could form a response. "I was trying to help them. You must see that. Now what I've begun can finally be fulfilled."

My fists clenched as betrayal burned in my chest. "You've been lying this entire — "

"And I regret you had to find out this way, amid all this distraction and chaos, instead of in the calm of my home with a soothing cup of rhosyn." He grasped my shoulders. "But you're their heroine, princess. Their savior. I'll make sure they know how indebted they are to you."

Curls whipped across my face as I shook my head. "Don't you dare. This was not why I helped you find the stele, and I have no wish for my name to be associated with yours." Shaking off his hands, I stepped toward the stele. "You cannot follow through with this. It is the property of the royal family, and I forbid — "

Shouts emanated from the crowd, agitated by our raised voices or simply the delay.

"Ah, but thanks to you, the royal family doesn't possess it anymore."

Sir Colin strode to the stele at the same moment someone grasped my arms from behind. I twisted to see Niles, his expression as bland and stoic as ever.

The shing of metal clanged behind me, bolstered by a pair of battle cries. Tassos and Petri?

Sir Colin yelled something in response, the beauty of the Delunian language fractured into harsh, angry syllables. Men, even boys, from the crowd pushed forward, zeal raging in their eyes.

I struggled against Niles, desperation and terror staking equal claims in my chest as I strained to see what was happening behind me.

More angry cries. A man whimpered in pain, followed by a hollow thud.

"No, don't hurt them!"

How had the world upended so quickly? We were supposed to be helping, not butchering, the villagers. I tugged at my arms again, but Niles's fingers pressed into my flesh like claws. Three of the stouter ladies surrounded me, their fierce grips locking my shoulders and hands in place.

"No! Please. You must listen to me. I want to help!" But how could they listen to me when I hardly spoke their language?

The motley group of men and boys marched into my field of vision, surrounding my scowling guards and hoisting their swords aloft.

Please, don't let anyone else get hurt, I prayed silently, pleading deep in my soul the Luminate would find my prayers worth listening to.

The women at my sides shushed my incoherent blubbering as Sir Colin reclaimed his elevated post, dabbing his brow with a handkerchief. Following a tight-lipped glance at me, he continued his speech, subdued at first but growing more animated as he went on.

No, no, no. The word pounded through my mind as quickly as the blood coursing through my veins. I strained against my captors' grasps as regret clawed my throat, nearly choking me.

I'd been trying to help—I'd thought Vander was blinded by his parents' wishes regarding the stele and his jealousy of Sir Colin. Sister Rochelle's concerns had seemed naive and simplistic. But I'd betrayed them. For this. For Sir Colin to release the magic among the people to wreak who knew what kind of havoc.

I'd allowed myself to be tricked, blinded by his impeccable manners and reminiscences of home. The irony pummeled me like a thousand blows to the head.

I was a traitor. Again.

I'd been taken in by another family who'd welcomed and cared for me. Another fiancé who'd treated me with kindness and respect, this time one I'd even . . . A sob convulsed in my throat, and I fought to stay standing.

Even with the best of intentions, with my guard up against being led astray—I was a traitor, through and through.

The villagers looked on with awe, almost hunger. My heart contracted as I surveyed their faces. So frantic for help, blinded to any consequences by the promise of an easy solution. Images of Lord Lessox assaulted my mind's eye—gaunt, crazed, delirious.

There would undoubtedly be a cost.

My chin dropped to my chest. *What have I done?* And what of Tassos and Petri? Would they kill us after the magic was released? They'd hardly let us saunter back to the palace to report what we'd seen.

Or would they accompany us to *Palati del Chrysos* and take out their rage on the entire royal family?

". . . with this power, you will finally be seen! Finally be heard!"

I jerked my head up. Sir Colin's words had been washing over me like a stream over a pebble, too swift and foreign to make any impact. Why could I now understand him?

"It has long been my dream to share this wealth with you, the way it was always intended!"

I narrowed my eyes. The sounds reaching my ears didn't quite match the movements of Sir Colin's mouth. And the gathered villagers continued to give him their rapt attention, sometimes murmuring, sometimes shouting in agreement.

He couldn't have switched to Sandrinian. Then what . . . ?

A flutter of black fabric caught my eye. I shifted my gaze, careful not to draw my captors' attention. Sister Rochelle knelt within a copse of trees, her hands folded.

Sister Rochelle? Yet another person who might be harmed —possibly killed—because of my folly. She had to get away.

Instead, she remained still, seemingly oblivious to the danger. Praying, of all things.

I shook my head. Perhaps she wasn't there at all, and my distress had advanced to delirium.

Sir Colin extended a hand into the air, his stature seeming taller in his exuberance. "I have shared your frustration, your grief at our past failures. But how much more glorious will those memories make our future triumphs!"

Behind him, the stele pulsed with otherworldly energy, almost as though it were trying to hurry Sir Colin along.

But . . . I blinked. It was moving.

Slowly, so subtle it would've been easy to miss, the stele hovered above the cart. Inching at a snail's pace, it slid in the direction of . . . I returned my gaze to Sister Rochelle.

Her eyes remained closed, but her fingers reached, almost as if coaxing something forward. Hope and disbelief tangled in my chest in an intricate dance. I'd heard stories of the mystics, but . . . could the Luminate truly give her such power?

I trained my eyes on Sir Colin, willing him to keep talking, to give her more time. The stele was halfway to Sister Rochelle now, hidden from the crowd's view by the circle of men keeping my guards subdued.

"Now, at last, it is our turn! Our time to rise!" Sir Colin started to pivot to where the stele should have been.

No. "Sir Colin!" No true plan had formulated in my mind, but I had to distract him. "Perhaps you're right. I'm beginning to understand what you're trying to accomplish, and if we—"

His brows lowered. "I appreciate your change of heart, princess, but there's no more time for discussion."

"But . . ."

He shook his head and turned, reaching for empty air. "*What?*"

The exclamation slapped the air like a crack of thunder. His cold, icy gaze rested on me. Then on Sister Rochelle, who'd drawn the stele within arm's reach.

"You! I don't care how holy you think you are, *Sister*, but you shall not interfere!"

Villagers craned their necks, their voices rising in anger and shock. Sir Colin swirled his hands, then pushed a coil of fizzling black sparks toward Sister Rochelle.

I gasped. *Protect her, Luminate. Please.*

Sister Rochelle raised her arms in a protective gesture, and a shield of glimmering white arced around her. The sparks battered against it but found no opening.

I strained against the hands holding me firm, but even the struggle between Sir Colin and Sister Rochelle didn't loosen Niles's iron grip. Soon my other captors' nails pinched my skin.

Tears welled in my eyes. *This is all my fault, and I can't even help her.*

Grunting, Sir Colin let the black sparks fizzle into nothing. With a tug that strained his muscles as though heaving a great weight, he brought the stele hurtling toward him.

Sister Rochelle cried out, allowing her shield to lapse and renewing her hold on the stele.

"Too predictable, Sister." Sir Colin's eyes held a cruel glint I'd never seen before.

Still pulling with one hand, his other arm snapped toward Sister Rochelle, sending writhing green ropes to circle her torso. She recoiled but couldn't free herself from the snake-like cords. Angry, red burns erupted each time her skin made contact with her magical bonds. Her head sagged against her chest, her fingers clenched into fists.

"No!" Nausea curdled the contents of my stomach,

phantom burns irritating my own skin. Why hadn't I confided in her? Why hadn't I listened to her?

Apparently satisfied with his work, Sir Colin settled the stele in place. Eyes wide with anticipation, he grasped a small rectangle protruding from the back corner.

He cried, "People of Leipon, fellow Delunians! Let nothing stop us! Let no one steal our moment!"

He gave one last tug to the sliver of stone, pulling it free. The chiseled labyrinth decorating the front took on an eerie glow as vapors hissed out from the hole left by the removed shard.

A strangled cry erupted from Sister Rochelle. I shuddered. Was the magic hurting her worse, or—

The ground rippled beneath me, twisting my ankle as I stumbled. All around, people cried out, arms flailing in every direction in futile attempts to regain balance. Another tremor shook the earth, producing a living sea of dirt and grass.

Tearing away the those who confined me.

In movements that felt too fast and uncontrolled to be my own, I lunged forward. Staggering as though on the deck of the *Ismena* during a hurricane, I made clumsy progress toward the stele.

I have to stop this.

The wisp of smoke from the narrow breach had thickened to black fog. So much damage already—I couldn't let any more dark power escape. With a last wild lurch, I threw myself onto the stele. My hands scrabbled for the opening, desperate to form a new seal.

Smoke poured over me—into me—in an endless barrage, stealing my breath. As though I stood in the depths of an angry, writhing storm.

"Princess, no! You mustn't—"

Sir Colin's wail reached me through the muffled haze, but my newly freed guards held him fast, forcing him to his knees.

Hands pulled and shoved from all directions, and screams

and shouts assaulted my ears. But the earth had stopped quaking, and my feet remained planted. I couldn't tell whether I was capable of movement, but I'd made my stand.

Futile as the effort was, I had to show them my betrayal was an accident, perhaps convince Vander . . .

But he'd never see. He'd never know. The dampness in my eyes condensed to tears. I'd be sent away again, in far worse humiliation than before. With a heart in even more fragments.

Unless this shroud of dark magic killed me first.

My heaving breath dissolved into a wheeze. A cough. No space, no air, only black. Then a bright flash, blinding and disorienting.

"Penelope!" The agonized cry of Vander's disembodied voice must've been a dream. A last hope . . . but no.

After all I'd done, all the harm I'd caused, I didn't deserve to be saved from the grim consequences of my actions a second time. Perhaps the best outcome would be for the world to be rid of me for good.

I sank to my knees as darkness overtook me.

CHAPTER 27

Smoke clogged my nostrils, my chest. I wanted to cough, but I couldn't move. My breath snaked in and out of my throat in the thinnest tendril of a lifeline, hardly sufficient to sustain me. Not nearly enough to expel the dark cloud from my body.

Where was I? What had happened?

My mind warred between opening my eyes and leaving them shut tight. Would restoring my vision merely confirm what I felt—that I lay engulfed in a fog I could never escape?

The magic . . . the stele pressed itself into my memory, spewing eerie black vapors. Released by Sir Colin?

No, that couldn't be right.

But then horror washed over me anew, too pungent to be imagined. It *had* been Sir Colin. He'd betrayed me, done precisely the opposite of what he'd promised. Just like I'd betrayed Vander . . .

A wave of guilt joined the horror, weighing me down as though to bury me alive.

Then I'd leaped forward—the dark magic had surrounded me. Entered me? Was that why I lay suspended in this coffin of fog?

I wasn't even worthy of death, just an eternity of gasping for breath, surrounded by blackness. Or did the magic control me now? Was my body performing evil deeds while my mind remained separate, trapped?

My consciousness trembled with a spasm that couldn't reach my limbs.

Footsteps padded into my awareness, seemingly near, yet so, so far.

"Poor dear, how I wish you'd awaken."

That voice, so much softer and gentler than my gloomy musings. And familiar . . . Sister Rochelle? She'd been there too, trying to get the stele away. Trying to undo the grim consequences of my mistakes.

But surely such a pure follower of the Luminate couldn't share my fate, could never be suspended in a purgatory of dark magic. Perhaps I merely dreamed—

A smooth cloth bathed my forehead with frigid water. I inhaled, loosening the mire coating my lungs. Coughs racked my body, closing the thin tunnel that provided my air.

"Oh, my child!"

My body was jerked into a sitting position, my back patted until the hacking subsided to a wheeze and I could gulp a rivulet of breath.

I collapsed back onto my pillows, shaking and rasping.

"I'm so very sorry, princess. I had no idea I'd startle you so. But praise the Luminate your consciousness is returning, even if it's rough going at first."

Tender hands brushed hair from my face and adjusted my blankets. My eyelids fluttered several times before I could keep them open.

"Sister Rochelle?" The words left my mouth in the merest whisper of sound.

Her movements stilled as her eyes sought mine. "Yes, princess. You're safe now, in the infirmary of *Palati del Chrysos*."

I was safe. Alive. "But you—are you all right?"

More coughs convulsed my lungs.

"I'll be fine. No injuries that won't heal."

A large white bandage was wrapped around her wrist, almost blending in with her nun attire.

A new wave of guilt and shame washed over me. "I'm so sorry. I didn't listen when you warned me, but you still came. And now . . ."

"There, there, dear. Please don't upset yourself." She waited until the worst of my coughs subsided. "If there's anything to forgive, it's forgiven. I should've known my advice would count for little when you'd already spent months establishing connections here. Sir Colin was more persuasive—and a more powerful sorcerer—than I'd anticipated."

Images of their battle slowly came into focus. "Your powers were—incredible."

The black smoke seemed to have turned to tar, coating my insides.

Sister Rochelle bustled to a table against the far wall and poured water into a thin glass. "My power is nothing. It is an immense honor the Luminate has chosen me as one of His conduits." She laughed. "The earthquake was remarkable."

"The earthquake was from you?" I'd assumed it'd been brought on by Sir Colin opening the stele.

"It was. Though I regret I could only free you, not spare you all this pain." The glass in her hand quivered. "I'm so grateful the Luminate gave me the foresight to pass that amulet on to you, or you never would've survived."

She returned to my side and tipped the water to my lips. The liquid cooled my throat, spreading a hint of life back into my chest. After a few sips, I gingerly raised my hand to the amulet still about my neck.

My shiver had little to do with the temperature of the water. The bright flash—had it come from this small, unobtrusive necklace? Would I truly have died without it?

Sister Rochelle's shoulders deflated in a satisfied sigh. "The Luminate knew just how much you'd need His protection."

The words I'd puzzled over so many times resounded in my mind. *Love surrounds you. My love will protect you.*

Love will protect you . . .

Fog encroached on my thoughts once more. No one loved me. No one here, anyway. My family was so far away, and Sir Colin's friendship had turned out to be every bit as duplicitous as Nicholas's professed love.

Could Vander—?

Heat tingled through my arms and legs, as though fusing them back to my body. Could Vander possibly love me, even after all I'd done? Was he here? A desire to see him—to meet his steady, admiring gaze, to feel his warm hands grasp mine— swelled the heat to an almost painful intensity.

I struggled to sit up, flailing against confining bedclothes.

"Easy, child. Easy." Sister Rochelle helped raise my shoulders and propped pillows behind me. "You've been asleep for days. Your recovery will take some time."

My eyes gave the room one last frantic scan but to no avail. *He's not here.* I swallowed slowly to avoid gagging on the lump in my throat. "Vander?"

With an effort, I resisted the impulse to cower beneath my sheets. Would her look turn sad, sympathetic? Had he abandoned me?

Sister Rochelle's face lit up. "He's hardly left your side. The poor man's been quite desperate. Watching you collapse like that, overcome by dark magic . . . but even devoted fiancés need a break once in a while. I insisted he get some rest. He'll be so pleased you've woken at last."

"He was there?" Perhaps I hadn't imagined his voice after all.

"Oh, yes. The prince brought a contingent of guards to Leipon shortly after the stele was opened. They were too late to stop Sir Colin, of course, but they got him safely transported to the dungeon and managed to subdue the townspeople."

I fingered the amulet once more, a swirl of hope expelling my inner darkness. "Then he was the one . . ."

"Ah. No, my dear." She squeezed my arm.

The spark died as quickly as it'd come, plunging me into inky blackness once more.

"You must understand, princess, no human love could be strong enough or pure enough to save you from such an onslaught of evil magic. Only the Luminate has that kind of power."

The pendant fell back to my chest. A mix of incredulity and awe warred within. "The Luminate's love saved me?" Doubts swarmed my mind at the very thought. "Why would He bother when it was my fault the stele was opened? When I've . . ."

I couldn't finish the statement. I'd done so much to repel His good opinion, to reject His influence.

Surely He'd given up on me ages ago.

Her probing gaze gave me the uncanny feeling my deepest secrets were being laid bare. "Was it your fault? Was that the outcome you intended?"

"That wasn't my intention, no. But—"

"Even if it was, the Luminate's kindness and forgiveness are far beyond anything we mortals can fathom." Sister Rochelle brushed a strand of hair behind my ear. "Nothing you've done or could do would ever cause Him to forsake you. His love will remain constant, regardless of the number or degree of your faults or mistakes."

I leaned my head back, my throat raw and sore from the short conversation. The Luminate loved me, had forgiven me. Saved my life.

Thank you?

The prayer felt so pathetic, so inadequate. I'd accused Him of abandoning me, had stopped seeking His guidance long ago.

But the softest radiance broke through the blackness clouding my mind, bringing warmth and hope.

Yes, even when I'd ignored or rejected it, that presence had never wavered. Never *would* waver.

Peace washed over me, unlike anything I'd experienced since meeting Nicholas. Since losing Mama. I breathed more deeply, letting my eyelids drift closed.

Thank you. I'll try not to turn away again.

The sound of poured water brought my awareness back to my surroundings. Sister Rochelle was transferring water from a kettle to a washbasin, humming to herself.

She set the kettle aside and glanced to me. "Now, my dear, you were asking about Prince Vander. I thought perhaps you might like to get freshened up before your fiancé visits?"

Her bright smile held a knowing quirk.

"Yes, please."

It'd be challenging to face him no matter what, but it couldn't hurt to smell less smoky and look less disheveled.

My incompatible longing and dread surrounding Vander's return pulled me in opposite directions like a torture device.

Would he be disappointed? Angry? Sad? Likely all three. But Sister Rochelle said he'd hardly left my bedside. Even if the Luminate was responsible for saving me through the amulet, was it possible Vander might — ?

"Here we are." Sister Rochelle's cheerful proclamation interrupted my jumbled thoughts.

She helped me slide to the edge of the bed, then dipped a cloth into water and pressed it to my face. How odd to be cared for so tenderly by a woman I'd only ever pushed away. Yet she acted as though we'd been the closest of friends all along. As though she truly had come to Delunia for me, not to scrutinize and judge but to guide and safeguard.

But even Sister Rochelle's soothing ministrations couldn't keep my patience at bay for long. "Did Vander say when he might come back?"

She paused, rolling up a sleeve of my nightdress. "I hope he's allowing himself a nice long rest. I'm certain he needs it." Her free hand squeezed my shoulder. "But don't worry. He won't be able to stay away for long."

"Did he say anything while he was here? About me?"

My face flared warmer than the water in the basin. I sounded more juvenile than Sophia.

"He said very little. He's been quite distraught."

"Of course." I almost wished another coughing fit would consume me.

"But you have nothing to fear, princess. Your journey together will not end here."

I jerked, nearly dislodging the washcloth from her grip. "How do you know? Have you seen something?"

She smiled and resumed scrubbing my arm. "Our visions are sometimes specific, but often merely a glimpse, or even a sense or feeling. Some are meant to be shared in full, others are meant to be kept within our hearts."

My posture deflated. She wasn't going to tell me. Yet, vague as they were, I found her references to her time spent in communion with the Luminate oddly comforting.

"The project that brought you to Delunia—was it successful? Do you plan to go back?"

"We made a promising start, yes. But now that I'm at the palace, I'd like to see what good I can do here before I venture out again."

I grasped her wrist, leaving a wet mark on her black sleeve. "Would you stay and advise me? For a time, at least? There's so much I don't understand about the Luminate, and I'd appreciate your counsel."

She squeezed excess water from the cloth, and my stomach gave a corresponding twist.

I couldn't meet her eyes. "I apologize that I haven't always appreciated it in the past."

"Some guidance takes time to appreciate." She hung the

cloth on the edge of the basin. "I should very much like to aid you in your goal of growing closer to the Luminate in any way I can."

"Thank you." My fingers locked together in my lap. "That is, of course, if I end up staying in Delunia."

Her exhale carried the faintest hint of a laugh. "Although he said little, the prince's vigil spoke volumes. He even asked me to pray with him." She brushed my hair back from my face, resting her palms on my cheeks. "Vander cares for you very much, princess."

Could he? After I'd betrayed the secret he'd so reluctantly shared with me?

Surges of heat and cold passed through me as Sister Rochelle settled me back into the bed.

How could I now dare to hope for—long for, even— Vander's love when I'd been pushing him away ever since I'd stepped foot in Delunia?

CHAPTER 28

*D*espite Sister Rochelle's strict instructions to sleep while she sought additional herbs, my rest was interrupted by every creak, every imagined footstep. When would Vander return? Would he return when he heard I'd awoken? Or would he avoid me, feeling his duty fulfilled?

The chance to scrub off some of the grime had been wonderfully refreshing, but nothing could fully soothe my anxious heart, the restlessness of my conscience.

A knock sounded at the door. Strong yet hesitant.

I sat up, attempting to straighten the robe covering my nightdress and spreading the blankets about my legs.

"Come in." I couldn't keep the quiver out of my voice.

The door inched open, first allowing Vander's face to peek in, then widening to accommodate his stocky frame. "You are awake! I hardly dared hope the sister could be correct. My great apologies I wasn't here upon your waking."

He hurried to my bedside and dropped to his knees.

Hope soared through my ribcage at his relieved, earnest expression. Surely if he'd lost all regard for me — if he was determined never to forgive me — he'd show more indifference about my return to health.

I fiddled with the sheets. "Yes. I'm still quite tired. A great deal of smoke or something like it seems to have taken up residence in my lungs. But I believe I will be well."

"I cannot express how happy it makes me to hear this." He lifted his hands as though wanting to take mine, then let them fall back. "When your Sir Colin opened the stele and such evil magic struck you, it made me fear . . ."

His voice turned husky as it trailed off. He looked down, a vein throbbing in his neck.

My coarse laugh sounded aged and gravely. "He's not *my* Sir Colin. Lying and underhanded, nothing like the gentleman I thought he was." I never could've dreamed my scholarly friend would have so much in common with Nicholas. "But how did you know to find me there?"

He rose to sit in the chair nearest my bedside, his lips pressed into a firm line. "After we confirmed the stele was missing, I suspected Sir Colin and feared for you. We could not locate you, even when Egan took us to Sir Colin's home. Leipon was the only additional place of which I could think."

He massaged his forehead. "But our arrival came too late to stop this monster. We could not prevent you from making your sacrifice—the most we could do was return your body to the palace."

His shoulders shook, whether from sorrow or anger or both, I couldn't tell. With a fortifying breath, I clasped one of his hands.

"I am so very, very sorry. For causing you such distress. For betraying your trust. Please believe I was not aware of Sir Colin's true intentions. If only I'd heeded your warnings." I swallowed a rising cough. "But he promised to destroy the stele and eradicate the dark magic. I was trying to help. He seemed to care so much for the people of Leipon, I never thought . . . I —I'm so sorry."

I made myself stop before tears could escape.

Vander stared at our intertwined fingers, his eyes unreadable. "I was most disappointed in your choice. I believed after I confided in you, we would . . ." He traced a thumb across my knuckles. "My parents were more angry still."

I winced but remained silent. I deserved every bit of their anger and disappointment.

He shook his head. "However, your reasons were not all bad, this I can see. Sir Colin's plan for the spread and use of dark magic was the worst possible outcome. But to hide it away, to hope it will never be found, never cause harm—this too is a problem. It was our responsibility to rid Delunia of such magic, and we failed."

"But I should've been honest with you and worked with you to find a solution." My chest compressed as though I'd been overrun by a carriage. "I feared you'd never forgive me for trusting Sir Colin instead of you. That perhaps it was better if the dark magic consumed me." I swiped my free hand beneath my eyes. "I can never seem to—"

His grasp around my fingers tightened. "No." He lowered his head until I met his gaze. "Even in poor judgment or betrayal, for you to perish could never be a good outcome. And your sacrifice made clear your intentions were noble. We have known each other only a short time. I hope perhaps in future we can have more trust, more communication between us."

"Then you . . . you still want to marry me?" A poorly timed cough ripped through my chest, forcing me to turn away.

"Of course." Vander rubbed my back in a slow circle until my coughs subsided.

Delicious tingles danced up my spine.

"That is, I—" Drawing back and relinquishing his touch, he set his jaw. "I have made a commitment to my country and yours, and I intend it to be fulfilled."

I leaned against my pillow, releasing my ragged breath slowly to forestall a sigh.

No one could blame the poor man for being scared to touch me, scared to betray any affection after all my coldness and rebuffs. After I'd used his attraction against him in the worst possible way.

How could I convince him I'd now welcome such overtures? Not to manipulate him, but because . . . My mind wasn't quite ready to put the sentiment into words.

"I'm glad to hear that." Reaching beneath my hair, I unclasped the amulet from my neck. "Did Sister Rochelle tell you how I survived the dark magic?"

He tipped his chair on its back legs, his brow furrowing. "She said something of her Luminate. Of special protection?"

I nodded and extended the amulet to him. "Yes. Do you remember this?"

He accepted it, squinting at the pendant. "This is the necklace from the Sister—Sister Rochelle, who has cared for you?"

"She's the same Sister who gave it to me, yes. She told me it has a special blessing from her and the other mystics she used to live with. The inscription says 'Love surrounds you. My love will protect you.'"

My heartbeat thudded in my ears. Could I really say it? I tucked my hands beneath the sheets, curling my knees to my chest.

"When I first awoke, I thought perhaps you had saved me. Your . . . love."

His eyes locked on mine, wide and uncertain. "I understand your wishes for our engagement and marriage, and I seek to respect—"

"I know."

Lightheadedness clouded my thoughts. I should've waited until I was better recovered to have this conversation. Perhaps never broached the subject at all.

"Sister Rochelle explained it was the Luminate who saved me through the amulet, and I'm so grateful. But my despair at the prospect of losing your respect and friendship followed by the hope that, in spite of everything, you might love me enough to trigger the blessing—it made me realize I've been wrong."

His mouth opened and closed in silent question. "I fear these few days have been a blur. So much worry, very little sleep. I don't believe I understand."

Heat scorched my cheeks. What a mess I'd created between us. But *this* was finally a mess I might be able to fix.

Laying my blankets aside, I pivoted until my legs dangled off the side of the bed.

"What I'm trying to say is that I've valued your friendship for some time, but lately . . . every time we've . . ." No attempt at serenity could keep me from gnawing at my lip. "I no longer think I would be satisfied with a marriage that is simply an alliance. Though I've been denying it—to myself most of all—I do care for you."

My heart hardly dared to beat in the silence. I couldn't meet his gaze.

"That is . . . but only if you think you could eventually trust or care for me. If not, I understand entirely—" My words came faster and faster, a dam threatening to burst.

"Penelope."

The whisper cut through the jumble of thoughts raging through my mind, directing my attention to him alone.

"Your error in passing information of the stele on to Sir Colin, it was grave. This I cannot deny. But if my admiration for you can be undone by one mistake, what kind of true feeling would this be? How could I be a man you can place your reliance on? I make many mistakes and shall make many more."

He grasped his knees, shifting his weight on the chair.

"I do care for you, and such feelings are much deeper than an unreasonable expectation of perfect conduct. You think so much about a people so new to you. You try so hard to adjust and show respect for my culture, when I know this is a challenge. Your treatment of me is gentle and kind, not full of scorn."

The huskiness in his voice constricted my stomach in an oddly pleasant sensation.

"Your beauty and grace affected me the moment we met. But since then I have seen you are passionate and vulnerable and spirited, and this makes you all the more lovely."

I slowly raised my head to meet his earnest gaze. Grasping his shoulder with one hand, I raised the other to touch his face.

"You are the sweetest, most generous man I could've asked for as a future husband. I'm sorry it's taken me so long to see it."

My thumb brushed the dark stubble shadowing his cheek.

A tremor ran through Vander's frame as his eyes focused on my mouth. I crept closer to the edge of the bed until mere inches separated us.

Then, without knowing whether one or both of us closed the distance, our lips met with the gentlest touch. The first rays of sunlight gracing early morning dew. But soon we drew nearer still, fervor etching cracks into our hesitance.

Kiss after kiss, learning the curve of each other's lips as we made up for months spent at arms' length.

When we finally parted, I leaned my forehead against his, struggling to slow my racing pulse. "I have a feeling we'll give our guests a much better show at the next ball."

His chuckle warmed my neck. "Indeed. Though it is best if we continue to practice, just in case."

CHAPTER 29

"M'lady!" Victoria rushed to my bedside in a swirl of chestnut hair and emerald fabric. She reached me and bowed her head, sniffling.

I pressed her hand, my chest rising as though another missing piece were clicked into place. "It's so good to see you, Victoria. I'm relieved you're well."

"Me?" Her eyes snapped up to meet mine. "Ye're the one who . . . and I . . ." A sob escaped her lips.

I edged closer to her. "I'm sorry I've given you such a scare. But I'm recovering, and all will be well now."

"But when I think of how I've been treatin' ye . . ." She took a long, gasping breath. "I've been so horrible the past few weeks, glarin' and angry, hardly speakin' a word. When I heard what happened and that ye wouldn't wake up, and they wouldn't let me see ye —"

She wiped the back of her hand beneath her nose. "I was so afraid that was how it'd end between us. That I'd never get to say goodbye, never apologize for actin' like such a childish, petty . . ." A new stream of tears assaulted her cheeks.

"Oh, Victoria. Please, sit down." I patted the bed beside me.

She blinked and took a step back. "Ye're very kind, m'lady, but I'm all right." She rubbed her fingers beneath her eyes and stood a little straighter. "I wouldn't want anyone to think I'm actin' too familiar, not respectin' my rank."

"Too familiar? You help me get dressed every day."

A smile twitched her lips, but she kept her distance.

"I'm requesting not as your princess, but as your friend." I tried to make my expression entreating.

She hesitated, then perched on the edge of the mattress. I pulled her into a hug. She melted into my arms, crying harder than before. I held her tight as my own eyes dampened.

I'd missed her even more than I'd realized.

After her tears subsided, she sat back, sniffling. "I don't deserve such kindness, m'lady."

A sentiment I understood all too well. "I've received many kindnesses I haven't deserved. It's refreshing to be the provider instead of the recipient." I blew out a breath and readjusted my bedcovers. "Besides, you had a right to be angry with me."

"Ye said yerself, ye were just tryin' to protect me."

For once, my sigh didn't turn into a cough. "That may be true, but I sought your protection for all the wrong reasons. I didn't want to see you get hurt, but it wasn't fair to burden you with my own fears and presumptions. I'm sorry."

A hint of her usual dimpled smile peeked through her tear-stained cheeks. "Please, think nothin' more of it."

"Thank you." I squeezed her arm. "How is Egan, anyway? You've still been able to see him even though he was reassigned?"

"Oh, yes, the servants take our meals together. But I've given him a hard time of it while ye've been ill. I felt it'd be a betrayal if I spent too much time with him while yer life was in jeopardy."

"Poor man. Make sure to show him some extra affection when you see him next."

Her responding bounce shook the mattress. "Does that mean you approve? We have yer blessing?"

Guilt tugged at my heart like an insistent puppeteer. To think she could've been this happy all along.

"You've never needed my blessing. I apologize for giving the impression that you did. But yes, if he's treating you well and you want to spend your lives together, then you have my full blessing."

Her wide smile made the stark room so much more cheerful. After weeks of her frowns, her joy warmed me like a blazing hearth in mid-winter.

Her eyes returned to me, filled with a new curiosity. "Not to pry, m'lady, but . . . could this mean ye might be open to embracin' a romance o' yer own?"

The implication in her question brought heat to my cheeks. "Perhaps. After Vander's visit this morning, I . . . I'm quite open to the possibility."

She squealed and grasped my shoulders. "I'm so thrilled for ye. And for him! The way his eyes have followed ye ever since we arrived . . . I understood yer hesitation, o' course, but I just hoped one day ye'd turn around and see the prince was so devoted and loyal to ye and nothin' like . . ." She heaved a dramatic sigh. "How wonderful that ye'll both get the happy endin' ye deserve."

I blushed and ducked my head. "I'm not sure it's deserved in my case, but I plan to embrace it anyway."

I pictured Vander's face so close to mine, the tender kiss he'd placed on my forehead before submitting to Sister Rochelle's entreaties that he return to his chambers to rest.

"The only thing worse than the mistakes I've already made would be to let them ruin my future."

～

Sister Rochelle turned to me with a mock frown. "Yet another visitor. Doesn't anyone around here know to allow an invalid some rest?"

I grinned. "I've rested plenty today."

Victoria had left hours ago, and Vander hadn't yet returned from his much-needed nap.

"I hope to eschew my invalid title altogether very soon."

"Very well, you may come in." She ushered Dionne into the room, giving her a wide smile to undermine her feigned disapproval.

Dionne's expression remained stony.

"Dionne! How nice to see you."

I reached for her as she stopped at my bedside, but she drew back. Odd. Perhaps she felt the need to keep up her quiet, docile façade in front of Sister Rochelle.

I raised my hand to get the nun's attention. "Sister Rochelle? I should like to write a letter to my family later today after all that's transpired. Do you think you could scrounge up some paper and a quill for me, please?"

"Of course, Princess Penelope." Her glance between me and Dionne implied she caught my true purpose. "It may take some time, but I trust Princess Dionne to keep you company in my absence."

After she bustled out of the room, I turned back to my visitor. "There, now we can talk just the two of us. How have you been?"

"You have recovered, it seems?"

I winced at the flatness in her tone but tried to keep my own light. "Well on the way, at least. Sister Rochelle is a kind, diligent nursemaid. And surrounded by her fervent prayers night and day, I think I had little choice but to recover."

She averted her gaze.

"Is something wrong? If there's anything I—"

"Why should anything be wrong? You bat your eyelashes, beg forgiveness, and he's more in love than ever, eh? He announces that you have the importance to him, that you do not know what you were doing, and we should all just treat you as though it never happened."

My jaw went slack. Vander had defended me so staunchly to his family?

"I truly regret my actions, Dionne. I apologized to Vander, and yes, he has forgiven me. But not because I flirted or toyed with him. I've come to fully appreciate what a good man your brother is, and I—I love him."

The words tasted foreign and exposed, but not inaccurate.

"I don't take his forgiveness lightly, or his affection. I plan to be completely faithful to him and to do my best to make him happy."

She folded her arms across her chest. "That is all well for Vander, I suppose. But what about others?"

"Others?" My mind spun, trying to comprehend this unexpected development in the conversation.

"You betray us all!" Her foot stomped against the marble floor as she turned from me. "Father and Mother welcome you into our home, provide everything you ask. We change our language so you understand. I give you lessons in Delunian. We talk, we laugh. I—I think we become the friends."

Her voice cracked on the last word, revealing the hurt behind her anger.

"Oh, Dionne. You're absolutely right. I did betray all of you, and I'm so, so sorry. I've been welcomed as part of your family from my first day in Delunia, and I'm so thankful. You've given me your trust, but rather than return it, I chose in favor of Sir Colin instead. Please, accept my apology and allow me to try again."

She peeked at me over her shoulder.

"And we are friends. Sisters, even."

As I spoke the words, I acknowledged their truth. Dionne was one of the few young ladies I could converse with in Delunia, and I'd enjoyed her company. She'd confided in me, and we'd giggled about visitors and fashion. And the times when her teasing rankled me—in a way, they made her feel all the more like family.

"Of course we shall be the sisters. It seems you will marry my brother."

"Yes, I'm going to marry him." Instead of foreboding, the statement now produced a delightful flutter of anticipation. "But I feel as though we're sisters already. And as such, I should've considered the way my actions and decisions would affect you in addition to Vander."

"*Rei.* Yes, you should." Her arms remained crossed, but she pivoted to face me.

"Please, let me know what I can do to make it up to you."

"Hmm." She continued to frown, but the twinkle in her eyes suggested I was well on my way to being forgiven. "Perhaps you could suggest to Father we hold a ball to celebrate after your recovery. And insist that handsome son of the governor of Eanraig be invited." She shrugged. "Rest of Maceo's family may come too, eh?"

I covered my grin with a formal nod. "Consider it done."

I paused at the top of the cold, dank stairway. Another dungeon. Another friendship gone wrong.

Despite the shiver tickling my spine, I kept my posture tall. I'd made mistakes, yes, but I was done wallowing in them. Done shouldering responsibility for the guilt of those who'd deceived me.

Egan darted a questioning gaze at me, and I descended behind my newly reinstated guard. Despite being almost half a world away, Delunia's dungeon was built in the same style as the one in Imperia. As though people of every nation had come to precisely the same conclusion about the appropriate living quarters for criminals.

The echo of my footsteps on the surrounding stone brought memories rushing back of my visit to Nicholas. The loss and confusion and guilt tearing through my chest, nearly stealing my breath. Hints of the same swirl of emotions lingered, but I kept them at bay.

This time was different. This time, the future presented itself as a clear path forward, not a jumble of uncertainty and doubt. I'd turn to the Luminate with my struggles and failings, no matter how great, knowing His love and forgiveness had never truly left.

I'd marry Vander and do my best to love him without secrets or reservations and use my position in the royal family to do good among the people of Delunia.

Vander. I smiled just thinking about him.

He'd lingered by my side throughout my recovery, a strong, reassuring presence. I'd been tempted to accept his offer to accompany me to the dungeon, but this was something I had to face alone.

A memory of Vander's goodnight kiss the evening before ghosted across my lips. Yes, visiting another fallen friend in the dungeon was hard, but in every other respect, this time was different. Better.

Egan paused at the third cell and extended a hand. "You find him here, *principela.*"

After a slight bow, he backed away a respectful distance.

"Princess?" The voice within the cell was eager but weak.

I shook my head to clear my thoughts, then approached. "Yes, Sir Colin."

He hardly deserved the title of "sir" anymore, but his name didn't sound right without it.

"Ah, my dear girl. It's good to see you well and unharmed." He clung to the iron bars, almost as though he needed them to stand. "I've missed our conversations, and I never meant . . . the magic was never supposed to harm you."

I'd had so many things I wanted to say to him. Questions,

reproaches, dismissals. But now, with him before me, I could only stare. Without the trappings of his impeccable home and fashionable clothing, he looked so frail. So defeated.

My pent-up fury and betrayal washed away, as though an invisible river flowed through the hall separating the cells, leaving emptiness in its wake. But not the emptiness of despair . . . more an abiding peace.

He sighed, leaning his head against the gray wall. "I suppose you want to know why."

I nodded and stepped closer.

"I never meant to deceive you, princess. Truly. I was your friend, giving you the wisest counsel I could."

He winced and passed his palm across his face. "But when it came to the stele, I feared you wouldn't understand. Your experiences in Trellich, and especially Imperia, the fall of Lord Lessox—they'd given you a prejudice against magic I knew couldn't be overcome through my own testimony. I hoped you'd see the good I could accomplish among the people once it was released and perhaps reconsider over time."

He slid his hands down to hang at his sides. "But things never do turn out quite the way we expect, do they?"

A confusing mix of pity, anger, and disgust seemed to accentuate the dungeon's nauseating stench. "No, they don't."

Renewed hope kindled in his eyes at my response. "I should've told you, I see that now. I should've let you decide for yourself whether to help with my plan rather than ensure your assistance through deceit. But that stele, I felt I had a claim to it." He clenched his fingers into fists.

I tensed, but his gaze held only sorrow and entreaty. Not the desperation of Nicholas or the madness of Lord Lessox.

"You see, princess, I was once a student of sorcery. My tutor, Lord Buros, took me in and treated me as more of a son than my own father ever had. The source of his magic was one of the spirits we used in the creation of the stele. Getting to be a part of that experiment—using the skills I'd developed to help capture and stabilize magic along with fully trained sorcerers—was the highlight of my transition from boyhood to manhood. When the royal family turned on us and took it away . . ."

His tired stance became rigid. "Lord Buros lost everything. They all did. As you saw with Lord Lessox, separation from a sorcerer's spirit addles the mind, crushes his very being. Every sorcerer who'd generously given up his power for the greater good became weak, useless, with no recompense for their losses. I cared for Lord Buros until his death. Confined to bed, when he should've been in his prime!"

His voice had risen almost to a shout. Egan started for us, but I gently waved him back.

Sir Colin hung his head, jaw tight. "I applied myself to other studies, but I never forgot. I vowed to find a way to release that magic, to make it available to the people of Delunia as it was always meant to be. Not hoarded by the royal family to use according to their whims."

Had he truly believed that falsehood? "But they don't— didn't—use it at all. They were trying to protect the people from it."

"Perhaps now, yes. But Emperor Ulrich, Tertius's father . . ." He opened his hands in a helpless gesture. "What does any of it matter? It's gone, all of it, gone. Restoring that magic to the people gave me purpose. Now I'll rot in this dungeon for my failed attempt. At least the royal family doesn't control it anymore—that's a small victory. I suppose most of it went into you, didn't it?" His brows rose with interest. "You could use it, if you had someone to teach you."

"I have no desire to use the magic that nearly killed me."

He nodded with a laugh that held no mirth. "I suppose I can't fault you for that." His gaze collided with mine. "Will they send you away for your part in all this? I do regret encouraging your involvement under false pretenses. You would've made a fine empress, Princess Penelope."

His words rang true. Unlike Nicholas's clear agenda and impudent demands, Sir Colin seemed defeated, resigned to his fate.

"Thank you. Fortunately, Vander is more magnanimous than anyone I've ever known. He has offered his full forgiveness and still wishes to marry me."

"I hope he'll prove a worthy husband for you, then." His smile brought back a hint of the friend whose company I'd so cherished. "It makes it a bit easier to accept my fate, knowing the people of Delunia will be in good hands."

I reached through the bars and patted his arm. "Take care, Sir Colin."

He opened his mouth, then closed it. "Goodbye, Princess Penelope. To be called *sir* one last time—you don't know what it means to feel there might be someone in the world who still respects me."

Sympathy wound delicate strands around my heart. He'd waited so long for a failed dream, spent so much energy on a misguided cause.

Perhaps I'd petition Emperor Tertius to have him escorted across the Toan Sea, to live out the remainder of his days in Trellich.

"Goodbye. May the Luminate be with you." I turned and followed Egan back up the winding stairway.

With any luck, I'd never have reason to visit a dungeon again.

CHAPTER 30

J wrung my hands. Every jolt of the carriage seemed to add a new knot to my insides.

In the two weeks following my recovery, Vander had encouraged me on numerous occasions to ride with him beyond the city gates to Leipon. I'd put him off with requests for extra rest, errands at the marketplace, lessons with Dionne, consults with Victoria and the palace seamstresses about new additions to my wardrobe . . .

But today, I'd run out of excuses.

Vander placed his palm over my hands, gently smoothing my clenched fingers. "They will be happy to see you, Penelope. Please trust me on this."

I soaked in his warmth. "I do trust you. But I don't understand why they'd be happy to see me."

"You sacrificed for them. And the baskets, the supplies— they have helped." He nudged my shoulder. "Just wait. You will see."

I closed my eyes and leaned against him. With Vander at my side, how terrible could it be?

Tension invaded my posture once more as we veered off the gravel road. My thoughts seemed suspended in mid-air, caught between a desire to crane my neck and peer beyond the copse of trees and the instinct to hide.

Beyond the trees waited a familiar sight: the same shabby tents and collections of sticks that passed for cottages, the same drab colors and stooped postures. But as we drew closer, a few variations caught my attention.

A fenced-off, rectangular area of freshly tilled soil hosting what appeared to be a burgeoning garden sat off to the side. Many garments still appeared ill-fitting and threadbare, but others were fresher, more vibrant. Three children ran to greet us, their cheeks and limbs slightly more rounded out. In the distance, chickens squawked and pecked.

My wide eyes tried to process every detail. "You're right. It is making a difference."

Vander squeezed my hand. "The changes take time. But yes, there is much, hmm, furtherance already."

More villagers noticed our arrival and made their way toward us. Madame Yalena waved and cried out, and soon others joined in a kind of chant. "*Ira! Ira!*"

Anxiety rushed back through me like a wave crashing over the beach. Were they happy to see us? Or angry? "Wh—what are they saying?"

Vander grinned and grasped my shoulder. "They call out for you. *Ira* means something like hero."

My gaping mouth wouldn't form words. Hero? Such a prestigious, monumental term for my bumbling efforts to help. But I didn't know nearly enough Delunian to explain their mistake.

We alighted from the carriage to a motley set of bows and curtsies. The guards started unpacking additional supplies we'd brought. Hopefully, soon everyone would have a new set of clothes and at least a rudimentary stock of food and medicine.

Vander mingled among the villagers, keeping me tucked close to his side. Although I couldn't participate in the conversations, I murmured greetings as an array of frail women, weary men, and excited children pressed my hands and clutched at my skirts.

Leda ran to us, huffing and beaming. She traced the edge of one of my draping sleeves. "*Bellante, principela.*"

I returned her smile and made a show of admiring her new dress. Simple and practical, yet much better suited to her than the rags she'd worn before. "*Rei, bellante.*"

Her cheeks flushed. After a pause, she gave me a quick hug around the waist before chasing after Basil.

When my hands were covered in sweat and grime and my face sore from holding a smile in place, Vander managed to extract us from the grateful villagers. He ushered me into the carriage, where I gratefully collapsed against the seat.

He joined me, then called instructions to the coachman.

Another shout rose from the ragtag assembly. Different than the earlier calls of *Ira*. I listened, straining to block out the clip-clopping of the horses' hooves and the scrape of the carriage wheels over rocky dirt.

Vander tensed, apparently comprehending the request at the same time I did.

"*Kise! Kise!*" The refrain seemed to traverse all walks of life among the Delunian people.

Heat inflamed my cheeks, but I turned to Vander.

His smile was radiant but gentle. "I know you are not yet comfortable with such traditions. If you prefer a kiss on the cheek . . ."

"I don't mind. After all they've been through, they deserve to share in our happiness."

A blend of mischief and longing darkened his eyes. "As you like."

Cupping my cheek, he placed a long, sweet kiss on my lips.

The crowd behind us erupted in cheers. I buried my face in his shoulder as he gave them one last wave.

The carriage bounced us along the gravel road. Vander gave a sigh of contentment, his arm resting around my waist.

"How encouraging to see such an improvement." I leaned my head against the seat. "Did they say anything? About the . . ." I couldn't bring myself to finish.

The light in Vander's eyes softened. "The dark magic, *rei*. It dissipates. They say it does not feel so present now." He shifted to look me in the eye. "They say because of their *ira*, they have made vows never to access such magic again."

"Truly? Because of me?" I blinked against the sheen of tears forming in my eyes.

"You are a genuine hero, Penelope. I have such pride in my future empress."

His words warmed my core. I longed to bask in his admiration and pride, but a last vestige of doubt strung across my mind like a cobweb.

Would he still consider me a hero if he knew my full past?

Vander shifted to face me. The strain in my mind must've betrayed itself in my posture. "What troubles you, my love?"

Knots twisted my stomach. I had to tell him sometime, and it'd only get harder the longer I waited. But would he ever call me his love again?

"If only I were a hero. I'm certain you wouldn't be proud of me if you knew everything."

"We have much time to share our histories, have we not? The rest of our lives." He placed a curl behind my ear and kissed my temple, a playful light in his eyes.

I reluctantly shifted away. "Yes, but there's a certain part of my history that you should know now. That I should've told you long ago."

"As you like." He folded his hands in his lap, his brows angled to a quizzical slant.

"You forgave me so readily for betraying you, and I'm so grateful. But I must confess"—the words lodged in my throat—"it's happened before."

A line formed on his forehead. "You have betrayed me on another occasion?"

"Not you." I fidgeted with the sash adorning my *etana*. "You know I was engaged to the Imperian prince, but I never told you the full story."

"You may tell me if you wish, but you do not owe me such explanation, Penelope. If you do not . . ."

My breath blew through my pursed lips. He was giving me an escape, but I couldn't let myself take it. "No. I'll never feel fully secure of your love until you've heard the worst."

He nodded, a new tension making his posture rigid.

Time to get on with it, before I lose my nerve. "When Papa arranged my marriage to the Imperian prince, I was in love with someone else. Nicholas Alberle, the Duke of Brantley."

"You were untrue to this prior fiancé." His tone was cautious but not accusing.

"If only that were the worst of it."

I shifted, overtaken by a sudden desire to pace. To move. To escape the confines of this carriage, which felt increasingly suffocating.

"Nicholas had arranged my marriage to Prince Raphael on behalf of Imperia, all the while courting me in secret. His intention was to bide his time until after my wedding, and then . . ."

I'd never spoken the words aloud. Never admitted to another person just how despicable his plan was.

Panic clutched my chest. "He wanted to take the throne for himself, so he arranged for a sorcerer to . . . to . . . to kill them."

Vander pulled me against his shoulder and laid his head on mine. I hadn't even realized I was crying.

"I didn't stop him. I didn't even tell anyone. I asked him if we could simply marry and give up his designs on the Imperian throne, but when he refused, I . . . I went along with it. I was going to let him . . . he said they were unfair rulers, and that was partly true. But they were kind to me. Especially Prince Raphael. How could I—?"

Sobs choked off any further attempt at speech. Vander held me as I wept, the remnants of my guilt and pain and humiliation drenching his shirt.

We sat in silence as the carriage rumbled through the palace city. I kept my face tucked against Vander, hoping to hide my red eyes and tear-streaked cheeks from curious onlookers.

He leaned forward to hold a quiet conversation with the driver in Delunian, keeping an arm curled around my back. I wasn't sure, but it seemed like we were taking a different route back to the palace.

After a little time, the jolting motion of the carriage stopped. Vander took my hand and helped me down.

I blinked, my eyes stinging and bleary. "Where are we?"

"I ask Yates to take us to a back pasture with little use. I hope you do not mind." He darted a nervous glance at my face. "I thought perhaps you would not wish for an audience as we continue to speak on such a difficult subject."

"Oh. Of course, thank you." I inhaled the fresh scent of grass and leaves.

Vander took my arm, and we began a slow, halting stroll.

"Will you send me away?" The question that'd burned in my mind since my revelation escaped without warning.

"Send you away?" He started. "Why? Do you have wish to leave?"

"No, but I thought perhaps—"

"Do you still love him?" His voice held a soft urgency.

"Nicholas? No." I gave a rueful laugh. "He was never deserving of my love. I see that now." I kicked at a tuft of grass. "And the Imperian royal family is alive and well, no thanks to me. One of my lady's maids—who is now Prince Raphael's wife—discovered the plan, defeated the sorcerer, and put a stop to the wedding."

A bit of the weight lifted from my shoulders. I could finally think of her without a trace of anger or resentment.

"This, I am glad to hear." Vander patted my hand.

"But I betrayed you, just like I betrayed the Imperian royal family. It happened again, even though I tried so hard to do better. How could you ever trust me?"

He paused. "But was it so similar?"

"Yes! I lied, went behind your back, put my confidence in someone who turned out to be deceitful."

I sniffled against the tears threatening to break down the fragile barrier I'd erected to keep them in.

"Nearly caused a disaster for you and your entire family. Your entire country."

"Ah, my Penelope. You never give yourself enough credit."

Because I deserve none.

He placed two fingers beneath my chin and slowly raised my head. "What you seem to ignore is how differently this situation ends. You trusted the wrong person, yes. But when you discovered the wrong, you did not stand back and watch. You did not allow corruption to continue. You put yourself in utmost danger to stop the evil, giving no thought to the cost to yourself. It is this that gives me hope."

My jaw worked as I processed this new appraisal. "Even so, what if I'm doomed to continue this pattern? To keep betraying the people I love even when I don't intend to?"

He stiffened, placing his hands on my shoulders. "Do you love me, Penelope?"

"I—" My mind whirled at the sudden change in subject. But I knew the answer, didn't I? "Yes, I do. Very much."

My cheeks flared as though I'd suddenly spent too much time in the hot Delunian sun.

His expression relaxed into a grin. "In such case, my love, I have no doubt we will learn this trust over time. But we must always be ready to talk, ready not to keep secrets. And have courage to steer each other down the right path when needed."

I pressed my lips together and nodded. That sounded surprisingly attainable. "You are so good, Vander. Kind and forgiving far beyond what I deserve."

"I can see forgiveness for yourself will be the hardest to obtain."

He stroked his thumb down my cheek.

"But this betrayal, it is a complicated matter, yes? Perhaps I betray my sister when I do not speak on her behalf to my parents. Or the villagers of Leipon, or others suffering in Delunia, when I do not seek more ways to ease their pain. I learn from these mistakes; I try to do better. But they do not make up who I am."

I had the forgiveness of Prince Raphael, of Vander. Even the Luminate had extended forgiveness for my many faults and welcomed me back into His embrace.

Perhaps it was time to forgive myself, to seize the new beginning I was being offered.

Vander tweaked my nose. "Now that we have established you must stay in Delunia with me, let us get you home."

Home. How startling, yet perfectly right, that the word brought forth an image of *Palati del Chrysos*. Of the chambers I shared with Victoria. Of being anywhere with Vander.

"Not just yet."

Before he could open his lips to protest, I claimed them with mine.

He swept me into his arms, pouring his love and assurance into the kiss. If I'd ever wondered whether the Luminate still cared for me, whether He still had a plan seeking my best interest, I couldn't possibly deny it now.

He'd given me yet another chance at a happy ending, in a country I was growing to cherish, with the best man I'd ever known.

Love surrounds you. My love will protect you.

I'd never believed those words more.

EPILOGUE

*D*ear Sophia,

    I ought to start with the proper salutations, but I can't hold back my news — we're coming to Trellich for your wedding!

    Vander and I worked out the travel arrangements, and we plan to stay an entire two months at Glonsel Palace. I can hardly sit still long enough to write when I think of it. How I miss you all! But the homesickness is so much more bearable knowing we'll be there with you in the spring.

    What fun we'll have, completing the last of your wedding preparations together! I look forward to getting to know Prince Gael much better, with plenty of time to ensure he will make a suitable husband for my dear sister.

    Now, on to my other news. Did I tell you Victoria is getting married as well? She and one of my personal guards became quite besotted with one another last year, and they have obtained the emperor's blessing upon their union. Victoria practically floats everywhere, much as I imagine your current state of bliss. She will continue on as my lady's maid, but another maid has been assigned to me as well so Victoria may move to separate quarters with her husband.

    Maya is quiet, hardworking, and very patient with my stumbling attempts at Delunian. Once you see her sewing and beadwork, you'll be tempted to steal her for yourself! I shall miss having Victoria as my constant companion, but I am truly thrilled that she has found happiness here as well.

If I'm not mistaken, another engagement may be in the works. Dionne has set her sights on Maceo, the handsome son of the wealthy governor of a northern province. She wouldn't say a word to the emperor and empress about it, no doubt fearing how Nadia might react. But after I hinted to Tertius time and again, he finally seems to have caught on to the potential benefits of such an alliance.

Dionne has become a good friend, and I will be sad to see her go when the time comes, but some distance from her parents to make her own way in the world will likely do her good. Hopefully we'll be able to visit often—I've heard the mountains in northern Delunia are stunning.

I am sorry to hear your report of Dominick. If he has already become such a spoiled, reckless terror, what will his future bring? And what of the future of our country? If only Papa could see how much Nicky needs his parenting in all respects, including discipline and boundaries, not just blind devotion and indulgence. I shall try my best to speak with him when we come in the spring, but I don't expect to make much headway.

I pray the Luminate will take Nicky under His own care and guidance, as the poor boy isn't getting it from his earthly father. I'm grateful you will be around a little longer to make what efforts you can with him.

Here at Palati del Chrysos, Vander continues to exhibit more constancy, patience, and good humor than I thought could exist within a single person. Marriage is so much harder than I anticipated, but at the same time, infinitely more beautiful. We'll have a great deal to discuss during my time in Trellich!

Our attempt to grow crimson bells in the garden didn't meet with success, but after consulting the gardeners, we've decided to try farendons and evening buds next year instead. Every reminder of home is so appreciated, yet I don't cling to them the way I used to.

And I'm pleased to report that Leipon is flourishing! Everyone is well-nourished and has proper clothing, and the guards have been helping the villagers construct better shelters. Sister Rochelle has even founded a church and a small school, teaching her adoring students reading and arithmetic.

Vander is so satisfied with our success there that he's commissioned scouts to find other villages in need of similar provisions. What a joy to improve the lives of the people around us!

I hope this letter finds you well. Give my best regards to Papa and extra hugs and kisses to Vivienne and Dominick. I so look forward to seeing you all soon!

With my love and best wishes,
Penelope, Princess of Delunia

THE END

Do not miss

Scarred

Book Three in the Tales of the Mystics.

Coming Soon from L2L2 Publishing.

ACKNOWLEDGMENTS

I've compared the writing of this book to riding a roller coaster, and for good reason! The path has been filled with slow, steep inclines and breathless tumbles forward, with a few meandering jaunts in between. And I never would've made it to the tops of the hills or back out of the valleys without my amazing family, friends, and readers!

So thank you, thank you, thank you to:

God, my heavenly Father, for putting another story on my heart and helping me see it through to its conclusion. There were so many aspects of this journey I didn't understand, but You stayed constant through it all.

My husband, for weathering every storm by my side with friendship and love. You endure all the piles of laundry and dishes, late nights, and ramblings about make-believe characters like a true champ, and I couldn't imagine life without you!

My children, for all the snuggles and grins and for helping me see life with a new perspective. I look forward to seeing all the incredible ways in which you'll bring your own creative ideas to life!

Mom and Dad, for believing I can achieve anything I set

my mind to and sharing about my book with so many family members, friends, and even acquaintances! Your love and support mean the world to me.

Jules, for always being a listening ear through life's ups and downs and making me laugh harder and more often than anyone else. I'm so lucky that my best friend happens to be my sister!

My in-laws, for being my first readers and among my biggest fans. Your willingness to drop everything to help out is an extraordinary blessing I never want to take for granted.

So many friends and extended family members who have provided love, prayers, and support in ways big and small. I fully believe every aspect of life takes a village, and I wouldn't trade mine for the world!

My writing community! Between the Ever Afters, my fellow Lands Uncharted contributors, the amazing Realm Makers tribe, and ACFW both here in Minnesota (they don't call us MN NICE for nothing!) and in the larger organization, I have found a wealth of knowledge and encouragement. You make writing less lonely and so much more fruitful and fun!

Michele Israel Harper, for setting the bar impossibly high for future editors. Your passion for helping authors, attention to detail, and incredible heart have blessed me in more ways than I can express, and I'm so grateful.

The rest of the Love2ReadLove2Write Publishing team, for being such a pleasure to work with and creating some of the world's most gorgeous books. I'm so proud to be an L2L2 author!

My Faith and Fairy Tales readers' group, for sticking with me even when I disappear into my virtual writing cave for months at a time. It has been such a pleasure to get to know each and every one of you, and your willingness to be on my team is one of my greatest sources of encouragement.

All my readers, for choosing to spend some of your valuable time in my imaginary worlds! Hearing how my stories have impacted you is truly the best part about being an author, and there aren't enough words in my writer's arsenal to fully express my appreciation. I can't wait to share more stories with you!

~Laurie Lucking

ABOUT THE AUTHOR

*L*aurie Lucking loves hoarding books, singing at the top of her lungs, playing games that don't involve too much strategy, and spending time with her husband and three energetic kids.

A recovering attorney, she now spends her days as a stay-at-home mom and has discovered writing young adult romantic fantasy is way more fun than drafting contracts. Her fairy tale–inspired stories combine the excitement of discovering a new world with the timeless enchantment of falling in love.

Laurie is the secretary of her local ACFW Chapter and a co-founder of Lands Uncharted, a blog celebrating readers and writers of clean fantasy.

Laurie's debut novel, *Common*, won the Christian Editor Connection's Excellence in Editing Award and was a finalist in the Young Adult category of the ACFW Carol Awards. Her short stories have been published in a variety of magazines and anthologies and are listed on her website.

Find out more about Laurie and her writing adventures at www.LaurieLucking.com.

Laurie loves to hear from her readers! Follow her on social media, check out her website, or drop her a line to let her know what you thought of Traitor. *Happy reading!*

www.LaurieLucking.com
Facebook: @AuthorLaurieLucking
Twitter: @LaurieLucking
Instagram: @LaurieLucking

REVIEWS

Did you know reviews skyrocket a book's career? Instead of fizzling into nothing, a book will be suggested by Amazon, shared by Goodreads, or showcased by Barnes & Noble. Plus, authors treasure reviews! (And read them over and over and over . . .)

Unsure of what to say? A review can be as simple as "I liked it," or as complicated as every deep thought and feeling about the book that you simply must share with the world, and should never reveal spoilers. Also, reviews are best when you share how you *felt* about the book instead of what was *inside* the book.

Whether you enjoyed this book or not, would you consider leaving a review on:

- Amazon
- Barnes & Noble
- Goodreads

. . . or perhaps your personal blog or website or fave social media account? Thank you so much!

—The L2L2 Publishing Team

More from L2L2 Publishing

If you enjoyed this book, you may also enjoy:

Half-faerie Caoine has no control over the banshee lament she sings each night, predicting the death of others. A senior in a brand new high school, she expects the same response she's received at every other school: judgment from fellow students over her unusual eyes and unnaturally white skin and hair. However, for the first time in her life she finds friends. Real friends. Life spins out of control when her lament comes out during the day, those whose death she predicts die right in front of her, and a dark faerie known only as the Unseelie prince blames Caoine. Her curse is not supposed to work like that. In a race against time, Caoine must uncover the Unseelie prince's identity and stop a spell before it unleashes hell on earth, all while trying to control her banshee song and finding a place among her peers.
Senior year just got real.

More from L2L2 Publishing

If you enjoyed this book, you may also enjoy:

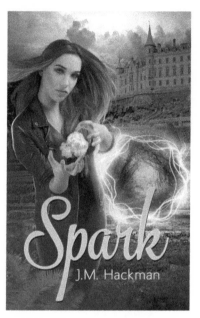

Brenna James wants three things for her sixteenth birthday: to find her history notes before the test, to have her mother return from her business trip, and to stop creating fire with her bare hands. Yeah, that's so not happening. Unfortunately. When Brenna learns her mother is missing in an alternate reality called Linneah, she travels through a portal to find her. Against her will. Who knew portals even existed? But Brenna's arrival in Linneah begins the fulfillment of an ancient prophecy, including a royal murder and the theft of Linneah's most powerful relic: the Sacred Veil. Hold up. Can everything just slow down for a sec? Left with no other choice, Brenna and her new friend Baldwin pursue the thief into the dangerous woods of Silvastamen. When they spy an army marching toward Linneah, Brenna is horrified. Can she find the veil, save her mother, and warn Linneah in time?

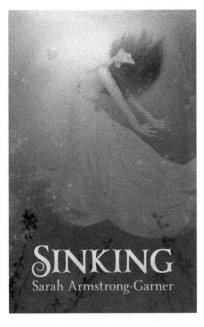

WHERE WILL WE TAKE YOU NEXT?

Reread *Common,*
Discover *Keen,*
Light a fire with *Spark,*
Drift into *Sinking,*
and Hunt with *Kill the Beast.*

All at
www.love2readlove2writepublishing.com/bookstore
or your local or online retailer.

Happy Reading!
~The L2L2 Publishing Team

ABOUT L2L2 PUBLISHING

Love2ReadLove2Write Publishing, LLC is a small traditional press, dedicated to clean or Christian speculative fiction.

Speculative genres include but are not limited to: Fantasy, Science Fiction, Fairy-Tale Fantasy, Time Travel, Alternate History, Space Opera, Steampunk, Light Horror, Superhero Fiction, Near Future, Supernatural, Paranormal, Magical Realism, Urban Fantasy, Utopian or Dystopian, etc., or a mixture of any of the previous.

We seek stunning tales masterfully told, and we strive to create an exquisite publishing experience for our authors and to produce quality fiction for our readers.

Traitor is at the heart of what we publish: a redemptive tale with speculative elements that will delight our readers.

All of our titles can be found or requested at your favorite online book retailer, local bookstore, or favorite local library.

Visit www.L2L2Publishing.com to view our submissions guidelines, find our other titles, or learn more about us.

And if you love our books, please leave a review!

Happy Reading!

~The L2L2 Publishing Team

CPSIA information can be obtained
at www.ICGtesting.com
Printed in the USA
BVHW080331210421
605392BV00003B/252